ALSO BY LAURA DALEO

Bound by Blood

The Vow

The Vampire Within

The Soul Collector

The Doll

Once We Were Witches

Immortal Kiss

By

Laura Daleo

AUTHOR LAURA DALEO

Immortal Kiss is a work of fiction. Names, characters, places, and incidents either are the product of the author's imagination or are used fictitiously. Any resemblance to actual persons living or dead, events, or locales is entirely coincidental.

Copyright © 1996 by Laura Daleo

Published in the United States by Author Laura Daleo, Tucson, Arizona

Print ISBN: 9780997846126

ebook ISBN: 9780997846133

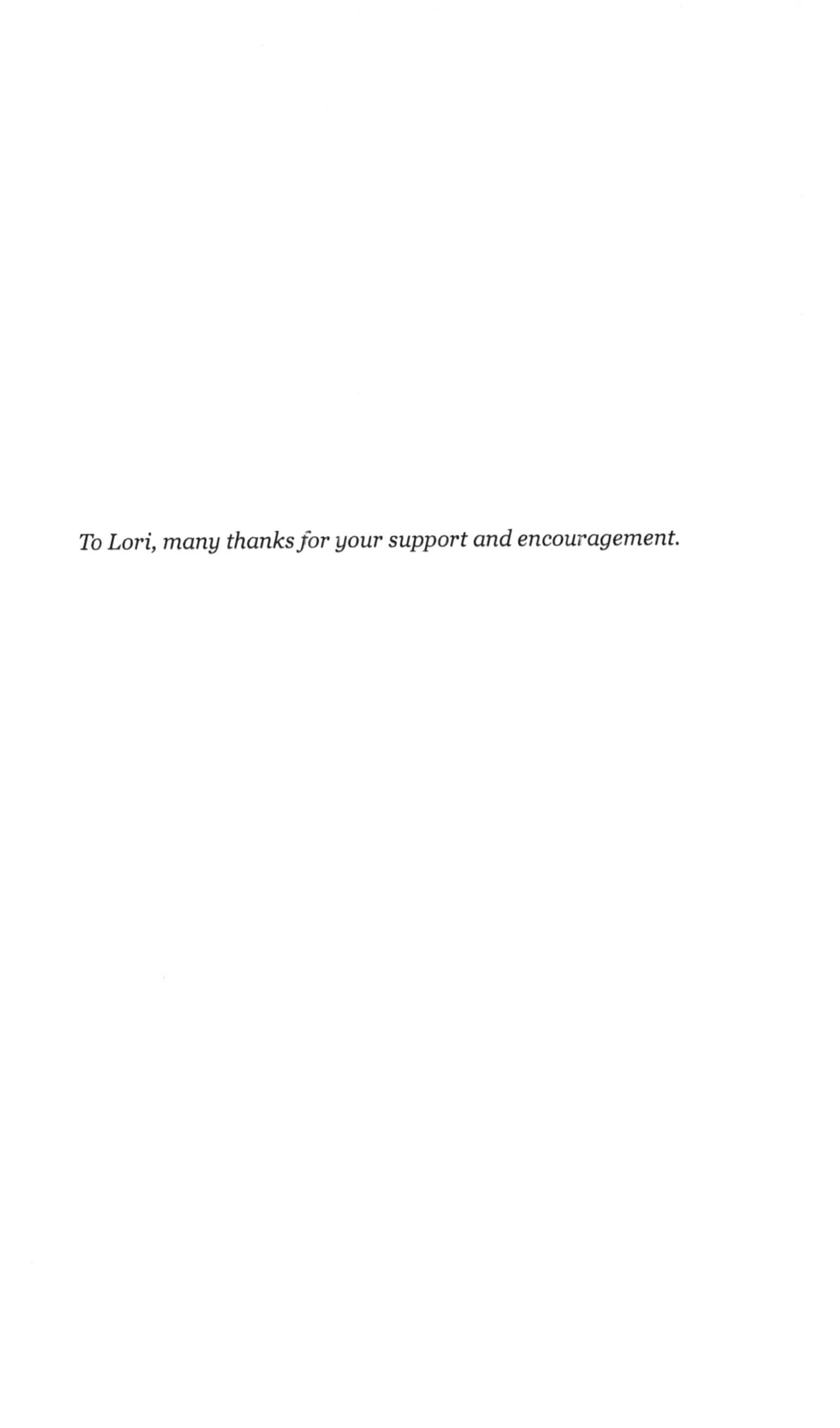

To Lori, many thanks for your support and encouragement.

PROLOGUE

Just after midnight, Danny's beat-up Mustang convertible pulled into my driveway. With a turn of the key, he silenced the soft rumble of the engine before leaning over to kiss my cheek. "Happy birthday, Beth."

A gust of humid summer air tousled my hair. As I tucked the strands behind my ears, I gave his shoulder a nudge. "That's number seven. You can stop now."

He grinned, calling forth a set of adorable dimples. "Seventeen is going to be epic. Feel any different?" Danny was such a dweeb.

"You're acting like I won the lottery."

He pursed his lips and gave a slow nod. "Now that would be truly epic."

"Yeah," I responded, my gaze drifting toward my open bedroom window. The moon hung low in the sky, peeking through the trees surrounding my house, but complete darkness lurked behind the curtains. I squinted. I could've sworn I'd left the light on.

"You're thinking about *it*, aren't you?" Danny mumbled, but his words emerged loud enough for my ears to catch their meaning.

His use of the word "it" scratched at my bones like nails on a chalkboard. I twisted in my seat to face him. "Don't call him that."

Tensing his jaw, Danny fixed his gaze on me. "What should I call it? It's mist, Beth. It's not human." He breathed a little easier, the rosy red returning to his cheeks. "I get it. It's been around for most of your life, but so have I, and you can see me, touch me, and talk to me."

I bit my tongue and swallowed my smartass remark. Danny was right, yet I didn't care. The mist's voiceless gestures had conquered my heart. Closing my eyes, I sat quietly, listening to the crickets sing like drunken fools. When we'd been kids, the mist had drawn Danny in, like an addict. He'd dubbed the shapeless mass Commander Vapor— his superhero. Every night of our childhood, Danny had camped out in front of my bedroom window, his eyes bulging from their sockets as he waited for the mist to appear.

"*It* can't give you what I can," Danny pressed, breaking through the memories.

You're wrong, Danny. Opening my eyes, I turned toward him. I didn't say a word, just stared at him in silence.

He squirmed and looked away, like a dog being reprimanded by his master.

I slouched down in my seat as I said, "The mist is part of me. I can't let go. I...I don't know how to."

Danny inched closer, narrowing the gap between us. "I'm not asking you to let go." He touched my hand. "Just give me a chance." The corners of his lips pulled upward to form a toothy grin. "You and I have things in common."

I blinked and cocked my head. "Like what? I collect shoes, you collect creepy bugs. I read poetry, you read comic books. I paint, you play paintball."

Shrugging his shoulders, he fired back, "We're both seventeen, next-door neighbors, and go to Emery High."

I smirked. None of those things were shared interests. "Nice try."

He lifted his chin and snapped his fingers. "Got it! We're near doppelgangers. My eyes are greenish-blue, and your shade mimics the sea. I'm covered in freckles, while you have just a few sprinkled across your nose. I'm a carrottop to your apple-red."

I eyed him, letting his words sink in. Danny's lips quivered, making it impossible to keep a straight face. Exploding with laughter, we fell into each other, our foreheads colliding.

He curled a strand of my hair around his finger. "Give me a chance."

I stiffened and pulled away. "I care about you, Danny, but we're—"

Bobbing his head, he finished my sentence. "Just friends, I know, but I may be able to change your mind." He tapped his temple. "I've been doing some research. Found some pretty interesting stuff in my comic books."

I clamped my lips shut. *Comic book research? This should be good.*

He held up his hand. "Hear me out. I mean, we're dealing with mist that forms into a man. Comic books aren't such a far stretch."

He had a point. "I'm all ears."

"I've narrowed the possibilities down to three types of beings." His expression screamed "wait for it," just like when our science teacher, Mr. Mayor, hesitated after every word, letting the anticipation build. "An alien...a warlock...or a vampire." He paused before adding, "In comic books, all three can turn their bodies into mist. You should ask *him* which of the three he is."

His words crept across the surface of my brain. The nagging itch to do just as he'd suggested filled me. *I have to know*, I thought as I pushed open the car door and stepped onto my driveway.

Danny flashed to my side, taking my hand. "Let me come up with you?"

I didn't look at him, my gaze fixed instead on my bedroom window. "No." I dropped his hand. "Go home, Danny. I'll see you tomorrow." As an afterthought, I faced him and pressed my hand over my heart. "Thanks for making my seventeenth birthday special."

His lips stretched into a goofy grin. "I love you, Beth."

I couldn't say it back, because I didn't love him. Forcing a smile, I backed along the drive and up onto the porch. As I turned and opened the front door, the Mustang's engine whined to life again. I waved to Danny as I slipped inside, closing the door behind me.

In the darkness, I climbed the drab, carpeted stairs. My mother wasn't one for color. Muted gray décor claimed every surface of our home. She called it modern; I called it boring. In contrast, my cotton-candy-pink bedroom screamed of my personality. Danny called it the "Pink Palace," and the space *was* my palace.

My bedroom door stood ajar, releasing the scent of dewy rosebuds. Inhaling the intoxicating air made my head spin. I inched closer, running my hand along the wall and peering through the partially opened door. The mist drifted past the opening, and my heart jumped into my throat. Pushing the door wide, I hurried inside and flicked on the light. Red rose petals cascaded like a waterfall of blood from my bed's comforter onto the carpet. I opened my mouth, but no sound escaped me, and my feet seemed rooted to the floor. He'd prepared this surprise for me, for my birthday. As I struggled to catch my breath, I shut the door, closing us off from the outside world.

The mist shifted to form the silhouette of a man, who glided across my room toward my bed. His translucent finger pointed to a pink sheet of folded paper resting on my pillow.

My palms tingled in anticipation of clutching up the filmy page. Could it be a love letter? I ran to my bed, scooped the pink note into my hands, and fell backward onto the silky blanket of rose petals. They fluttered around me, caressing my skin as gravity called them back. I bit my lip as I stroked the coarse paper between my fingers before opening it. My gaze roamed over the page.

If I had to choose whether to breathe or to love you, I would use my last breath to tell you that...I love you.

The paper trembled in my grasp, his words blurring inside my tears. He loved me and I him. I rose to my feet to face the mist, my mouth dry as a jarful of cotton balls. I forced out each of my words. "What...are...you?"

He waved his hand over the petals, spinning them faster and faster. As they came to rest upon my bedding, a letter began to take shape, becoming a V. Others followed, creating sense from chaos. My small human life shrunk into the background. All that remained in that moment was the word...VAMPIRE.

CHAPTER 1

A flurry of winter wind snarled around me. Shivers ran down my spine, crawling back up to explode into goose bumps across my flesh. I buttoned up my coat in response before slipping my arm beneath Danny's as we strolled along the ocean cliffs.

"It's friggin' freezing," he muttered, tightening his scarf.

"Wanna turn back?"

He shook his head and gripped my hand as he charged forward. "Our bench is just ahead." He glanced at me with a sparkle in his eyes. "The ocean's orchestra is playing our song, and we have front row seats."

I gave his hand a playful squeeze. "And what song would that be?"

He leaned in and brushed his lips softly over mine. "We don't have a song, but so what? Lots of couples don't."

I shuddered, but not from the cold. Four years together, and the word "couple" still didn't fit our situation. Our relationship had evolved out of convenience. Danny had always accepted me, even though I knew I was damaged goods. I mean, no guy wanted a crazy girlfriend who prattled on about mist and vampires. Danny knew my secret, so if I slipped and revealed crazy-sounding details about my past, it didn't matter. For that reason alone, I loved him, but it wasn't the earth-shattering, edge-of-your-seat, heart-pounding, make-you-ache-all-over love. That corner of my heart belonged to the mist.

Danny rubbed his hands over my arms and asked, "Get a chill?"

I soundlessly snuggled up to him in response.

His arm came around to hold me close. "I see our bench."

The rickety old thing came into view, perched inches from the cliff's edge and just a foot behind the safety railing. Danny scooped me up in his arms and sprinted to the bench where he plopped me down into his lap. The bench moaned like an old man at the sudden burden.

I slid off onto the wooden seat and said, "This thing's on its last leg. The park should really replace it."

He raised his brows. "Are you kidding? They can't get rid of this baby. It's got character."

"Character? It's giving me splinters."

He frowned, grabbing my hands and turning them over. "Did you get pricked?"

"Not yet, but it's only a matter of time before it sinks its claws into my skin."

"I'll protect you," he responded, enfolding me inside both arms and settling back against the bench.

"That's sweet," I told him, resting my head against his shoulder and tucking my hands into his coat pockets.

Huddled together on the decaying bench, we listened to the crashing waves serenade us from below. A blast of seawater soared above the cliff, perfuming the air with its tang. When I breathed deeply, I could taste the salt on my tongue.

"I've been thinking," Danny said, reaching inside his pocket and lacing our fingers.

"That's never good," I teased.

He nudged me playfully. "I'm serious."

I returned the gesture with a nudge of my own. "Me too."

He stared at me, troubled, his brows knitting together.

I laughed and kissed him. "Kidding."

He cracked half a smile and cleared his throat. Twisting his shoulders, he faced me. "Move in with me, Beth."

My jaw dropped just a hair. "What?"

"Move in with me," he said again, this time with his head held high.

My gaze drifted away from him to the ocean's restless horizon. How could he ask such a thing of me? Danny had been spending most nights with me, keeping my bedroom window closed so he could shut out the mist. I knew that living with him would drive a permanent wedge between me and the mist.

He cupped my chin in his hands, forcing me to look at him. "I know this is a big step, but I feel like we're ready."

I shook my head in slow motion. "I can't do that to *him*."

Danny remained silent, his glare burning heat straight at me.

I wanted to flee, but I clung to his hand instead. "I'm sorry," I said softly.

His breaths rushed out noisily. "Beth, we're not kids, or even teen-agers. We're adults now. Start acting like one."

I scooted away from him, dropping his hand. "Because I have feelings for him, a being who's been with me for nearly my entire life, I'm a child?"

He sprang to his feet. "You're almost twenty-five, and you still live in a fantasy world, believing in mist and vampires."

Even in the cold of the winter night, the heat rushed to his cheeks. Struggling to avoid snapping at him, I gripped the rough edge of the bench. "Why should my age make him any less real? I'm not making this up. You've seen him too."

He threw his hands in the air. "I don't know what it is I've seen."

I leapt up from the bench, hot tears stinging my eyes. "Don't do this. Don't pretend like you think I'm crazy all of a sudden."

His brows twisted together, and he trembled. "I would never think that of you, but you can't keep allowing the mist, vampire, whatever that thing is, to rule your life."

I remained silent for a moment as tears streamed down my face. "I didn't realize you thought my life was no longer my own."

With the edge of his scarf, he dabbed at my tears. "He never plans to show himself or he would've done so by now. I'm right here, and I love you. Don't push me away."

I laid my head against his chest and hugged him. "Maybe you're right." Out of the corner of my eye, a soft shape flickered in the distance. Pushing myself free of the embrace, I peered into the darkness. "Did you see that?"

Danny turned. "What?"

Again, a flash of light lit up the night, closer that time. "There." I shouted.

The brightness intensified, becoming too brilliant to hold my gaze.

Squinting and shielding his brow with his hand, Danny wondered aloud, "What is that?"

I backed away, shaking my head in confusion. "Don't know."

The glittering mass spiraled upward, twirling like a tornado in the dark sky before plummeting toward us.

Danny pushed me behind him, shielding my body with his. "What the hell?"

I clung to his coat, feeling my body go numb, but I couldn't look away.

After whooshing through the air around us, the glowing cloud glided to a graceful stop mere inches shy of me and Danny. Its blinding illumination dimmed, like the overhead lights in a movie theater at the start of the show. A sheer fog rose from the light and transformed into mist.

My breath caught in my throat, goose bumps pinching my flesh. It was him. Our visits had always been confined to my bedroom, and he'd never ventured outside its four walls. What had changed? And how had he found me? Had he followed us that night?

Danny's shoulders slouched, and he hung his head. "Really?" He turned and squinted up at the intruder. "Jesus, Beth. It's bad enough he pops in and out of your bedroom whenever he pleases, but following us here to our bench?" He clenched his jaw in anger. "That's crossing the friggin' line."

I swallowed hard. The mist's appearance wasn't my fault, and I had no idea why he'd come or what he wanted. I took a step backward, shaking my head in disbelief. "Don't you yell at me, Danny. I'm in the dark the same as you. I don't know why he came here."

The mist whirled between us, encircling me, and I did nothing to discourage him. A warm sensation penetrated every cell in my body, like an electric blanket set on high, easing my mind into sedation. If only I could reach out and hug his insubstantial body in return. I did the next best thing, wrapping my arms around my own waist, closing my eyes, and swaying back and forth.

"Beth!" Danny snapped, his voice bitter.

My eyes flew open.

Danny stood rigid before me, his arched brows almost converging in anger, his colorless lips forming a taut, thin line. He ground out his words. "I'm done."

The weight of the meaning behind his words sank heavily into my gut. I was his girlfriend after all. I wouldn't hurt Danny. *Make things right*, my brain screamed at me. Breaking free from the mist's enchanting embrace, I ran to Danny and grabbed his arm. "You can't mean that."

He brushed my hand off his arm like it was a stinging wasp. "Make a choice, Beth. Me..." He pointed at the mist. "...or him."

My gaze darted back and forth between the pair. How could I choose? I needed the mist like I needed oxygen. Without him, I would surely breathe my last breath and waste away into nothingness. Danny offered me grounded reality and a sense of security. Any semblance of certainty would vanish from my life without him. Nonetheless, I chose to stand up to Danny. "I won't make such a choice."

His posture stiffened, and a malicious smile spread across his lips. "Fine. Whatever." He locked his gaze on me before bolting, with large, quick strides up the walkway.

As the distance grew between us, a prickling sensation raced across my scalp, lifting the hairs from my neck. Tugging at the scarf wound around my neck, I dashed forward, shouting, "Danny, wait!"

He didn't turn when he replied by waving his hand in the air in dismissal as he trekked farther and farther away from me.

I stared after him, a part of me certain he would return to me. He didn't.

The mist drifted toward me, encircling me again. Heat radiated throughout my body, and my fingers tingled, aching to touch him. If only I could. I began to back away and poured conviction into my voice. "You can't keep coming between me and Danny. We're together now."

The mist darted forward, coiling like a snake.

I placed the palm of my hand over my heart, and in a softer tone, I said, "I wanted it to be you—needed it to be you." The tension brought on by my words gripped my neck and shoulders, and I raised my voice when I spoke again. "But you don't trust me enough to show yourself, which means things will never work out between us."

The mist slowed its movement, hovering before me and brushing against my cheek.

A flutter of excitement drove me forward to lean into his caress. I closed my eyes. "My first memory of you is from when I was six years old, and a strange, dewy mist appeared at my bedroom window. I let you in." I opened my eyes, and my lips curled into a slight smile. "Eighteen years later, my bedroom window is still open to you."

The mist surrounded me, moist droplets covering my skin. My mind scattered in a million foggy directions. I reached out, my fingers grasping at damp air. "Don't you know I would die for you?" I whispered into the fog.

My words, steeped in heartbreak and self-pity, rang in my own ears. Danny had been right. I'd given up everything else about my life except the mist, for the mist...and he'd only kept me in the dark. After all those years, I knew nothing about him, not even his name. If he wanted me, loved me in return, he needed to prove it. Breaking myself free of his charm, I stepped back, nodding curtly in his direction. "Show yourself, or I walk away...for good."

The mist lingered in front of me, unchanging, as if to mock me.

A dull twinge of pain nipped at my heart. Hunching over in response, like an old man, I stared at my upturned palms as if their pale surface held some kind of answer. They didn't. I used them to hide my face as I shuffled backward, slowly walking away from my mysterious, commitment-phobic suitor.

"Wait," he called, his voice rich and smooth, like melted chocolate.

At the sound, time stopped. The breeze fell silent, leaves froze in mid-air, and even the moon's glow seemed to darken. I couldn't move, nor could I breathe. Excitement swirled in the pit of my stomach, the way it might before the first drop on a roller coaster. After all that time, *he'd* spoken to me! My body caved in on itself, gasping for oxygen.

A single crimson leaf blew toward me, softly brushing my hand as it fell at my feet. The wind snatched it up, blowing it over my shoulder toward him.

"Beth, I'm here," he whispered inside my head.

When he soundlessly spoke my name, chills exploded down my arms. Weightlessness claimed me. The tenor of his voice lingered inside my head, seducing every cell. Slowly, like a scene captured by a camera lens freezing each frame, I turned to face him.

He stood mere inches from me, clad only in a simple pair of faded blue jeans and a gray sweater, instead of the mythical black suit and red-lined cape. Moonlight played over his pale skin and shimmered like glitter through his dark wavy hair. A dazzling smile came to life on his wine-colored lips as he looked me over. "A beautiful redhead with eyes colored like the sea has captured my immortal heart."

My heartbeat drummed its way into my throat, sweat beading my palms. As I gazed into his blue-gray eyes, the world melted away, leaving only him. I stumbled toward the bench, plopping down before my knees failed me. "You're real."

He tipped his chin and raised his perfect brows. "Quite real."

"Then I'm not crazy."

He sat next to me, clasping our fingers together, and squeezed my hand. "Of course you're not."

I gaped at him before saying, "I don't even know your name."

He placed his hand on his chest and announced, "I am Philippe, Philippe Delon."

I had to say his name out loud. "Philippe," I murmured, touching my lips.

His gaze glowed, and he sat very tall as he smiled at me. "Finally, we meet in the flesh."

I just stared at him, unable to speak.

"It's cold out. Come with me to my home and warm yourself by the fireplace." He gestured toward the opposite side of the street.

The house he'd indicated was the stuff of legends—an enormous, castle-like mansion that occupied an entire block. The original owners had passed away years ago, leaving the structure empty and unloved... until the present moment. I crossed my arms and pursed my lips. "So... we're neighbors. Apparently, revealing that tidbit to me slipped your mind."

He scratched his temple as he said, "I've only just moved to Castle Beach. France has always been my home."

"You're French?"

Stroking his neatly groomed mustache and goatee, he responded, "Je suis."

I swept my hair behind my ears. "What does that mean?"

"I am."

I wanted to bounce off the bench and shout to the world that my mist had actually turned out to be a French vampire; nevertheless, I forced myself to remain composed, my gaze transfixed on him.

He rose to his feet and held out his hand. "Come, let me show you my home. I'll tell you everything you want to know after we're seated by the hearth inside my study."

When I took his hand, rose petals fluttered in a vivid dance inside my head. The memory awakened the love-struck seventeen-year-old who still lived inside me. After all the years spent waiting, there he was—not a hallucination or mist. A real, live, corporeal being. I didn't hesitate to stand on my wobbly legs and accept his invitation.

As we approached the massive structure which served as his home, I saw that a towering brick wall, combined with a massive wrought iron gate, guarded the entrance. Trees reinforced the stone barrier, creating a canopy of greenery on all sides. In a romantic way, their branches interlocked to conceal the front of the mansion as though they wished the estate to remain hidden from prying eyes.

Gazing in awe of the property's solitude, I touched his arm. "It's beautiful."

"It is, isn't it?" he asked before vanishing from my side.

The whirl of cold air stung my cheek. I flinched and turned my head to gawk at the empty space where he'd stood only a moment before.

Like a flash of lightning, he reappeared, landing behind the gate and swinging it open. I staggered backward, my gaze locked on his form.

He returned to my side immediately, steadying me with his arm. "Are you all right?"

Was I? Maybe...yes. I managed a slow nod.

He studied me. "I realize this is all new to you. I must be more careful to avoid overwhelming you with my powers."

How many more did he possess? A handful? A dozen? Too many to count? I frowned as we pushed forward through the gate.

"There is much to discuss. Come."

That was a gross understatement. Why me? Why hide behind the mist for so many years, and what was the reason behind his sudden reveal? Why...why...why? I rubbed my aching temples. My head was filled with too many questions, but more kept rising to the surface of my mind. Glancing over, I searched his eyes. "Will you be truthful, no matter what I ask of you?"

The corner of his mouth twitched before his lips spread into a genuine smile. "Of course."

When we reached the gate, he bowed slightly and said, "After you."

As we crossed the estate's threshold, the three-story stone structure peeked through the trees, revealing colosseum-like archways and elegantly carved pillars. Beams of moonlight danced across the terracotta roof, but not a single light burned forth from the multitude of windows.

Though I'd gazed upon the building many times from afar, something about the way it appeared under the glow of the moon filled me with inner peace. My arms hung loosely at my sides, and a strange feeling of oblivion washed over me, as if I were dreaming. But I was awake, and all my sight beheld was real. He was real. Turning to him, I grabbed both his hands in mine. "Take me inside."

He laughed aloud and squeezed my hands. He ushered me past the circular brick drive, up the stone steps, and onto the massive stone porch at a human pace. Upon opening the front door, he stepped aside and said, "Please, come in."

My pulse fired beneath my numbed skin like a machine gun. Hesitant, jerky steps delivered me through the doorway and into the house. Standing in the center of the empty foyer, I turned in a slow circle.

A grand marble staircase dominated the room. A pair of medieval suits of armor stood at attention on either side, swords in hand, as if they were prepared to spring to life and defend on command. An elegant crystal chandelier, which I guessed to be hundreds of years old, hung from the cathedral-styled ceiling, shooting prisms like multicolored diamonds across the travertine floor.

I shuddered involuntarily. I was standing inside his home. I'd fallen asleep many nights fantasizing about such a moment. My fantasy paled in comparison to the reality.

Again, he took my hand. "The study is this way."

As he guided me through the dimly-lit hallway of the first floor, we passed several closed doors. Images of coffins filled with earth flashed through my mind. Giggles rose and tickled my throat. *Get a grip. This isn't Hollywood.* As our eyes met, the ridiculous images vanished from my thoughts.

He came to a halt in front of the second to last door and opened it, leading me into a large study. Scores of books lined the walls, ranging in age from ancient to modern, not a single cover filmed by dust. Obviously, he took pride in the room, which was decidedly a man's room, bedecked by brown leather furniture, a full bar, numerous trophies, and a display filled with antique swords—and all those books. As promised, a crackling fire glowed from within the hearth. The deliciously warm heat drew me closer and closer to the fireplace.

He stood at the opposite side of the room, brightness lighting his eyes as he looked at me. Gesturing toward one of the high-backed chairs surrounding the hearth, he said, "Have a seat."

I chose the one closest to the flames.

He sat across from me, clasping his hands over his knee. "Here we are, together at last."

All I seemed capable of answering with was, "Yes."

Crossing his legs, he queried, "Where shall we begin?"

I shrugged my shoulders. "I really don't know."

Appearing puzzled by my response, he stared up at the ceiling as if he were at a loss as to how we might proceed. He refocused on me in the space of another breath. "Surely, you must have questions."

My words rolled off my tongue as if I were caught in a trance. "Yes, but as I sit here, I find I've forgotten them all."

He cocked his head quizzically. "Are you frightened?"

I narrowed my gaze, wondering what might have prompted his question. I did not fear him. Maybe I had the first time he'd appeared at my window, but I had only been a child of six. Fear hadn't existed as a part of our relationship. "I'm not afraid. You know I'm not."

He stiffened in his chair and swallowed hard.

Was that apprehension? Seemed an odd reaction for a vampire. Had I imagined it? I must have. Fear shouldn't be any part of his nature. I went to him, kneeling at his feet. "Here you are, sitting in front of me, one-hundred percent real. I can see you, touch you, and no I'm not frightened."

He didn't speak, the same taut line drawing at his mouth.

His actions hadn't rung true. After revealing himself, he'd led me to his home, inviting my company. Did he feel vulnerable now that he'd taken on his physical form? Had the mist been a shield behind which he'd hidden? *No, definitely not.* Persistence, arrogance, and elegance better suited his personality, but I didn't know what to make of his current expression. But should I call him on it? I decided to return silently to my chair.

His face relaxed visibly. Clapping his hands, he rose from his seat and asked, "Would you care for something to drink? A glass of brandy, perhaps?"

"I've never tasted brandy before."

He approached the bar, his lips curling into a charismatic grin. "No time like the present to take your first drink of the stuff." After setting a glass on the bar, he uncapped a bottle and filled the glass halfway. As he handed it to me, he said, "Enjoy."

I held the glass under my nose and breathed in deeply. The spicy, burnt-amber scent awakened all my senses. I swallowed a mouthful to find it burned like fire. I set the glass down on the hearth as I choked the liquid down.

His eyes gleamed with silent laughter, as if my actions greatly amused him. Once he'd regained his solemnity, his powerful gaze studied me. Using his vampiric dominance, he interlocked our minds, extending his formidable reach deep into my memories. He'd never invaded my privacy before, and at present, I certainly hadn't given him permission. Rudeness didn't become him. I glared at him and shouted, "Stop!"

He released me at once.

I bolted straight up, crossing my arms. "More vampire powers? So, you possess the audacity and skill required to invade a human mind. What else can you do?"

"Shall I list them for you?"

"Yes, do list them," I demanded.

He tugged on his goatee and peered up at the ceiling. "Well, let's see..." His gaze darted back to me, a proud smile forming on his lips. "There's preternatural eyesight and hearing, coupled with superhuman strength and speed." His grin grew wider. "My movements occur too quickly to be followed by the human eye, which makes for the most enjoyable games of cat and mouse." He leaned forward in his chair and winked at me. "But my most favorite power of all is the control exerted by the vampire mind. You see, I can put you in a trance while I manipulate your mind and control your thoughts, or I can simply read them." He sat back, clasping his hands behind his head. "My mind can also move objects...and so on, and so on."

I scooted to the edge of my seat. "What about flying?"

"Only when I'm inside an airplane," he chuckled.

"So the part about being able to fly isn't true?"

Closing his eyes, he nodded. "It's true, I just choose not to."

I rattled off another question. "What about turning into a bat?"

He threw back his head and roared with laughter. "Completely ficti-tious." He rose and went back to the bar. "More brandy?"

"Still have some."

"Very well," he responded, pouring a glass of red wine and taking a generous swallow.

I blinked and did a double take. "You can drink alcohol?"

He grinned deviously. "When I was made vampire, I was provided with rules I must follow, as well as a list of things I would never be able to do again." He tilted his head for emphasis. "The rules are meant to be followed. The list, on the other hand, is something with which I've toyed, discovering two things I am still free to enjoy."

"Which are?"

"While we no longer require food or drink, I still thoroughly en-joy red wine." He studied the contents of his glass, turning the liquid this way and that in the warm glow of the fire. "Yes, I do love wine." Breaking free of the liquid spell, he added, "Secondly, I choose not to sleep in a coffin. I rest peacefully in my bed like everyone else."

I took in every word yet craved more of him. "How old are you?"

"When I was born into this new life, I had aged twenty-five years. That was seven hundred years ago."

My mouth fell open, and I almost dropped my glass. Seven hun-dred years! *My God, he was twenty-five during the thirteenth century.* "How do you do it? Doesn't it weigh on you, living so long, I mean?'

A gaze of longing overtook him, as he donned a slight smile. 'It's not as difficult as you might think. For an immortal, time becomes meaningless. We aren't bound by it as humans are; therefore, we don't much consider it."

I pressed my lips together, eyeing him. "By meaningless, are you referring to the fact that vampires don't taste death and humans do?"

His eyes widened at my words. "That's not at all what I meant, and I would never allow death to touch you."

I unbuttoned my coat, shedding it and throwing the garment over the arm of the chair. "But that's not your decision to make."

He winked at me. "But it could be."

I leaned forward to stare at him, memorizing every detail of his face. I'd had enough of the casual questions, feeling it was time to toss out some pointed ones. "Why did you pick me?"

He shifted in his chair, crossed and uncrossed his legs, and then leaned back in a carefree manner. "How could I not?"

I arched a brow. "That's not a real answer."

He placed his hand over his chest. "One cannot control the choices of the heart."

I crossed my arms stubbornly across my chest. "Again, not an answer. You promised to be truthful with me."

He gave me a firm nod. "That I did. Your beauty captured me, even when you were a child."

"Too vague. I need more. Where did you see me? How did you find me?"

"At the beach, just after sunset. You were with your family," he retorted, his tone crisp.

As I dug through mental pictures, a handful surfaced. Before my father had left, when we'd all still functioned as a family, my parents had taken me to the beach where I'd played in the sand, discovering seashells and sand crabs, leaving only after the sun crept below the horizon. I bit down on my lip and took in a deep breath. Happy times had been few and far between with my parents. They'd always seemed to be at odds with one another, placing me, unhappily, at the center of all the turmoil.

"Beth," he said, dragging me out of the past and back into the present.

I fired off another tough question. "Why did you disguise yourself by appearing only as mist?"

"Fear of rejection," he stated bluntly.

"I don't understand how you could think such a thing? I begged you to show yourself so we could be together. I gave my heart to you. I would've never rejected you."

He ran his hand over his face and then through his hair. "I didn't know that for certain."

I grabbed the glass of brandy, took a large swallow, grimaced, choked, and swallowed some more. "So, why now? What changed? Why are we sitting here staring at each other?"

He released a long, low sigh. "Danny forced my hand. He asked you to live with him. You were going to walk away, so I had to reveal myself."

Sounded reasonable; I'd give him that one. The last question rolled off my tongue, lifting the weight of all the whys. "Why did you leave France to make a new home in Castle Beach?"

He raised his brows. "Don't you know? Why, to be near you, Beth."

The objects in the room distorted, twisting and contorting around me. The spinning inside my head intensified, swirling faster and faster. Dizziness infected my brain, and a wave of nausea crashed over me. Was it the brandy or the conversation? Slowly, I stood, swaying before sinking back into the chair. Dropping my head into my hands, I moaned out my misery.

"Are you all right?" he asked, his voice heightened by concern.

A thick fog surrounded my brain. His voice sounded distant, even though he knelt at my side. Had he moved away as he'd spoken? He must have, again, too quickly for my human eyes to comprehend.

His hands cupped my face, his chilly thumbs swiping over my cheeks. My lashes fluttered and I tried to focus, but his image warped and swam before my eyes.

His form shifted at the speed of light, placing him back at the bar, and then again at my side before I'd drawn another breath. "Here, take a sip of water," he said, guiding a glass to my lips.

My dry throat craved the water. Tilting my head back, I allowed the cool liquid to fill my mouth and then swallowed gingerly after. Several sips later, my vision began to clear, and I looked into his eyes. My soul seemed to vibrate due only to his close proximity. I could feel my heart open itself up to him, as it thumped helpless and vulnerable inside my chest. I didn't understand this powerful connection which drew us together. Maybe he couldn't either.

His eyes glistened in the firelight as they searched mine. "Just as you wished to be with me, I, too, wished for your companionship. I've longed for this moment with you for centuries. Please don't deny me. Say you will stay the night," he pleaded.

My heart fluttered. I couldn't leave him, not when we'd only, truly, found each other that night. "Yes, I'll stay."

He laughed aloud and kissed both my hands. "Thank you." He helped me from my chair with a gentle touch. "Let me show you to one of the guest bedrooms."

He led me out of the study, past the lifeless medieval guards, and up the marble staircase. I glanced back at the ancient suits of armor and wondered why he'd placed them there as if on guard? Did he fear someone or something? Did the guards signify some type of warning? Could they come to life if he worked his vampire magic on the pair?

He put his arm around me, resting his hand in the small of my back. "They represent a part of my past I enjoy holding onto."

He'd read my mind. I squeezed his hand and said, "Someday, I hope you'll tell me all about your past."

He smiled back at me. "Someday, I will."

We climbed the grand staircase arm in arm. Paintings, which looked to have originated from the Renaissance period, hung side by side inside delicate gold frames along the wall facing the stairs. Every corner, in fact, was occupied by ancient treasures which must have captured a special place in his heart.

The second floor was swathed completely in darkness. Shadows escaped from every nook and corner, toying with my imagination before he switched on the hallway light. Beneath our feet, a majestic tapestry rug spanned the length of the corridor, causing me to envision kings and queens bearing candlesticks, gliding across the woven fabric and disappearing into one of the many rooms.

He pulled me closer, bending down to whisper into my ear, "You're quite the romantic."

As I became drawn into his gaze, the room began to spin. His presence utterly intoxicated me, but I ached for more...much more. "Why must you keep invading my thoughts?"

A charismatic smile adorned his lips. "Yours is a lovely mind. I can't seem to help myself." Once more, his hand came to rest on the small of my back as he continued to lead me down the hallway.

Antique silver mirrors hung in deliberate patterns along the wall, varying in size and design—perhaps more representation from his past. As we passed by, I caught his reflection in several of the glass surfaces, making me jump and clutch at my throat. "You cast a reflection!"

He chuckled. "That I do. Mankind can be blamed for the erroneous belief we do not." He peered into a mirror and smoothed his hair. "We're incredibly vain and enjoy admiring ourselves. I believe it quite possible mirrors were invented to serve the vampire above all others."

I touched his arm and laughed softly, still under his spell, despite his excessive vanity. "You may be right."

He interlocked our fingers, his eyes filled with adoration as he gazed at me while pulling me forward. "Come. Your room is here on the right."

I stared in stunned silence at the room's beauty. Heavy, hand-carved mahogany pieces furnished the elegant room. The contrast of delicate lace curtains framed each window, matching the coverlet and flowing canopy, the delicate fabrics adding a touch of innocence and purity to the space. A fire burned inside the hearth in the far corner, inviting me inside and enhancing the atmosphere with its soft, homey glow.

"In the morning when you wake, Betty will see to your needs. She's my human caretaker." He winked at me. "She will make you breakfast and anything else you may want, but please don't leave afterward. Wait for me to rise. Promise me this." His voice teetered on the verge of begging.

Entranced by his gaze, nothing else mattered but him. "I promise."

Without another word, he vanished, disappearing into thin air.

My eyelashes fluttered before I turned in a complete circle, staring at the empty space he'd left behind. *Probably something I'll have to get used to.* I shrugged my shoulders and closed the door, a yawn escaping me in a rush. Exhaustion slowly crept over me. I dragged myself to the ensuite bathroom and stepped inside. Opal sconces occupied the space above the porcelain sink, flanked by ivory towels neatly folded and ready for my use. A matching robe draped the back of the bathroom door, hanging by a hook, inviting me to pull it on. I stripped off my clothes and slipped into it, hugging the plush cotton against my skin. After pulling my hair up, I splashed water on my face and glanced into the oval mirror. A girlish giggle rose inside my throat. *I'm the luckiest girl in the world.* I blew a kiss to my reflection before skipping into the bedroom.

I turned off the light on the nightstand and sunk into the luxurious softness of the mattress, where sleep drew me down into its depths.

CHAPTER 2

I woke the next morning with an image of Philippe etched onto my brain. *I'm in his home.* Stretching my arms overhead, I sank back into the down pillows and breathed in the crisp scent of fresh linen. I tossed back the covers and jumped out of bed, a squeal escaping my lips as my feet touched the floor. A ravenous growl erupted from my stomach, demanding my attention. I tied the sash of my robe over my body and left the room in search of the mysterious Betty.

I padded softly across the tapestry rug, humming in time to my footsteps thumping through the dead quiet of the deserted hall. No voices, television, music, or even white noise sounded to indicate any other signs of life within the house. I didn't question the solitude. Vampires kept secrets, so the fewer people kept close who might expose those secrets, the better. Yet, he'd invited me into his home, so he must trust me. My heart swelled, and I stood a little taller. I would never betray that trust.

I bounced down the staircase, breezing past the guards before skidding to a stop in the center of the foyer. My eyes examined the vast hallways. Betty could be anywhere. Should I search every room?

As if I'd summoned her somehow, footsteps echoed at the rear of the foyer. A plump gray-haired woman, glasses balanced on the edge of her nose, ambled toward me. I raised my brows, believing her sudden arrival at the height of my bewilderment to be anything but coincidence. Had Philippe alerted her to my presence?

In a cheery tone, she said, "Hello, there. You must be the guest Mr. Delon told me about. I'm Betty. What's your name, dear?"

I tugged at my bathrobe and cleared my throat. Heat burned across my cheeks, spreading onto my ears. What must she think of me running around the house wearing nothing but a robe? I swept my hair over my ears and held out my hand. "That would be me, Beth."

She smiled wide as she took my hand and squeezed it. "Would you like some breakfast, Beth?"

My stomach rumbled, answering for me. I laughed and said, "Yes, thank you."

"The kitchen's this way." She bobbed her head to the right to indicate the direction, leading me down yet another dreary hallway and into any chef's dream kitchen.

Sunlight poured through the French doors, brightening the spacious room, shining off the pale walls, granite countertops, gleaming pots and pans, massive gas stove, and the other stainless steel appliances. Philippe had no use for such things. This room belonged to Betty.

She stood at the center island, her hands resting on her rounded hips, and asked, "What'll it be, Beth? Scrambled eggs, waffles, or maybe pancakes?

I mulled over my choices and decided, "Scrambled eggs would be heavenly."

As she reached overhead for a pan, she asked, "How about some bacon and toast too?"

Imagining the scent of sizzling bacon, I answered, "Mmm...yes, thank you."

Betty chuckled, turned toward the stove, and glanced out the French doors. "It's such a beautiful morning. Why don't I serve you by the pool?"

Wow. "Sounds amazing."

She pushed the doors open and waved me forward. "Come, dear."

I followed Betty across the slate-brick patio to a set of wrought-iron tables which faced a black-bottomed pool. A babbling fountain fed the pool from the right, the soothing rush of water over rock easing away all the residual tension in my body.

Betty pulled out a chair for me. "Enjoy the view, and I'll be back in a jiffy."

I gazed past the pool at the blanket of greenery. Forest-green, Granny Smith apples, and olive-toned trees painted the landscape in a way Philippe could never bear witness to in the daylight. *Seven hundred years without sunshine.* I brought my knees to my chest and hugged them.

Forever he'd overshadowed my life, but what details did I know about his own? The previous night's conversation had revealed very little, and I desired every last tidbit of information about him. I stared at the sunlight glistening on the water's surface. *If I'm going to become like him, I need to know everything about him.*

Betty broke through my thoughts when she delivered a plate of fresh fluffy eggs, smoked bacon, and buttered sourdough toast. "Here you are," she said, setting a tall glass of OJ beside the plate.

"It looks delicious. Thank you." I stabbed my fork eagerly into the eggs.

"You're most welcome. Enjoy your breakfast," she responded, turning to leave.

"Betty?" I called out, stopping her forward movement.

"Yes?"

I asked, "How long have you worked for Philippe?" digging for answers.

"Twenty years," she answered, short and sweet—and seriously lacking in detail.

I couldn't help myself and pressed further. "Surely, you must have some help. Are there others who live with you and Philippe on the property?"

She nodded and wiped her hands on the hem of her apron. "Mr. Delon employs a full staff, but only Jon Paul and I live on the estate."

"Jon Paul?"

"Mr. Delon's personal driver." She cut our conversation short by asking, "Is there anything else, dear? I must return to my duties."

"One more thing. Philippe asked me to stay and wait for him, but he didn't inform me of the hour I should expect him."

"I usually see Mr. Delon shortly after sunset. My guess is that he will appear at that time." She stepped toward the kitchen. "Do let me know if you need anything else."

"I will. Thanks, Betty."

As she walked away, I studied her. Did Betty know the truth? I laughed under my breath. Of course she knew. She lived in his house with full access to every room. Was she paid to look the other way? Maybe Betty also served as his protector, but what kind of physical threat could an older woman present? I cocked my head thoughtfully. *Batman did have Alfred.* I chewed at a piece of bacon, dismissing my harebrained theories.

After breakfast, I returned to my room. A long, hot, relaxing shower sounded like a wonderful idea. After hanging the robe on the bathroom door, I cranked the hot water, letting it flow for several minutes. Steam filled the bathroom, lingering close to the ceiling like a thick fog. As I stepped into the tub, wet beads of warmth rained over my body, caressing my skin, and I closed my eyes, leaning into the swirling stream. I lost focus, lingering somewhere close to sleep. How long I remained in that state, I couldn't say. Maybe five minutes, fifteen, a half-hour? Finally, I shut off the water and changed back into my clothes, settling on the bed after.

Thirty minutes ticked by at a snail's pace, and the nagging itch of boredom sent my thoughts spinning in a thousand dangerous directions. *Sneak through the house and find his room*, was one of them. The idea teased my brain and challenged my body. I fell back onto the bed, closing my eyes and shaking my head, but the urge to find him remained, coaxing me to my feet. Biting my lip, I hurried toward the door, slipping off my shoes before I exited the room. My stomach fluttered as my hand grasped the knob and swung the door wide.

I glanced left and then right down the long hallways. Which path would lead me to him? I waited for some magical force to pull me in the right direction. When nothing summoned me, I shrugged my shoulders and decided to try left. My reflection pursued me, jumping from mirror to mirror as I traveled down the dimly-lit corridor. My mind drifted, envisioning him lying in bed, his long dark locks flowing over his pillow while I stood over him. He awoke and reached for me, and willingly, I fell into his arms. He kissed me, his lips nuzzling down my neck to my breasts. Swept up in his passion, I pressed against him as he sunk his fangs deep into my flesh.

I jerked my head backward, shattering the fantasy. Becoming a vampire's victim wasn't an item on my bucket list. I stood completely still, contemplating while I ran my hand over my throat. *Return to my room or continue on?* Strengthening my resolve, I lifted my head high and decided, *I'm moving on.*

As I crept down the hall, a door came into view, beckoning me to invade its privacy. My pulse surged and thumped inside my head like war drums. I rushed forward to grab the knob and thrust the door open.

Sunlight broke into the room through the partially drawn curtains. Black furniture with hard lines dominated the cold, colorless suite. The temperature plummeted inside the room, and I felt the cold advance as I crossed the threshold. Shuddering, I attempted to rub the chill from my arms. Along with the drop in temperature came the eerie sensation I was being watched. I listened intently, cocking my head to the side. Only the sound of silence kept me company in the room. Was my mind playing tricks on me? I turned in a circle, squinting into the gloom. Unable to shake the feeling, I left the room and closed the door, my gaze lingering on the wood even after it had closed. I backed away carefully until several feet separated me from the room, before continuing my search for Philippe.

I stood before the next door, tapping my finger against my leg. I chewed nervously at my lip as I inched the door open. Sparse, delicate white pieces, full of purity and innocence stood before me, a complete contrast from the black room I'd just visited. How could two rooms of such contrasting good and evil share a common wall? Was this interior decorating representative of real life? Had Philippe acted as the designer, exposing his opposing natures in a physical manner? *Find him.* A rush of adrenaline spiked my blood. After pulling the door closed, I ran to the next room.

A pitch-black wall greeted me when I entered. After gently pushing the door closed, I stood with my back resting against its frame, waiting for my eyes to adjust. Bit by bit, shapes formed, a draped bed coming into view. A hazy form, barely visible through the sheer curtains, lay upon the mattress. I peered closer. My mouth went dry, and sweat trickled over my palms. *I'm in Philippe's room.* My legs suddenly felt composed of gelatin. What if he awoke, drained my blood, took my life? I held my breath and focused on our conversation the night before. He'd never threatened me, displaying only kindness and hospitality. I found in my heart that I trusted him.

Feeling along the wall, my hand found a light switch. I hesitated before flipping it on. The warm glow of the bulb illuminated a room furnished with large, bulky, 14th-century furniture. Louis the XIV in-spired, perhaps? The king-size canopy bed posts met the ceiling, and off to its right stood a massive writing desk, and to its left, an empty hearth. A candlestick placed at its center caught my eye. I crept to the desk on my tiptoes, like a thief. With a shaky hand, I lit the candle with the lighter resting at its base and hurried back to the light switch to snap it off.

Holding the dancing yellow flame before me, I inched along the hardwood floor to his bedside. After I'd set the candlestick on the night-stand, I grabbed the edge of the curtain, my breaths coming hurried and restless. I fought to steady my nerves, exhaling before easing the curtain open.

Philippe lay with his arms folded across his chest, a tranquil ex-pression written into his face.

A cold wave crashed over me, and I struggled to breathe. My legs brushed up against the mattress as I gazed down at him. I brushed a strand of hair from his pale forehead and whispered, "I found you." And I lost all reason in that moment. I felt I could never leave him, this vampire. Leaning over, I softly touched my lips to his. Immediately, lust pumped through my veins. I came alive with a hunger I'd never known. My mouth lingered on his, reluctant to leave his behind, want-ing more...so much more. My heart demanded I curl up next to him and never leave his side; nonetheless, I blew out the candle and hurried from his room.

I ran back toward my own room, lust-driven fantasies of his fangs sinking into my neck tormenting me. When I reached the door, I bolt-ed inside and slammed it shut. I collapsed onto the bed, dizzy and intoxicated, visions of Phillippe taking my human life playing behind my closed lids.

A distant tapping, which steadily grew louder, pulled me from my dreams. With a jerk, I sat upright. The sound came from the other side of my door. I glanced at my watch and blinked. Five hours had slipped by effortlessly.

The knocking sound persisted.

Smoothing my hair, I called, "Come in."

Philippe sauntered through the door, sending my heartbeat leaping into my throat. He came to my bedside, frowning. "You were asleep?"

I glanced around the room as if some corner of it held the answer. "I guess so."

The color of his eyes brightened as he gazed at me, a charming smile set on his face. Gesturing toward the door, he said, "Come. I'll have Betty prepare dinner for you."

The five hours of sleep had returned some sense to me. I had a life I needed to get back to. "I can't stay," I said, but my tone lacked conviction.

A deep wrinkle creased his forehead. "What? No, you must stay."

I shook my head. "I don't belong to your world. You and I are too different."

A pained grimace spread across his face. "You're wrong," he argued, his tone sharp. *You* and *I* are the same. You mustn't leave; you can't. There is so much more for us to explore."

We weren't the same at all. I was human, he was not. We would mix like oil and water. "Danny's probably worried sick about me. I have to go."

Yet again, he moved with a speed too quick for my human eyes, landing in a spot beside me on the bed. "I have known you for your entire lifetime. I cannot let you go." He took my hands into his. "Come and live with me."

My posture stiffened, and my mouth fell open. "What?" I didn't wait for his reply but pushed off the bed and hurried toward the door.

He blocked the doorway before I'd closed half the distance and declared, "We are meant to be together."

As I stared into his blue-gray eyes, my resolve weakened. My heart ripped wide open, bleeding out sheer agony at the thought of leaving him, but as a mortal, how could I possibly live in his immortal world?

His gaze turned fierce, and he blurted out, "You were in my room today."

A heated blush stung my cheeks. I released a gasp and backed away.

A sense of urgency permeated his voice, and he clasped his hands in desperation. "I wanted nothing more than to open my eyes and look upon you while you stood there, but I feared I would frighten you. Instead, I lay listening to your thoughts. And then, you kissed me. The sweet touch of your lips felt like I had truly died and been sent to Heaven."

The heat spread from my face to flood my entire body. I ached for him, but he held me at a great disadvantage with his ability to read me and learn my secrets, while I could rely only on my intuition.

"True," he said, grinning.

I folded my arms across my chest and glared at him. "Will my thoughts ever be my own again?"

He placed his hands on my shoulders, forgiveness softening his face. "I must apologize. I hold no intention of invading your privacy. Reading you simply happens so that, at times, I don't even realize I am doing so. I respect you, all humans in fact, but I'll admit my curiosity does get the better of me now and again," he said, attempting to explain himself.

For some unknown reason, I chose to believe him. Most likely, he was only behaving in accordance with his nature.

His expression took on a haunted look. "I have yearned to be embraced by love. You can't imagine what it's like to experience never-ending rejection. Humans would see me only as a monster. My loneliness has made me long for death, wishing to end my misery, my pain. I closed the door to the living world until I met you."

My pulse throbbed under my fingertips as I stroked my neck. A deep yearning to be near him drove me closer to his body. "You said we were the same, but how could that be possible?"

"My human soul has been awakened once again, and you are the reason for the change. From the moment I looked into your eyes, I knew you and I shared but one heart. I let you in, knowing my life would no longer be empty with you to fill it. We are the same at our cores because our souls are both human."

His words didn't make complete sense to me, but the love-struck girl inside my body didn't need them to. I stepped closer until our bodies touched. "I can't deny it; some part of me deep inside longs to be with you. I do feel connected to you somehow. I believe you're right, and we're destined to be together."

The color of his eyes brightened, twinkling like jewels. "Then come and live with me."

His request made me tingle all over. *He* made me happy. "Yes, I will."

"Thank you." The way he breathed the words out sounded more like a sigh of relief. "When can I expect you?"

"I have to take care of some things first...like Danny. A week, maybe two."

He shook his head stubbornly. "That's too long for us to wait. You must come sooner. We must not be parted for any considerable length of time."

"I'll try."

"Very well," he answered, seemingly satisfied for the moment.

We stared at each other for a moment, drawn out into forever, before he guided me out the door and toward the staircase. A dull pain tugged at my heart. I felt the discomfort intensify with each step I took, which would draw me away from him.

"I'll have my driver, Jon Paul, take you home," he told me as we reached the foyer. A heartfelt, yet confident smile claimed his face. "I promise to offer you a life you will find unforgettable."

Every cell in my body believed him.

When I emerged onto the front porch, a slate-colored BMW with darkly tinted windows pulled up the brick drive. The driver parked inches from the porch and opened his door. A tall man of European descent with dark hair, fair skin, and deep blue eyes stepped out of the car. He straightened the jacket of a very expensive gray suit and nodded curtly at Philippe.

Philippe escorted me to the car. "Jon Paul, please, take Beth home."

With another brief nod, he opened the rear passenger door. "Right away, Mr. Delon."

As I turned to leave, Philippe grabbed me and pulled me into an embrace. He gazed down at me. "Beth, your beauty dazzles me. Your features remind me of a hand-painted porcelain doll, striking, yet delicate."

He clutched at me with such urgency, his touch set my soul on fire. After burying his hands in my hair, his lips lightly brushed my neck, inviting me to roll my head backward in surrender.

We held each other a moment longer before I pulled away and slid into the back seat. As Jon Paul pulled away from the driveway and onto the road, Philippe faded into the distance. My heart ached for him already.

CHAPTER 3

I stumbled backward when I reached the top step leading into my apartment. Danny sat huddled by my front door, holding his head in his hands. My fingers turned icy at the sight, and I shoved them inside my coat pocket. The chills spilled throughout my body, and I shuddered. The temptation to flee crossed my mind. I'd lacked the time to rehearse a breakup speech but putting off *"It's over"* didn't make any sense. I knew I had to tell him. After all we'd been through, he deserved the truth. I heaved out a heavy sigh and stepped forward.

Danny's head jerked up, his eyes widening. After scrambling to his feet, he threw his arms around me, squeezing me hard. He pressed his lips to my cheek, then murmured, "Beth, thank God you're all right. I was so worried."

I swallowed, my throat painfully dry. "I'm sorry I worried you, but don't forget that you left me behind. You did leave me there, alone with the mist."

He took a step back to study me, shaking his head. "I went back to our bench to find you. I must've walked up and down the beach a hundred times. I thought something terrible had happened to you." He pointed in the direction of my front door, a scowl forming on his forehead. "And *she* was no help. Anna wouldn't even let me in." He folded his arms aggressively and demanded, "Where have you been?"

I dug my keys out of my coat pocket with trembling hands, nearly dropping them as I attempted to shove the house key into the lock. "Let's go inside."

Pushing the door open ahead of me, he finished with, "And talk."

I nodded. "Yes, we do need to talk."

My roommate, Anna, paced the living room carpet inside. When her eyes met mine, she released a shrill gasp, running her hands through her pitch-black hair as her dark-brown eyes glossed over with relief. "Damn it, Beth, you scared the crap out of me." She arched a brow at Danny. "Him too."

Danny threw his hands in the air. "I have a name, ya know."

She glared at him, tapping her foot. "Beth, he left you there alone. He doesn't deserve an explanation from you."

"Stay out of our business," Danny snapped.

I thrust my arms out in both their directions, as if holding each of them at bay. "Don't you two start." I turned to face Anna. "I'm sorry. I'll explain everything later. Right now, I really need to talk to Danny. Could you please give us some privacy?"

The two of them had always loathed one another, each vying constantly for my attention. The girl before me with dark hair and eyes and dimpled cheeks had been my best friend since college. When Anna and I had lived on campus, we were right across the hall from each other. We'd always shared all our secrets with nothing to come between us... except Danny and the mist. What would she think of my latest rash decision? Would she be able to understand the sense of destiny I felt so strongly driving my heart?

Anna's face softened. "Anything for you, Beth." She marched down the hall and entered her bedroom, closing her door behind her.

I entered the kitchen, dragging my feet, and grabbed two glasses, along with a bottle of wine—a must for the upcoming conversation. After filling them to the rim, I handed one to Danny and took a generous swig from my own.

He swayed side to side, shifting his weight, his gaze glued to me.

"Danny, relax. Take a sip of wine."

He chugged the entire contents and placed the empty glass on the counter. "Where were you?"

I rubbed the back of my neck, nervously scraping the fingers of my other hand through my hair. "Where doesn't matter. *With whom* does."

He scrunched his eyebrows together, a storm building behind his eyes. "What?"

I took his arm and led him into the living room, pulling him down beside me on the couch. My voice quivered when I said, "I—I met him, Danny. He finally showed himself."

He sat motionless, his jaw locked. He dipped his head when he spoke next. "*Him*?"

"Yes."

He looked away from me, staring off at nothing. His hands fell into his lap. "You spent the night with him?"

"Yes."

When he turned his head to look at me, his eyes were full and sad, like an abandoned puppy's. "Did you sleep with him?"

I jerked my chin up in disbelief. "No, Danny."

He gave me a half-hearted smile. "At least that's something, but the hold he has over you…is something supernatural. I–I'm only human. I can't compete with him, Beth."

My heartbeat slowed, mournfully thumping out a melancholy rhythm inside my heaving chest. "I don't expect you to, and I'm so sorry. I love him. You know I've always loved him."

The color drained from his face as he slowly nodded his head. "I do know." Gripping up a fistful of his shirt like he was having a heart attack, he let out a strangled breath and rose to his feet. "I have to go. I can't be here…be around you. It hurts too much."

I slumped forward as I bore witness to his pain, my arms wrapping around my shoulders. Tears burned behind my eyes. As he staggered toward the door, I jumped to my feet and cried, "I do love you too, Danny."

He stopped and turned to face me. Spasms of agony gripped his shoulders. "Don't say that. Don't ever say that to me again." He tore open the door and disappeared.

Violent shudders ran through me again and again. I couldn't stop shaking. Tears blurred my vision before streaming down my cheeks. I'd just wounded and lost my best friend, who'd put up much less of a fight than I would've ever expected. I fell back on the couch, staring at the patterns in the ceiling.

As if from under water, I heard Anna's door open and her feet scurry through the hall, delivering her into the living room. She sat by my side, wrapping her arms around me. "What happened?"

I clung to her, burying my face in her T-shirt. "We broke up."

Soothing her hand over my back, she asked, "Are you okay?"

I shook my head in response—the only one I could manage.

My cell's ringtone, "Me and My Broken Heart," blared too loud inside the room. *How fitting.* It sounded twice more before I released Anna and reached inside my coat to retrieve it.

Crossing her arms defiantly, she muttered, "It's probably Danny calling with a change of heart."

As I brushed away tears, I cleared my throat and peered at the screen. Restricted. I glanced at Anna. "It's not Danny," I told her as I tapped the screen. "Hello?"

"Beth," Philippe queried, his rich, velvety voice floating into my ear.

My heart fluttering, I cradled the phone and pressed it against my cheek. "How did you—"

He finished my question. "Get your number?"

Anna, still seated next to me, whispered, "Who is it?"

I waved her question away, my eyes begging for her silence.

"Is someone with you?" he asked.

"Anna. My roommate, Anna. But, again, how did you get my number?"

"I'm a vampire. I have...connections." Glee danced amidst his words.

I sank into the cushions, my pain drifting away at the mere sound of his voice. Wishing he were beside me, I plucked a pillow off the couch and held it close. "I really needed to hear your voice right now."

"Are you all right?" He paused and then softly added, "You've been crying."

I stroked the pillow. "I'm better now."

"I can't stop thinking about you." A sense of urgency bled through his words. "Move in tomorrow. I can't wait another day."

I sat upright, dropping the pillow. "That's impossible. I have a job, a roommate...all my belongings."

Anna grabbed my arm, tugging at it. "Who is it? What's going on?"

I covered the phone and whispered, "I'll explain everything once I hang up."

She let out a huff that reminded me of a two-year-old initiating a tantrum and crashed back against the couch cushions.

"Anna again?"

"Never mind about Anna. Twenty-four hours isn't enough notice. I have to pack. I need boxes to hold all the stuff. And tomorrow's Sunday, so there's no way I could find movers who weren't already booked. And then, Monday, I'm back to work." I took in a breath before continuing. "And my friend, Anna, will need to find a new roommate. You can't expect her to find one in just a couple of days."

He fired back, attempting to shoot holes in all my excuses. "I can have a moving company on your doorstep first thing in the morning, and they'll bring all the boxes you require. They'll even pack for you. You may return to work or choose not to, your choice, but I can provide all you will ever need, as well as cover Anna's expenses while she searches for another roommate." He paused, before adding, "This resolves each of your concerns, yes?"

His words made my head buzz with incredulity. Could I do something so impulsive? Change my entire life and return to him?

"Yes, you can," he purred in his charismatic voice.

Again with the mind reading! "Okay, we need to set some boundaries. If I wanted you to know what I'm thinking, I would say it out loud. You need to respect that."

"Forgive me," he said, his voice deeply sincere. "I will try to abide by your wishes, but I cannot promise I will succeed. Reading minds has become a part of my nature."

"Fair enough."

"I'm forgiven, yes?"

"Yes."

"What of my proposal? Will you come to me tomorrow? May I arrange for the movers?"

I bit my lip and squeezed the pillow. "Yes."

"Wonderful," he replied, the pitch of his voice raising an octave. "I will inform Betty. Is there anything else I can do?"

"Yes. Tell me how much you miss me."

"Words cannot describe the emptiness I feel when not in your presence," he remarked, his tone both gentle and heartfelt. "Tomorrow, I will hold you in my arms, even though tonight will undoubtedly feel like the longest night of my immortal life. Goodbye, my love." With those words, he ended the call.

I held my phone against my ear, refusing to let go of the comfort of his voice. Anxiety twisted in the pit of my stomach, making me nauseous. I had committed to becoming his companion, his lover. I fanned myself with the pillow momentarily, before dropping my phone and rising to my feet. My thundering heart seemed to propel a flood of questions to race through my mind. Did vampires have sex? Was the desire for sex replaced by that of draining another's lifeblood? Perhaps the drinking of blood was all they knew of sexual pleasure?

Anna grabbed my shoulders, shaking me as she blurted out, "Spill already. Who was that? What's going on? Why would I need a new roommate?"

I flopped down on the couch and sank into the cushions. I felt my chest cave in on itself as I uttered, "Philippe." How would she ever understand my rash decision? I barely understood what I was feeling myself.

"Who the hell is Philippe?"

I opened my mouth to explain and then quickly snapped it shut. Anna had never taken the whole mist/vampire thing seriously, even though she'd born witness to countless gifts appearing magically on my bed and heard all my late-night conversations when she'd thought me to be alone in my room. She'd blamed my obsession with vampires on Danny, insisting he was a bad influence with his own brand of overactive imagination influenced by constant comic book reading.

I searched her face—a firm wrinkle creased her forehead. No, I couldn't tell her who Philippe *really* was...not at that moment. For the time being, it seemed more reasonable to fib. "I met him a few months ago. We kept it secret, but things recently got serious. He just asked me to move in with him."

Her mouth dropped open in shock. "What?"

Just the thought of living with Philippe spread a warm fuzziness throughout my body. I couldn't stop smiling, sitting upright and taking her hands in my own. "Oh, Anna, he's everything I've ever dreamed about. I can't stop thinking about him."

She sat stone still and arched a brow at me. "Who is this guy?"

If I said he was a seven-hundred-year-old vampire, she, of course, would never believe me. But I had to tell her something. Shrugging my shoulders, I went with succinct truth. "The one."

The wrinkle furrowed deeper as she regarded me.

I held my tongue, leaving her in the dark. Her expression told me she knew what I was doing. We'd never kept secrets...and I'd broken our code.

"Does your soulmate have a last name?"

"Delon, Philippe Delon."

She searched my eyes, hers narrowed. "Do you love him?"

His blue-gray eyes flashed behind my eyes. A pang stabbed at my heart; his absence painful. Touching my finger to my lips, I said, "Yes." In actuality, I'd loved him for most of my life.

She blinked in slow motion. "You're really caught up in this guy."

Yes, Anna, I am, and he's a real live vampire, not just a figment of my imagination. One day I'm going to tell you that. "Like I said, he's the one."

"So, when's the big move?"

"He said movers will be showing up tomorrow morning. I need to start getting my things together."

She sprang to her feet. "Jesus, Beth, nothing like waiting until the last minute."

I fixed my gaze on her and sat silently, yet my mind was awhirl, shouting internally of all I wanted to say, but couldn't breathe a word of. *No, Anna, it's not last minute. I've waited almost my entire life for this very moment—the moment I would finally be with the love of my life. To an outsider looking in, my actions may seem hasty, rushed, inconceivable, irrational, and foolish, but to me, they are so very right, like connecting that final piece of the puzzle. No one, not you, Danny, or anyone can know the utter loneliness, the heartrending sadness, the gut-wrenching pain I've felt over the years separated from my one true love. So yes, I will drop everything, sacrifice everything, throw caution to the wind to rush into his arms and not wait a second longer. The only opinion, conclusion, or judgment that matters now are my own and Philippe's.*

She pursed her lips at me. "You're going to go forward with this no matter what I say, true?"

"I've made my decision, Anna. You can sit back and watch or you can help. Either way, I'm doing this."

She grabbed my hand, pulling me down the hall and into my bedroom. "I think you're crazy, but I know you. You've made up your mind, and I'm not going to be able to change it, so let's get busy."

The open window inside my bedroom brought me to a standstill. An open window had been part of my life, like a limb, and had controlled me for so many years. With Philippe's appearance, it had lost its power over me. A sense of relief ran through me, like warm water, relaxing every muscle under my skin. For the first time in my life, I was able to close a window.

I turned to Anna. "Keep the furnishings. All I really need are my personal belongings."

She frowned. "You're sure?"

"His house is full of stuff. There's no reason for me to bring more." I wrapped an arm around her shoulders and pulled her close. "Besides, you partly own all the furniture. Most of these things we bought together."

Her eyes moistened with tears. "Thank you. I just hate to see you leave. It sure will be quiet around here without you."

My chin trembled. "Don't start crying or you'll get me started. Come on, help me get my stuff together."

She swiped at her eyes and nodded, opening drawers and stacking my clothes for me a minute later.

We didn't get to sleep until after three in the morning. Piles of clothes, shoes, jewelry, toiletries, CDs, papers, books, and knickknacks cluttered my room. We crashed on the floor at the center of it all, sharing a blanket and pillow.

The next morning, I awoke with a start and ran into the bathroom to splash water on my face, tie my hair into a ponytail, and throw on a T-shirt and pair of leggings, all just minutes before the doorbell chimed.

Stepping over a still sleeping Anna, I hurried to the door and yanked it open.

Four men wearing canary-yellow shirts and khakis crowded on my doorstep, each armed with a tall stack of boxes.

Anna shuffled up behind me, rubbing her eyes, and mumbled, "Let them in. I'll make some coffee."

I showed them into the mess my room had become, climbing over scattered items while pointing and instructing. "All of this is coming with me. What can I do to help?"

The tallest of the bunch addressed me. "Mr. Delon gave us instructions, ma'am. We will take care of everything."

I smiled. Philippe taking care of me already. I had to admit, I kind of liked that. I nodded in acknowledgement. "Would anyone like some coffee?"

The tallest man answered again. "No thanks, ma'am. We're fine."

I left them alone in my room so I could join Anna in the kitchen for some coffee.

The packing went rather smoothly, taking less than an hour for all my belongings to be secured inside cardboard. After they were all loaded onto the truck, Anna and I stood in front of our apartment building with our arms around each other. "On to bigger and better things," I said, letting out a nervous laugh.

Anna gave me a squeeze. "Get in your car, and I'll follow you. I'm dying to meet the man you'd drop everything for."

My stomach clenched. My friend couldn't have chosen a more horrible set of words, but then, she didn't know she was about to come face-to-face with a vampire. I forced a smile before climbing into my car. Slowly, I backed out of the driveway and onto the street. Our apartment building filled my rearview mirror, as if it were saying goodbye. I blew it a kiss, determined to never look back.

As I neared his street, I searched among the treetops for the terra-cotta roof. A hint of the red brick peeked through the trees as I rounded the corner. Excitement churned within my stomach as the wrought-iron gate stood open, anticipating my arrival. I didn't slow down, zooming through the opening and onto the property I would now call home. After parking the car on the circular drive, I sat gazing at the mansion, the blaring thud of my heartbeat blocking out all other sound. In the light of day, the enormous stone walls of the castle seemed to come alive, throwing out a strange energy. Every flower, tree, and blade of grass bathed in the sunlight and painted the grounds with vibrant color.

Anna pulled up alongside me and parked. She stumbled out of her car, her mouth hanging open as her large dark eyes roamed over the mansion. I climbed out of my car and stood next to her.

She turned, a smile forming on her lips, and uttered, "Beth...oh my God. No wonder you were in such a hurry to move."

The movers arrived, parking several feet from the front door. The same man who'd spoken to me back at the apartment jumped out, lead-ing the way for the others up the steps to the door and ringing the bell. Anna and I followed behind.

After a few minutes, Betty appeared in the open doorway. Her face lit up with joy as she took both my hands into her own. "Beth, dear, Mr. Delon informed me of your impending arrival. I'm delighted to hear you'll be staying with us."

While standing at the front door, my heartbeat finally slowed, find-ing its rhythm. A sense of peace filled me, as if the mansion had always served as my home. I suddenly remembered my friend standing at my side. "Betty, this is my friend, Anna."

Betty shook Anna's hand. "Pleased to meet you."

Anna nodded and smiled but didn't say a word.

"Please, come in," Betty said, her tone bubbly. "Your room is wait-ing for you." She turned to the men, focusing on the tall one who seemed to be in charge. "Mr. Tibbs, please, follow me. I will show you where to place Beth's things."

The movers and I followed Betty upstairs, while Anna waited in the lobby. The sight of the beautiful mansion, staffed with people who wished to take care of one's every need, had left her speechless. I giggled. She would totally freak once she laid eyes on Philippe. The beauty and elegance of the man who owned such a lavish home would surely send her over the edge.

Betty led us into the same room I'd slept in the night before. "I'll take care of this, dear. Go visit with Anna," she urged, shooing me out the door.

With Betty in charge of the movers, I returned to Anna. She appeared trapped in a daze as she stared up at the exquisite chandelier. "Are you all right?" I asked, placing my hand on her shoulder.

She slowly bobbed her head up and down. "Can I move in too?"

We both burst out laughing.

She grabbed my hands and asked, "When can I meet him, Beth?"

"Soon." The truth was that I had no idea when he might appear.

"The movers should be done shortly," Betty informed us, treading lightly down the stairs and past the guards.

"Thank you," I told her with sincerity. Then, I glanced over at Anna. She was eyeing up the suits of armor and rubbing her arms as if caught in an unexpected snowstorm without a coat. I fell back a few steps and reached for her hand.

Staring hard at the two metallic sentries, she whispered, "What a weird thing to place on either side of your staircase."

I gave her hand a squeeze and pulled her forward. "Just ignore them."

"Girls, I put some brie and mini toasts in the TV room for you," Betty announced.

I realized I was lost in my own new home. "Where *is* the TV room?"

She smacked her palm against her forehead and shook her head. "Silly me, of course you'd have no idea yet. Please, follow me."

Betty ambled down the hallway of the first floor, and we followed. Three doors in, she stopped to open a door on the right, revealing the mysterious TV room. I gawked at the interior, my jaw dropping open. "TV room" had not accurately described what lay inside. Movie theater would've been a more befitting label.

"Make yourselves at home," Betty said, gesturing toward the massive velvet sectional. "Would you girls like some wine?"

I shook off my stupor so I could manage a reply. "That would be great, thank you."

"Red or white?"

I looked at Anna, already knowing her preference. "White."

A moment or two after Betty had left us, Anna embraced me and released a high-pitched giggle. "This place is too good to be true. I mean, look around, Beth."

I spun in a circle, examining every corner of the room. A black velvet sectional lined the back and the right wall, but there were also giant throw pillows spread across the surface of the plush carpet. A wide, theater-sized screen claimed the entire center wall. Speakers hung in every corner. A delicious-looking tray of brie and mini toasts lay waiting for us on the L-shaped coffee table.

"I must be dreaming," Anna said, shaking her head.

I pulled her toward the sectional so we could plop down. The TV controls were built into the arm of the massive couch. When the picture flickered into being, I flipped through the channels.

Betty returned, carrying a bottle of wine and two glasses. She popped the cork and poured a glass for each of us. "Do you need anything else, girls?"

I smiled and said, "We're good. Thank you, Betty."

"Enjoy," she said before retreating and leaving us alone.

Anna and I gorged on the brie, mini toasts, and wine. Betty checked in on us, bringing more food and a lot more wine. By sunset, drunkenness had claimed us both. We slid off the sectional and onto the throw pillows, laughing uncontrollably.

Then, Philippe entered the room.

My heartbeat skyrocketed, sending my pulse into a throbbing frenzy and driving adrenaline through my veins. I struggled futilely to reclaim my composure. He had sent my emotions—my whole body—spiraling out of control.

Anna gripped my arm, her dark eyes growing vast and pensive.

Philippe's eyes met mine. He didn't speak aloud. Privately, he declared, "I've missed you beyond belief. I am elated to see you."

I filled my mind with words. *I'm happy to see you too.*

His face lit with delight, and he flashed me a charming smile.

Anna jumped to her feet and thrust her hand out. "I'm Anna."

I pushed to my feet, swaying, before catching my balance, and gestured to my bestie. "Philippe, this is Anna. Anna, Philippe."

He took her hand and kissed below her knuckles. "I'm enchanted to meet you."

Anna stared...then blushed.

I nudged her forcefully.

"It's nice to meet you too," she blurted out.

Philippe took my hand. A wrinkle creased his brow as if he were troubled. "I'm sorry to inform you that I must go out for a short while. I'll be back as soon as I can."

Was he going out to hunt and feed?

He bent over, softly touching his lips to mine. I died and went to heaven all in the space of those few precious seconds. Instinctively, I wrapped my arms around him, pulling him close and refusing to let go.

"Beth, I must leave," he whispered urgently into my ear.

I hugged him fiercely, feeling his heartbeat against mine. I drew in a breath, as if I could draw his essence into my body, before allowing him to pull away. We gazed at each other, a moment frozen in time, before he turned and strode gracefully from the room.

Anna punched my arm playfully. "Damn it, Beth. He's frigging gorgeous. You definitely found yourself a prince." She frowned and tilted her head. "He's a little on the pale side, but still absolutely gorgeous."

In a dreamy voice, I answered, "He is, isn't he?"

Winking, she asked, "Does he have a brother?"

I laughed before rubbing at my brow in honest bewilderment. Did my intended have a family, and if so, were they an immortal family? The hairs on the back of my neck stirred to attention, and I broke out in a cold sweat. I wanted to tell her the truth, tell her everything. "Philippe, he's…" I took a step back, clamping my mouth shut. My longtime love's deepest, darkest secret had almost slid from my tongue so effortlessly. Would Philippe agree to the sharing of such a secret? I couldn't tell her, not yet. I had to speak with Philippe first.

Anna came to me and took my hand, her brows knitting together as she whispered softly to me, "You can tell me anything, you know that."

I looked to the floor. "It's the wine. I should lie down."

"Do you want me to stay?"

"I'll be okay. I just need to rest. I'll have Philippe's driver take you home, and one of the other staff members can follow in your car. I'll call you tomorrow."

The motherly look on her face said it all. She didn't believe I was fine at all.

CHAPTER 4

After Anna left, I finished off the last of the wine. In one gulp, I emptied the remainder of the bottle. My shoulders slumped forward like an old man's, and I heaved out a sigh. I'd lied to her, kept her in the dark. Blurting out the fact that my lover was a vampire would require validation. Anna had always been a skeptic, requiring proof, hard facts, a visual—like Philippe exposing his fangs. How could she refute immortal teeth the size of daggers? I'd figure out the particulars later with a clear head. After setting my empty glass—and the empty bottle—on the coffee table, I staggered out of the TV room, down the hall, and up the staircase. It was all I could do to lumber up the stairs, making my way to my room.

In the bathroom, I somehow managed to stumble into my pajamas. I tapped the faucet on and let the cold water run while I rested my head against the mirror. Slipping my hands under the stream, I gathered up enough water to splash on my face and neck. The cool water gave me a jolt, and I shuddered. Icy liquid ran through my hair, dribbled down my face, and into my mouth as I stuck my head in the sink. I rolled the cool liquid over my tongue like a thirsty dog. It was several minutes later before I turned off the water, combing out my hair while it was still wet.

Refreshed, I drifted down the hallway and stopped at Philippe's door. My pulse surged when I turned the knob, but I gathered my courage and charged inside. My fingertips prickled, aching to touch everything belonging to him which fell into my sight. I climbed atop his bed, sinking into the mattress as I listened to the beat of my lovesick heart pummeling my eardrums. I latched onto his pillow, pressing it under my nose and breathing in his spicy musk cologne. The room spun and my eyelashes fluttered. I felt as though I were floating above the clouds like a bird and clung to the pillow for some semblance of stability, imagining the firm shape to be his body. I couldn't determine how much later it was when I stirred and hopped off his bed.

Double doors on the opposite side of the room called to me. I couldn't resist throwing them open and strolling inside the gigantic walk-in closet. Rows of dark suits hung neatly on the left, while jeans, sweaters, and T-shirts claimed the right. Countless pairs of shoes covered the bottom shelf. Excitement swirled in my belly as I stroked my fingers over the fabrics, lighting my skin afire. Sweat trickled between my breasts as I imagined him in every outfit my hands explored. I blew out a heated breath and fanned myself.

The gray sweater he'd worn the other night caught my eye, making the tiny hairs on my arms rise at the memory. I rolled the soft wool between my fingers, plucking the sweater off the hanger with a swift jerk and slipping it over my head. I spun in circles, laughing and hugging the fabric close with my own arms. In his stolen garment, I paraded back into the bedroom.

A writing desk with overhead drawers caught my attention. The possibility of learning his secrets or details about his past drew me forward. I pulled out the chair and sat down, as if I'd lived with him for years, and he felt no aversion to such intrusions.

Photos, journals, and newspaper clippings tumbled down to litter the desk when I yanked one of the drawers free. I scooped the pile into my arms, intent on returning the contents to their shelf. Like a statue, I froze, reconsidering. Shouldn't I take a peek? Shouldn't I study up on my vampire history where my new living partner was concerned? After all, I really knew no details about his past other than his fine taste in gifts.

After hauling the stack in front of the fireplace, I plopped down and spread everything out. Where to start? I hadn't a clue. I shrugged my shoulders and picked up the newspaper clippings. The articles ranged in date from 1986 to 1989, all referencing a man by the name of Dana Karan—an FBI agent who had apparently been obsessed with cases involving possible vampirism. One article included a photograph Dana had snapped, one in which he claimed a vampire could be seen draining a human of his blood. I squinted, straining to make out details of the image. I didn't see a vampire feeding on his prey. The blurry picture displayed, at best, a struggle between two mortal men.

Despite the photo's lack of clarity, the media had hungered for his story, eager to get their hands on the original photo. He'd made numerous appearances on talk shows, and for several months, his story was the headliner in the news, but then the story's popularity had died away rather suddenly. The last article in Philippe's collection told the story of an obsessed Dana, constantly struggling to defend his reputation, and how he'd hauled in would-be suspects, grilling them for hours about possible vampire sightings. His harassment of said suspects had led to his resignation. Gazing at the article, I scratched my head in confusion. Why had Philippe followed his story? Were they somehow connected? Had he learned Philippe was a vampire? My heart jumped wildly inside my chest, and I dropped the clipping on the floor. Could Philippe be the vampire in the photo? My hands swept through the clippings, searching for more, but I'd already read them all. I sat wallowing in disappointment for a moment before shifting my focus to the photos.

Four photos lay in my lap, but Philippe appeared in only one. A twenty-something, auburn-haired man with pale flesh and diamond-like hazel eyes posed in all four, his scarlet lips flashing the same wicked grin in every shot. In the photo he shared with Philippe, they appeared to be friends, their arms around each other, laughing as the photo had been snapped. Who was this mystery man? What was his relationship to Philippe? More importantly, was he human or vampire? I flipped the photo over, hoping to find a date—1957? Fifty-three years ago, Philippe had looked exactly the same as he did at present. Only the style of his clothing and hair had changed. Seven hundred years of constancy, while the rest of all life continually evolved around you. What kept him sane in the midst of all that flux? Goose bumps pricked at my skin. I pushed the photos onto the floor as I attempted to brush the chill from my arms.

Only the journals remained to be studied by my prying eyes—six in total. Perhaps the identity of the auburn-haired man and the relevance of Dana Karan in relation to Philippe would be found inside. Flipping open the first journal, I discovered its inability to reveal any new information to me. The words scribbled across the page weren't written in English. I snatched up the second, but again, it was written in a language I couldn't understand. Tossing it aside, I searched the third, and finally the fourth. I couldn't find a single legible word, just gibberish. My shoulders caved inward as I audibly groaned.

"Interesting reading?" Philippe asked, a touch of glee in his tone.

My body collapsed further in on itself, a chill scampering down my spine and tightening my skin. The articles, photos, and journals lay all around me, incriminating me.

He knelt down beside me and lifted my chin. With a wink and a grin, he said, "I like your sweater."

My cheeks grew fiery. "Oh God, I'm so sorry. I didn't mean to...I know how this must look." I pulled the sweater over my head, blushing more fervently as I lowered my head.

He chuckled and waved dismissively. "I'm nothing more than amused." He leaned closer. "You've discovered my darkest secret. Why would I hide anything else from you? If you want to know more about me, you have only to ask."

I sat upright and blurted out, "I *do* have lots of questions."

He settled himself by the fire. "Ask away."

I snatched up the photo of him posing with the auburn-haired man. "Who is he? Is he a vampire?"

He took the photo and stared at their faces for a moment, stroking his goatee. "His name is Caleb Keith, and he is my maker."

I leaned forward, my words escaping in a rush. "Where is he? Does he live here, in Castle Beach?"

"Right now he is visiting Paris, but yes, he does live here."

"In this house?"

He wrapped his arm around me and stroked my hair. "He owns a house nearby, though he does spend a considerable amount of time here."

Living with two vampires, practically! I'd be outnumbered. "When will I get to meet him?"

A deep line creased his brow. "I'd like to put that off for as long as possible."

I searched his eyes. "But why?"

"He won't approve of our relationship," he said matter-of-factly. "He will consider you to be inferior and tell me I shouldn't waste my time cohabitating with a mortal." His gaze drifted up to the ceiling. "He's always had a hand in choosing the women I see...vampire women, I mean." He shook his head. "None of them have ever piqued my interest, and he chooses to disregard my wishes."

I lifted my chin stubbornly. "I'm not worried. I'll make him like me."

His lips spread into a confident grin. "I don't doubt that, but in truth, Caleb's opinion doesn't matter to me." He kissed my cheek. "You're the one for me."

My heart gushed like a waterfall, spilling love out into my body. "As are you for me."

He leaned forward, covering my mouth with his, and softly kissed my lips. An electric jolt passed through me, igniting every nerve, but my absolute need for the truth tugged at my core. "Why did Caleb turn you? Did you want to be a vampire? Did he offer you the choice?"

He angled his body in front of me and raised a brow. "Shall I tell you a story of adventure, love, and danger?"

"Only if it's yours."

"It is. Would you like to hear the long or short version?"

I scooted closer. "Long. I want all the details."

He smiled and patted my knee. "I had a feeling you'd say that. This calls for a bottle of wine. Be back in a moment." He rose to his feet and vanished.

A sour taste coated my mouth. My third bottle of wine in one night! I'd never had so much to drink at one time in my life, always being a one glass kind of girl—and only on weekends. Technically, Sunday night was still considered part of the weekend, but I was way past my one-glass rule, and I wanted to keep a clear head for whatever story he had planned to tell me. Cringing, I fell backward, sprawling my legs and arms in every direction in front of the fireplace.

Philippe returned, carrying a dark-green bottle in one hand and two glasses in the other. He popped the cork, poured the wine, and handed me my glass. After seating himself opposite me, he took a sip, his gaze focused on the hearth before traveling back to me. The muscles in his jaw clenched and relaxed. "I guess my story really begins at the time my father sent me away to train for my knighthood as a page."

Interrupting him, I asked, "You were a knight?"

He grinned and brushed his knuckles over his chest. "Yes. I was born of nobility. My father wanted the best for me, so at the age of seven, I was sent to a castle of my father's choosing to serve as a page."

Like a schoolgirl experiencing her first crush, I sighed, gazing at him with visions of Philippe cast in the role of knight in shining armor dancing about inside my head.

"My pagehood was completed alongside several other boys, and I quickly became friends with Paul, who was one of them. Like brothers, we spent nearly every moment together. During our initial training, we learned how to sing, play backgammon and chess, ride a horse, wield weapons, swim, and hunt. Every waking hour was spent learning a valuable skill. Paul and I competed against each other fiercely, driven all the harder by the most dangerous scenarios. If our lesson involved even the slightest risk, we were thrilled to no end.

"At the age of fourteen, we both advanced as squires—those who shadow a knight in all aspects, from the dinner table to the battlefield. The more advanced our training became, the more we enjoyed ourselves. We were ruled by fearlessness, nothing standing in our way, and we wanted to achieve all that was possible.

"Part of becoming a knight meant the choosing of a lady. Of course, you might guess that we fell in love with the same girl. I was the fortunate one she chose, and the rejection devastated Paul. It became evident that he felt less of a man and our friendship suffered, but I was infatuated with her. I couldn't choose to abandon her just to spare his feelings."

As he spoke of her, a flash of anger hardened my stomach into a tight ball. It burned deeper, tunneling into my bones. For God's sake, I hadn't even been born at the time when he'd loved another, but I couldn't shake off the bitterness the knowledge inspired. He was telling me about another woman he'd once loved. I scooped up my glass to fill my mouth with wine and swallowed hard.

He stroked the back of my hand with his fingertips before kissing each knuckle, seeming to glean the jealousy building inside my chest. "You must understand that I have lived for centuries. Along the way, I've experienced my share of love, but never have I felt a love so deep and powerful as the one I harbor for you. I have watched you grow from innocent child to a sophisticated, beautiful woman. It has created a bond between us unrivaled by any other." He cupped my chin within his palm, holding me with his gaze. Sheer determination laced his tone when he said, "With all the others, I knew there must come a day when we would part, but with you...I cannot let you go. You have become an essential part of my very makeup. We must be together forever and ever."

A sense of calm overtook me, my breath flowing more easily. As long as I remained at his side, mortal or immortal, nothing would ever matter, only love, trust, and devotion.

"Shall I continue?"

"Yes, of course."

"Very well. Paul kept his distance, refusing even to speak to me, and he would hear no justification regarding my decision. In fact, his last words spoken to me carried a warning that, someday, he would carry out his revenge. They say time heals all wounds, right? I honestly believed he would eventually heal from the pain I'd caused him and forgive me."

"How could he just cut you out of his life like that?"

The weight of the past seemed to wilt all the strength in his shoulders. "In his eyes, my choosing to be with Tessa instead of him was nothing short of betrayal." He scowled. "If the tables had been turned and she'd chosen him, there remains no doubt in my mind that he would have gladly accepted her hand and tossed our friendship aside."

As I lightly stroked his forearm, I said softly, "He behaved badly, not you."

He nodded half-heartedly and pressed his lips together before continuing. "When the day of our knighting ceremony finally arrived, we all felt as though the world was ours for the taking. We drank, feasted, sang, and danced—all with the magnificence of a king well into the wee hours of the morning. After the celebration, we each went our separate ways to serve different lords and aid in the protection of their lands.

"Five years passed by with no word from Paul. I'd given up hope of ever mending our friendship. On the sixth year, a messenger arrived, sent by my long-lost friend. Devastation had befallen Paul's lord, and the titleship to his land lay in jeopardy. Paul had requested my aid. Without hesitation, I explained the situation to my lord, said goodbye to Tessa, and set out on my journey with my most trusted squire.

"Two days into our journey, we were ambushed. Ten men on horseback, including Paul's messenger, attacked from all sides."

My throat burned, and I clenched my jaw. I wished Paul harm, even though I'd never met the man.

"My squire was murdered straightaway, leaving me to battle ten men alone. The odds were stacked heavily against me, so I turned my horse around and fled. As I raced through the woods, my enemies drew frighteningly closer. With each glance over my shoulder, they narrowed the gap between us. When my horse reared abruptly, I was sent flying into a group of trees, striking my head and falling unconscious."

I grabbed onto his arm, my heart thumping inside my throat. "Were you captured?"

His gaze narrowed and darkened as he nodded slowly. "I awoke chained to a dungeon wall, stripped of all my armor and most of my clothing." He swallowed and grimaced. "Paul stood before me, clenching a leather whip in his fist. I didn't want to believe his summons had been employed solely for the purpose of revenge. I asked him to what end did he hold me prisoner. He said nothing, merely sending the whip flying across my chest and drawing first blood. I shouted at him. 'Was this revenge you spoke of so many years ago?' Again, the whip struck me in answer.

"He kept me chained to the wall like an animal, offering me neither food nor water. He gloated as he tormented me, wanting nothing more than to watch me die a slow death."

My chin trembled, tears gathering behind my eyelids. How much more could I bear to hear? I was trapped with him inside my mind—weak, starving, terrified of dying.

"Blocks of time slipped away from me, and strength abandoned my body. The chains were all I had to keep me from collapsing. I began to give up my will to live. When I'd grown dangerously close to death, I met my maker, Caleb.

"A bright light shone down to me from the top of the dungeon stairs, glowing brighter and brighter as it neared me. I wondered if the glow was real or merely hallucination. But Paul had noticed its descent as well. Leaping to his feet, he grabbed up the whip, ready to attack. The sheen had come from a man bearing a torch as he descended the stone stairs. The blaze of the flame obstructed his face, leaving his features unrecognizable.

"Paul had called out to the man, demanding he state his intentions, but he received no reply. As Paul had raised the whip to strike, the man vanished like a ghost. In the time it had taken me to blink, I found him standing before Paul. The man ripped the whip from Paul's hands and coiled it about Paul's neck, constricting the leather as a snake would their victim. The brittle crack of Paul's bones, coupled with his painful shrieks, pierced my ears. I struggled feebly with the chains restraining me, cold sweat lacing my body. I was sure the hour of my death had arrived."

Philippe's account weighed heavily on my heart and I struggled to breathe. This wasn't a story constructed of fiction. All the elements were real. Paul had been swiftly executed as Philippe had looked on.

"The man dropped Paul to the ground and drew near to me, his breath so cold, it stung my face. Holding the torch before me, he remarked, 'Look what he's done to you.'

"I said nothing. I couldn't. Fear crippled me as it does the lamb brought to slaughter. In a low voice, he added, 'You will not survive the night. You, my friend, are dying.'

"I blubbered. In fact, I wailed. I did not feel ready to die, so I screamed from the depths of my lungs, 'I want to live! Live forever.'"

I clutched at Philippe with one hand, slipping my other arm under his. "He turned you."

His gaze fixated on the fire as he disclosed the truth. "Yes. The torch flew away from my face, falling to the ground and igniting the dungeon walls. His hands effortlessly snapped the chains binding me. When my weakened legs buckled, his arms tenderly enfolded me, cradling me against his body. As he gazed deeply into my eyes, he drained my mind first. I fell limp in his arms, surrendering as he sunk his fangs into my neck.

"A crazed heat swarmed into my blood, coursing through my veins like lightning. I clawed at him like an animal, every sane trace of my existence escaping from every pore. My gaze darted about the dungeon, searching for something, anything which might free me from his clutches, but I couldn't fight the preternatural strength contained within that being, that thing, that monster. I'd become fated to meet death. The room dimmed around me..."

The gentle tapping of my pulse mounted as I sat stiffly, my gaze glued to Philippe's face, taking in every word he spoke.

"Violent hunger clenched within my gut when I woke. I held my attacker in my arms, my teeth embedded in his neck, drawing life from his jugular. Rich, thick blood spilled into my mouth, driving life back into my body. Every nerve inside me lit up, lifting me off the ground and filling every cell with ecstasy—ecstasy called forth by his blood. I couldn't drink from him fast enough to satisfy my limitless thirst

"At some point, he pushed me away. I could taste the blood spilling forth from my mouth and dripping onto my chin. 'You are a vampire now,' he told me, 'a human no more. I am Caleb Keith, and I am your maker. You will remain by my side as I instruct you in the ways of your new life.'"

Philippe gestured to himself. "And here I am."

Mesmerized by his tale of knights, dungeons, and vampires, I found no words to speak. I embraced him with all my might, pulling him close and allowing our hearts to pound, one atop the other.

"I can feel the sun beginning its ascent," he whispered into my ear. "I must sleep now."

I shivered, feeling as though I could never leave him. If I walked away from him at that moment, I knew I might shrivel up, breathing my last breath. "May I stay with you?" I asked, my voice strained and edgy.

He brushed the back of his hand across my cheek. "Beth, you may stay with me every night."

My hands trembled; my breath quickened. I would fall asleep in his arms, but how could I possibly sleep? I still had so many questions. What about Dana Karan? "Can you resist the sun's Sandman effect just a little while longer?"

He laughed lightly. "I sleep as you do, only when the sun and moon are reversed. The rising sun tells me I should be tired."

I clasped my hands in desperation. "Just one more question?"

"One," he countered firmly.

"Who is Dana Karan?"

His mouth twisted into a grimace. "Dana Karan is a complicated subject. He cannot be explained away with one brief answer."

"Please, I have to know."

Placing his hands on my shoulders, he said, "You can't expect to find the answers to all your questions inside the space of one night, especially when the one providing the answers has lived for centuries. When the time is right, I will tell you all about Dana."

I frowned at him as I folded my arms across my chest.

He chose to ignore my displeasure, kissing the top of my head and disappearing into the bathroom. He returned wearing pajamas and turned off the light, leaving only the warm glow of the fire to light the room. Philippe took me by the hand, leading me to his bed as tiny fireworks exploded inside my stomach. I ached all over, hungry for his touch. I lay down next to him and gazed into his eyes.

He pulled me close, kissed me, and said, "Good night, my love."

CHAPTER 5

I opened my eyes to a pitch-black room. Did the hour belong to the day or the night? I couldn't tell. I turned toward Philippe, who was sound asleep, his arm resting on top of my stomach. Gently, I lifted his arm and slipped out of bed. I tiptoed over to the window and peeked through the curtains to find a brilliant shade of powder-blue filling the sky. The sun's golden rays reached down and glistened across the pool below.

Oh God, it's Monday! I dropped the curtain and fled his room, quietly closing his door behind me. I ran down the hall like a crazy person and sprinted into my bedroom. I flew into my clothes, threw my hair up in a ponytail, and charged out of my room to descend the staircase. Taking the steps two at a time, I dashed toward the door, only to collide with Betty at the bottom.

I grabbed her arms, attempting to steady her before bolting once more for the door. "Sorry, I'm in a rush. Please, tell Philippe I left for work. Not sure when I'll be home."

In a motherly tone, she called out, "Drive careful, now. Be safe and take your time, dear. I will let Philippe know."

"Thank you!" I called over my shoulder.

Once I'd settled in the driver's seat, I gunned the engine and spun the car around, zipping through the gates. I sped down the road like I was filming a car chase scene for a movie, weaving in and out of traffic while checking my rearview mirror for cops. I maneuvered onto the freeway, racking my brain as I tried to come up with an excuse to satisfy Ron, my boss. The water heater blew. A family emergency came up. Flat tire. Got locked out of the house. All good reasons, but none would explain why I hadn't called in. There was always the option of telling the truth. I got drunk and overslept. I shook my head. That would definitely piss him off. As I turned into the parking lot, I still didn't have a clue as to what I might say. I'd have to wing it and hope for the best.

Ron's administrative assistant, Vicki, greeted me as I entered the building. Her pale, panicked face told me all I needed to know. "Ron wants to see you right away." She touched my arm and whispered, "He's pissed."

The saliva in my mouth evaporated. *I don't have a reason. I need a reason.* I cleared my throat. "Thanks, Vicki."

She hurried back to her desk while I walked the proverbial plank down to his office, my mind a complete blank. I stepped into his open doorway, clutching at my purse in fear. "You wanted to see me?"

The vein in the center of his pasty forehead pulsed. His nostrils flared as he jerked his head to the right. "Close the door and sit down."

A cold wave swept over me as I closed the door. Listening to my pulse throb against my eardrums, I made my way to the chair. I looked him right in the eye, holding my head high and asked, "Yes?"

He glared at me over the top of his glasses and pointed at the clock. "More than half the day is gone." He paused, eyeballing me. "Did the meeting with Masters and Colby slip your mind?"

Nausea churned my stomach. *I'm done. It's over.* Shifting uncomfortably in the chair, I blurted out, "Ron, I'm sorry. Something came up. It won't happen again." I cringed. How lame had that sounded?

He swiped his glasses from his nose and nodded curtly. "You're damn right it won't. You're fired."

All the blood in my body rushed to my head. I stiffened and gripped the chair arms. "What? You can't be serious, right? You can't just fire me."

"I can, and I am," he stated calmly. "Masters and Colby is our largest account." His brows came together, his mouth twisting into a nasty scowl. "Or should I say, they were."

Radiant heat replaced the cold of the moment before and sweat coated my palms. "Were?"

"Yes." He leaned forward, placing his hands on the desk. "For God's sake, Beth, you know how they expect to be pampered. *You* didn't show. *You* wasted their time. Now they're taking their business elsewhere."

My throat started to close, so I swallowed rapidly. Somehow, I had to dig myself out of the hole I'd fallen into. "Ron, let me call them. I can fix this."

He sighed in frustration. "They're done. They closed their account. The funds have already been transferred."

I stared at him in stunned silence, shaking my head.

His face relaxed, his tone softening. "I'm sorry, Beth. I hate letting you go, but this loss was substantial, and the whole mess could've been avoided. Here is your final paycheck."

I sat with my hands resting in my lap. I'd never been fired before. Now what? In a small voice, I managed, "I'll clear out my things."

He nodded in answer.

I left his office and staggered down the hall like a zombie into my office. I stood still enough to feel my hands trembling. A box waited at the center of my desk. I walked over and plopped down in my chair one last time. Completely numb, I somehow collected my personal items, placing them gently inside the box as if they could shatter at any moment, just like my heart.

"So, how's the handsome prince?" Anna asked, popping her head in my door.

I looked up at her and opened my mouth, but no words came out.

After rushing inside, she closed the door and rested her body against the frame. "Did Philippe break things off?" Her gaze shifted to the box on my desk. "Why are you packing?"

I looked away for a moment, before meeting her eyes. "Philippe and I are fine, but I just got fired."

Deep lines furrowed her brow. "What?!" She threw her arms up in the air and exclaimed, "But I covered for you. When you didn't meet me for our usual morning coffee, I figured you and the prince had a late night. I told that bastard, Ron, you weren't feeling well and would be in late, or maybe not at all."

"I missed the meeting with Masters and Colby. They pulled their funds, and we lost the account."

She pressed her lips together, the blood draining from them. "Geez, Beth, I'm so sorry."

I gathered the last of the knickknacks from my desk. "I feel broken."

Anna put her arm around me, offering me a reassuring squeeze. "I'll blow off work. Let's go across the street, have an early dinner at Rock Bottom, and then go downstairs and get drunk in the nightclub."

I gagged and clutched at my stomach. "Please, don't mention alcohol. I'll throw up."

She laughed and waved my worries away. "Axe the booze. We can still have dinner and dance our asses off, right?"

I gave her what I hoped was a happy smile. "We can."

"I'll meet you outside in ten." She turned and left me alone to collect the last physical reminders of my former career.

A dull ache spread throughout my chest as I glanced around the office one last time that I'd worked in for four years. I lifted the box and stumbled out of the building in a daze. Once I'd climbed into my car, I placed the box on the passenger's seat. Leaning back in the seat and closing my eyes, I massaged my throbbing temples. In the span of two days, I'd lost both Danny and my job. Still, I knew that even if everything from my past life slipped between my fingers, the losses would be worth what I would gain—Philippe. I loved him that much.

A knock on the window pulled me back to reality, and I opened my eyes. Anna stood by my car, grinning, her dimpled smile infectious. I smiled back before climbing out to stand next to her. She turned toward the building and gave it the finger before dragging me forward. "Forget about this place, and let's go have some fun."

"Sounds wonderful."

As she pressed the walk button at the corner, she mused, "You know what? It's Ron's loss."

I nudged at her shoulder. "You're right. Let him suffer through some of those nightmare clients without me." I glanced over at Rock Bottom, and then back at Anna. "Wanna share a basket of fries?"

"Oh, you know I do." She shifted her feet impulsively, as if she might dart out into traffic.

The pedestrian WALK signal finally lit, though I was sure it had nothing to do with Anna's impatience. We crossed the street arm in arm, strolling up to the front doors of Rock Bottom. Voices buzzed, filling the packed, shipwreck-themed restaurant with exuberance.

A bubbly hostess greeted us. "Hey there, welcome to Rock Bottom. Table for two?" Anna nodded. "It's your lucky day. I've got one table for two left, and it's right by the window. Follow me." She led us to the galley-inspired table, anchors serving as its legs, and handed us our menus with a cheerful smile. "Sam will be your waiter. Enjoy." She spun on her heels, bouncing back in the direction of the front door.

Anna glanced up from her menu. "Are you sure you don't want a drink? The Marooned Margaritas are to die for."

I curled my lips and shuddered. "Iced tea for me. If you want one, though, go for it."

She rolled her eyes toward the ceiling, considering. "Iced tea sounds good, especially the peach flavored one." She perused the menu again. "Hmm...basket of fries...a panini or a burger?"

I scanned my own menu. "The Tomato Pesto Avocado Panini sounds sinful."

"It really does. Sold." Anna clapped her menu shut.

Not two seconds after we'd laid our menus on the table, Sam appeared. Decked out in a red and black velvet uniform, our dashing pirate winked at us brazenly. "Arrrgghh! What'll it be, gals?"

We rattled off our orders, and the pirate scribbled them onto a notepad before hurrying away, disappearing into the crowd. In only a couple of minutes, he returned with our drinks, setting them on the table and rushing off again.

Drinks in hand, Anna and I clinked our glasses together, simultaneously blurting out, "Good riddance, Ron!"

We exploded with laughter. Who needed that stupid job anyway? Certainly not me, I had Philippe.

Ten minutes later, Sam was settling scrumptious plates in front of us.

Anna dug into the basket of fries, shoving a few into her mouth. "Mmm, so good. Have some." She generously held the basket out to me.

While we ate, she chattered on about all the boyfriends who had come and gone. The image of Danny walking out of my life for good played out inside my brain, his words stinging me anew. *Don't say that. Don't ever say that again.* Could he ever forgive me? The urge to call him burned within my heart, but what good could come of it? He'd made it clear he wanted nothing to do with me, even though he'd always been my best friend. How could either of us shut the door on such a connection?

"Earth to Beth. Are you listening to me?" Anna queried, waving her hand in front of my face.

I took a huge bite of my sandwich and executed an exaggerated nod. "I'm listening."

"You need to set me up with one of Philippe's friends."

Did my new boyfriend have friends? The only person I knew to be a part of his life was Caleb, and from what Philippe had told me, Caleb despised humans. "We'll find someone for you." I winked at her. "Who knows who you might meet tonight in the club."

She threw her napkin at me. "As if."

"What? Mr. Right can't be discovered inside a bar?"

Sam came up, interrupting her unspoken reply. "Anything else I can get you gals?"

"We're good, thanks," Anna replied.

He laid the bill on the edge of the table. "No hurry. Stay as long as you like."

"Thanks, Sam," I said.

As soon as he was out of earshot, Anna whispered, "A normal nice guy in a bar? Yeah, right."

I arched a brow. "We'll be in the bar and *we're* normal."

She tilted her head in acquiescence. "You have a point."

Literally taking Sam up on his offer, we settled back in our chairs, requested several iced tea refills, chewed the fat, and waited for the club doors to open. Every half-hour or so, Sam passed by, giving us a *"get off your butts and get the hell away from my table*" sneer. So much for, "*stay as long as you like.*" We played dumb, batting our eyelashes and smiling at him. He'd stomp off, and we'd snicker. Several rounds later, the humor of it all dwindled, and truly, we'd outstayed our welcome. Besides, Happy Hour was in full swing downstairs.

Looking at Anna, I said, "Ready to go scope out Mr. Right?"

She shook her head. "I'm ready to go into the nightclub. Scouring through a bunch of desperate barflies for Mr. Right...not so much."

I laughed so hard that I snorted, which made my friend collapse in on herself with the force of her own. A flurry of giggles took us both over, and we couldn't stop them. Holding our aching sides, we managed to slide from the table and stumble down the stairs like a couple of drunks.

The invasion of fluorescent lights lit the nightclub, casting an unnatural sheen on everything in sight. Purple skin and glowing teeth crowded around each of the three bars, spilling out onto the split-level dance floor, which hovered below the DJ booth situated high in the far-left corner. Soft music piped through the speakers, setting the stage for Happy Hour, unlike later when the DJ kicked off his multicolored light show to a mixed blend of blaring techno. The Happy Hour flock, eager to save a buck, paled in comparison to the club's late-night inhabitants. Swarming in after ten, they'd spread out drugs in bathrooms, proposition strangers in every dark corner, and arrive in an array of outrageous and shameful attire, but we'd be long gone by then.

Bodies crammed together in a solid line surrounded the bar. Thrusting a hand into the air and waving cash, they hollered at the bartenders for drinks. Anna and I pushed our way through the alcohol deprived maze and managed to snag a couple of bar stools overlooking the dance floor. The couple smack up against me locked lips in a steamy kiss, sending my heart into a frenzy and aching for Philippe.

Anna wrinkled her forehead. "Please, tell me you're not thinking about that jerk, Ron."

I spread my fingers over my heart through my shirt. "Every inch of me, from my fingertips to my toes, misses Philippe."

Anna gave me a playful nudge. "I think he misses you too."

I stared at her, frowning. "What makes you say that?"

She grinned and pointed. "Because he's standing right behind you."

Goose bumps prickled my flesh. "What?" I spun around to find him mere inches from me. He stepped closer. Our bodies touched, his lips caressing my ear.

Anna grabbed her purse and hopped off her stool. "I'll leave you two alone. Beth, call me tomorrow."

"I will," I choked out, my voice breathless.

His eyes burned into mine, sparks appearing to fly across the surface of his irises. Feeling drunk with love, I wrapped my arms around his neck and pulled him into my heated embrace, running my tongue over his lips. He opened his mouth so our tongues could dance, and I kissed him harder.

I spoke my demands directly into his ear. "Take me home and into your bed."

He picked me up and whisked me out of the club, being careful to curb his vampire speed. Out on the street, we groped one another's bodies like teenagers. As he slid his arm around my waist, he thrust his groin against me. Heat surged between my legs, extending out into my limbs.

"I didn't drive. Where are you parked?" he asked, taking a nip at my ear after he'd spoken.

I pointed across the street. "That parking lot," I said, my breath coming fast and furious.

At the speed of light, we landed in the parking lot next to my car. As soon as I fastened my seatbelt, I gunned the engine, shoving the car into reverse and screaming onto the street. We raced over the road, Philippe lightly running his tongue up and down my neck, driving me insane. At every red light, we kissed with a sexual hunger, hunger I'd never imagined myself capable of.

The car roared up the circular drive, forcing me to slam on the brakes when I parked recklessly in front of the mansion. Philippe swept me into his arms as soon as the car doors flew open, bolting into the house, up the stairs, and inside his bedroom. We stumbled toward the bed, clumsily shedding our clothes in the process. As his body covered mine, my heart beat out a rapid fire, driving my heated blood through my veins like a raging river of liquefied earth. His hands caressed my breasts, and I lost all reason. Nothing mattered, other than taking him inside me.

"Make love to me, now," I begged.

He pulled away, his forehead a wrinkle of worry.

I grabbed desperately at his shoulders. "Why are you stopping? Don't stop."

"Before we go any further, there's something I must tell you."

My eyes searched his. "What is it?"

His frown deepened. "There is no subtle way to say this."

I stroked his face. "You can tell me anything. You know that."

"My bodily fluids are…blood."

I frowned and shook my head.

"*All* of them," he said with insistence.

The meaning behind his words finally sunk in. I giggled, struggling to stifle my juvenile behavior immediately after. His vampire blood entering my body would be like air entering my lungs. I didn't care, because I loved him. "That only makes sense. Blood is the one sustenance you require now. It's what you're made of. I'm not afraid."

Relief flooded across his face. Philippe snatched me up in his arms and whispered in my ear, "I want you."

"Then take me," I demanded, pulling him down on top of me.

I gasped softly as he entered me. Our bodies molded together, our hearts pounding one atop the other, urgency swirling amidst in our breaths. We moved as one, our passion taking us past the point of no return.

Only after we'd made love four more times did we fall asleep, locked tightly within each other's arms.

CHAPTER 6

For the next few weeks, Philippe and I locked ourselves in his bedroom—which had become *our* bedroom—making love morning, noon, and night. We barely came up for air. Our hungers for food or blood was all that forced us apart. While I raided the kitchen, Philippe prowled the streets in search of human blood. I didn't allow myself to dwell on thoughts of his victims. I couldn't. Those considerations I buried deep inside my brain.

Each night, I paced the bedroom like a caged animal, my gaze glued to the bedroom door, awaiting Philippe's return. The second he crossed the threshold, our clothes found the floor. Trembling, sweating, panting, we fused together like magnets, making love in bed, on the floor, in the shower, time and time again, never seeming to get enough of each other. Of late, a sluggish sensation had begun to confine me to the bed, long after our moments of pleasure had ended. My dry, bloodshot eyes burned, and fits of chills plagued me more often than not. Convinced I'd caught the flu or a stubborn cold, I loaded up on over-the-counter remedies and supplements, even downing myself in hot tea, yet nothing brought me any relief.

After three days of nothing but lounging around, I dragged myself out of bed, threw on a robe, and ventured downstairs for a glass of fresh-squeezed orange juice, hoping a jolt of vitamin C would do me some good. When I'd reached the bottom stair, my chest heaved, refusing to draw breath. Wheezing uncontrollably, I fell to my knees on the rug, clinging to the banister and fighting to catch my breath. An army of maids bustled about on the first floor, cleaning every surface of the front hallway. After smoothing my tousled hair and closing my robe, I nodded in the direction of the closest maid.

An olive-skinned, black-haired young woman, freckles scattered across her nose, strode up to me. "Good morning, Miss Ryan. May I help you with something?"

I'd never met any of the new maids before. How could she know my name? Philippe or Betty must have provided them with instructions. "Good morning," I choked out. "Yes, thank you. Some orange juice would be great."

"Yes, Miss Ryan. I'll be right back, and then I'll help you back to your room."

As she vanished down the hallway, the doorbell chimed. My legs wobbled beneath me as I tried to stand. I sat staring helplessly at the door.

A tall, skinny maid with strawberry-blonde hair hurried past me. "I'll get that, Miss Ryan. You look as though you need to rest."

I laid my head against the cool railing. "Thank you."

As the second chime sounded, she opened the door halfway. "May I help you?"

Anna's vivacious voice filtered through the crack. "Hi there. Is Beth around?"

Blocking the doorway with her body, the maid responded, "Who may I say is calling?"

"It's okay," I croaked out. "Please, let her in."

The maid pushed the door wide. "Please, come in."

Anna pulled off her sunglasses and stepped inside. As her gaze focused on me, she scrunched up her nose and narrowed her gaze, making a beeline for me. "You look like you just woke up."

I laughed, wincing as I rubbed the back of my neck. "I did."

She glanced at her wristwatch. "Are you serious? It's almost noon."

"I'm not feeling well. Came down for some OJ."

The olive-skinned maid had returned, bearing a tall glass of orange juice. She glanced at Anna and smiled before stooping in front of me to hand me the glass. "May I help you back to bed now, Miss Ryan?"

"Not just yet. I'm going to visit with my friend for a little while." I turned back to Anna. "Let's go out by the pool. The fresh air might do me some good."

The maid reached for me. "Let me help you, Miss Ryan."

Anna offered her aid as well, gripping me under the arms and lifting me to my feet. "I'll take care of her from here, thanks."

The maid backed away. "Yes, ma'am."

Anna propped me up with her arm, and I rested my head on her shoulder as we hobbled down the hall.

"Did you come by to see if I was still alive?" I asked with a small laugh.

She shot a stern look my way. "Stop kidding around. You were supposed to call me, remember? So I called, and then texted you. Three weeks with no reply. What the hell happened to you?"

My eyelashes fluttered. "Philippe happened."

She smirked, a devilish gleam brightening the color of her eyes. "So, spill. One to ten, how good is he?"

It was my turn to smirk. "Definitely a twelve."

She raised her brows in response. "That good, huh?"

I fanned myself, releasing a breathy, "Yes."

She giggled. "Well, where is he? Why isn't he taking care of you?"

A lie flew too easily from my mouth. "He's working."

When we shuffled into the kitchen, we found we weren't alone. Betty greeted us, carrying a stack of freshly laundered kitchen towels. She hung a couple on the rack above the sink and said, "Good afternoon, Beth, and it's nice to see you again, Anna."

Anna flashed a charming smile. "Good to see you too, Betty."

Betty placed her hands on my shoulders and peered into my eyes. "I heard you're not feeling well."

Anna planted a hand on her hip. "Philippe should be taking care of her."

I gave Betty's arm a light squeeze, depositing my OJ on the kitchen island, and narrowed my gaze. "I was just telling Anna that Philippe's working."

Betty nodded discreetly before turning to Anna. "Mr. Delon is tied up with an international conference call. Unfortunately, he cannot be disturbed and asked me to look after Beth."

Her voice held such steadfast conviction, even I believed her, knowing her words to be untrue.

Still, Anna let out an agitated huff.

"Are you two heading out to the patio?" Betty asked, steering the conversation away from Philippe.

"Yeah, I feel like I could use some sun," I answered, grabbing onto the edge of the island and inching toward the French doors.

"I'll mix up a batch of iced tea and bring it out with your juice."

"Thank you. That sounds wonderful," Anna said. She wound her arm around me and ushered me out the doors.

Once we were outside, she lowered me into a lounge chair, easing me down like I was ninety years old. "Are you comfortable?"

I squinted in the glaring sunlight beating down on me. "A little more umbrella, thanks."

"Sure." She gripped the chair arms and dragged me to the left. "Better?"

I nodded, but even beneath the shade, the sun's rays raked across my skin, stinging like a swarm of angry bees.

As she sat opposite me, she leaned forward, staring intently at my face. "You're right, you don't look so good."

I waved her concern away. "It's just a cold. I'll be fine."

The double doors swung open, and Betty trotted a tray of drinks and finger sandwiches over to the table. As she set the tray on the glass tabletop, she said, "I couldn't let you girls go hungry. I made some sandwiches for you too. Enjoy."

Anna let out a sigh as Betty vanished back into the kitchen. "You're so lucky. I love it here, and Philippe is an absolute dream—when he's not ignoring you to take an international business call."

Ignoring the last part of her statement, I mused aloud, "I am lucky, aren't I?"

"Totally."

Being with Anna began to take my mind off the pain a little, like I was a sick child holding onto her favorite blanket. She stayed with me a little over an hour before rushing back to work. After she left, I sat outside alone, letting the warm, stinging heat of the sun soothe my sore, stiff muscles.

"Miss Ryan."

I looked up to find the olive-skinned maid standing just outside my umbrella, her hands clasped before her.

"Yes?" I asked, shielding my eyes from the sun.

"I came to see if you would like to return to your room now."

"Yes, thank you." I paused and peered at her. "I don't know your name."

She smiled sweetly. "I'm Karina."

I nodded curtly, as if I were royalty, and said, "Please take me to my room, Karina."

She covered her mouth, but a snort slipped out as she laughed at my joke.

I laughed with her, which initiated a coughing fit. After choking down a sip of OJ, I cleared my throat and stood. Sweat drenched my pajamas, making the warm breeze frigid. The landscape blurred and I swayed, crumpling back into the chair.

Karina rushed to my aid, slipping her arms around my waist and hoisting me up. "You're too weak. Lean on me."

I latched onto her, allowing her to lug my feeble, feverish body up the stairs to the bedroom I shared with Philippe.

She turned the knob and pushed the door open. "I can't help you inside. We're not allowed to enter."

"I'll be okay. Thank you." I shut the door and crawled back into bed with Philippe. My head barely touched the pillow before I fell into the deepest sleep of my life.

****

The next afternoon, I sat perched on the edge of an exam table, staring into Dr. Hughes' brownish-green eyes and rattling off my symptoms. "I have no energy. Food makes me nauseous. I ache all over and get constant chills. My eyes hurt. My skin burns, and today, this annoying ringing started in my ears."

Leaning forward in his chair, he scratched his bald head and studied me. After a long, uncomfortable silence, he rose to his feet and took out a tongue depressor. "Say ahhh…" He proceeded to give me a complete physical exam, sending me off to the lab afterward.

A male lab technician with a horrible case of acne called my name. "Beth Ryan."

I followed him into a small room, with chairs you would find inside a classroom. He pointed to one in the middle of the row and said, "Have a seat and lay your arm on the armrest."

I rolled up my sleeve, placing my forearm against the cool wood. The unnatural feeling of my blood flowing out of my vein and into a glass tube had always made my skin crawl. Bolting from the room crossed my mind, but I managed to remain seated.

"Make a fist for me."

The tip of the needle pierced my skin, disappearing inside my vein. A flurry of butterflies swarmed my stomach, pushing a foul taste up and into my mouth. The scent of rich, salty blood perfumed the air. I felt my breath quicken and sweat trickle down my brow. I licked my lips anxiously as my blood spiraled upward into the clear glass.

"Are you all right?" he asked, touching my hand.

I nodded, transfixed by the color and smell of my own blood. The beauty of the crimson fluid mesmerized me. My mouth watered as I imaged the taste rolling over my tongue and sliding down my throat to feed my body. What a rush. *What?* Was Philippe's lifestyle influencing me and altering my brain? Could this sudden craving be a subconscious attempt at pleasing him? I shook my head. *Most definitely not.* I would never compromise my values. I wouldn't kill, not even for him.

The tech dabbed at my forehead with a towel. "Not a fan of blood tests, huh? Good news is that we're done." He pulled the needle from my skin and replaced it with a Band-Aid. "I'll get you some water." He returned with a cup of cool liquid. "Sit here as long as you like."

"Thank you."

He patted my hand with a smile in place before exiting the room.

As I sipped at the water, I focused on the beige grout surrounding each clean white tile until the peculiar blood craving faded away.

Dr. Hughes popped his head in the door and pointed a finger at me. "Get some rest, and don't worry. Probably just the flu. I'll call you once I get the lab results."

As I stepped outside the doors of the urgent care clinic, a sense of calm washed over me. Nothing more than the flu. I could live with that. I breathed in the fresh air, strolling toward my car like I didn't have a care in the world. Before heading home, I drove to the beach to watch the sun set, my mind tranquil and at peace with the world.

I entered the mansion a few minutes after nightfall. A gnawing pang twisted my gut, awakening some sort of starvation craving, but not for food—for blood! I skidded to a halt, my scalp pricking in disbelief.

Philippe descended the staircase and began slipping into his coat. His expression darkened, and he hurried forward to draw me into his arms. "Beth, what is it?"

I held him at arm's length, fixing my gaze on him. In a low, raspy voice, I said, "I want to go with you tonight. I want to watch you feed."

His eyes grew large with surprise. But then he cocked his head and frowned. "Why now? What happened for you to want this?"

I shivered and rubbed my hand over my arms before shrugging my shoulders. "I don't know...something in my body, my brain. I have to go with you."

He regarded me, shaking his head. "I don't think it's a good idea."

I clasped my hands in front of me in desperation. "Please, Philippe."

He stared as if he'd never met me before.

"Pleeeassse."

He stroked his goatee and narrowed his gaze. "You're sure?"

I gripped his hands and squeezed them. "Yes."

"Then come along." He led me to the door.

Outside, Jon Paul was waiting. His lips parted, and a flicker of shock shone on his face. His professional stony-faced expression swiftly returned as he opened the car door for us.

I situated my body as close to Philippe as I could, holding his hand as Jon Paul drove us to a dive bar on the other side of town. He pulled the car around the back, parking in the alley and leaving the engine running. As he opened the door, he asked, "Same as usual, Mr. Delon? Pick you up in an hour?"

"Yes, thank you," Philippe answered, offering his hand to help me from the car.

"Of course."

Philippe guided me inside the bar, his hand resting on the small of my back. Thick smoke polluted the room, gathering in a smothering haze. I gagged and attempted to wave enough away to draw a couple of breaths. Men sporting shaved heads, goatees, leather, chains, and hostile scowls had laid claim to the bar. We wove between the groups of unruly locals, headed to the back of the establishment, and slipped into one of the booths. Philippe pulled me close, circling my shoulders with his protective embrace.

A waitress with a weathered face and bleached blonde hair approached. She popped her gum before speaking to us. "What'll it be?"

"Two glasses of the house wine, please," Philippe answered, his gaze darting over the crowd.

She nodded, blowing a small bubble, before heading back toward the bar.

Scanning the faces as well, I asked, "How do you pick one?"

"I read their minds."

"And what do they have to be thinking to get chosen?"

Without emotion, he answered, "They must want to die."

An icy cold tunneled into my bones.

The waitress returned and set the glasses on the table. "Here ya go."

I grabbed my glass and gulped it down immediately. "Can I have another, please?"

The waitress grinned, showing her pink wad of gum. "Sure thing." She looked to Philippe. "How about you?"

"I'm fine, thank you."

She tapped her pen against her temple. "How about a carafe?"

"Yes," I blurted out, "that would be wonderful. Thank you."

"Be back in a jiffy."

Philippe touched my face, turning it toward him. Deep worry creased his perfect forehead. "Are you sure you want to go through with this?"

I swallowed the lump in my throat and pushed his hand away. "Yes, I'm sure. Stop asking me."

He clenched his jaw. "Beth, this isn't a game. Watching me take a life is something you can never unsee."

The waitress returned, interrupting us. She refilled my glass and set the carafe within my reach. "Just give me a holler if you two need anything else."

"We will. Thank you," Philippe said.

As soon as she was out of earshot, I fired back, "I'm well aware of what I'm getting into. This is part of your life. I'm part of your life, so I need to know everything about you. Even this."

His face relaxed, and he replied, "Very well."

I lifted my glass and took a generous swallow. Philippe turned away from me and focused on a group of men clustered around the bar. Within a matter of minutes, he nodded toward a rough-looking character leaning against the bar, chugging down a beer. His leathery skin hid behind dark sunglasses resting atop his lumpy nose. A huge birthmark peeked through the sparse gray hair sprouting from his scalp, and he wore a tattered black leather jacket.

Philippe narrowed his gaze as he fixated on the man. At once, the man removed his sunglasses and shoved them in a pocket of the raggedy jacket. He stared dead ahead before placing his glass on the bar and staggering toward the exit. Pushing drunkenly through the door, he left the building.

"He's leaving," I said, sliding to the edge of the booth.

Philippe grabbed my arm. "Wait. We'll follow in a few minutes."

I drummed my feet on the floor, my gaze glued on Philippe.

"Now," Philippe said, nudging me gently.

My pulse fired rapidly as I jumped out of the booth, shadowing Philippe as I followed him out of the bar.

The man waited in the alley where Jon Paul had dropped us off. His eyes had glazed over, and he stood with his mouth slack and open, his body completely motionless.

Philippe vanished from my side, seizing the man and dragging him behind a dumpster. My gaze darted to the spot where they'd disappeared. I couldn't see either one of them. Surely, he wouldn't start without me! I bolted forward, charging behind its rusted metal frame. Philippe had the man cornered, pressing his body into the wall, his hands thrusting his head to the side and exposing his neck. The man hung limp, not an ounce of fight within him. Philippe's eyes blazed like hot coals; the humanity erased. His mouth flew open to expose dangerously sharp fangs dripping with saliva. As his teeth plunged deep into the man's neck, Philippe groaned and flattened his prey further into the wall, his eyes rolling back into his head as he guzzled greedily.

Dark crimson seeped down the man's neck and commanded my attention. My pulse flew into a rage as I stood terrified, captivated, and sickened by the bloodthirsty act. Heat rippled through my core, awakening a hunger unlike any other I'd experienced. I lunged forward and pressed my lips over Philippe's, kissing him hard. The man's salty-sweet blood dribbled into my mouth, causing sexual heat to engulf me. I slammed my body into Philippe's, shoving my tongue into his mouth so I could get a better taste of the blood. Philippe let his victim fall to the ground. Savagely, we tore at each other's clothes before he entered me. With only the dead man to bear witness, we made love, growling like wild animals in heat.

During the drive home, we sat on opposite sides of the car. The thirst for blood I'd felt had rendered me speechless. Philippe had been right; I couldn't take back any of the night. I was no longer the same girl who'd walked onto his property that very first night. What had happened? What dark need had overtaken me? Was I losing my mind, becoming some kind of psychopath who craved blood and violence? Would the mysterious illness plaguing me provide a reasonable explanation?

Because this certainly hadn't been brought on by the flu. I hoped with all my heart that Dr. Hughes would have answers.

Back in our bedroom, we avoided the issue, maintaining a safe distance from each other while getting ready for bed. Did Philippe find my reaction disturbing? Did he still love me? I laid down next to him and stared at the ceiling, unable to sleep. I broke the silence by muttering, "I'm sorry."

He swept me up in his arms and kissed me. "My love for you grows with every beat of my heart. Your behavior this night did not disturb me. On the contrary, you made my hunt all the more enjoyable...seductive. My concern is only for how my behavior has affected you."

A chill crept beneath my flesh. I rubbed it away as I explained, "When I saw his blood, I had no control over my own body. I had to taste it."

"But why tonight? What changed?"

I hugged my pillow. "I'm not sure. Maybe I wanted to see what it was like. Maybe I wanted to share this part of your life. Or maybe I just wanted to taste the blood." I glanced at him, and then turned away. "The same thing happened to me today at the doctor's office. When they drew my blood, I wanted to drink it. That's crazy, right?"

He brushed my cheek with the back of his hand. A hint of sadness laced his voice when he said, "It's my blood. It must be changing you."

I tossed the pillow aside and bolted upright. Why hadn't I thought of that? His blood had entered my body every time we made love, and there had been so many times, too many to count, but that couldn't be it. I was human. The blood in my veins was human blood. I barked out a laugh and shook my head. "I'll wait for my doctor's call. He'll have the real answer."

Philippe offered me a half-hearted smile. "I hope he does."

I searched his eyes. "Promise me tonight hasn't changed anything."

The color of his eyes twinkled like jewels. "Oh, but it has."

My stomach dropped and my heart fluttered wildly. "How?" I cried.

He kissed me softly and brought his lips to my ear. "Marry me."

I jerked my head back. "What did you say?"

Beaming from ear to ear, he repeated, "Marry me, Beth."

He'd stolen the breath right from my lungs. Had I heard him right? Had he just proposed?

Reaching over me, he pulled open the nightstand drawer and grabbed up a small box, flipping the lid open. Right under my nose sat a canary diamond set in the center of a thick gold band.

"This was my mother's wedding ring. Before she died, she gave it to me and told me to place it on the finger of the woman I loved. That woman is you."

Tears welled in my eyes, and my hands flew to my cheeks. "Yes!" I blurted out with delight. "I will marry you, Philippe."

He leapt from the bed and lifted me up, whirling us both around the room. We fell to the floor laughing, and he smothered my face with kisses.

What did it mean to marry a vampire? Would I be governed by the same set of rules as he? *Well, rules were meant to be broken.*

CHAPTER 7

When I reached across the bed, I grasped only air. I forced my eyes open, rubbing away any lingering sleep. Philippe was gone, and a note lay on his pillow instead. *Couldn't wake you. Left to feed. Be back shortly.* A twinge tightened around my heart, but I shrugged it off. There'd be plenty more nights to join him.

Fully awake, a sense of awareness tapped at my skull. I was no longer covered in sweat or plagued by chills. I brushed my fingertips over my arms. No tingling or stinging on the surface of my skin. The crackling sizzle of the fire rang crystal clear in my ears, no longer muffled by the irksome ringing. I threw back the covers and set my feet on the floor. The room spun in a distorted whirl. I swayed, but quickly steadied myself. Could I be cured? More importantly, was I ready for breakfast? Nausea swelled inside my stomach and rushed up my throat. I swallowed hard. Though definitely not ready for food, my body decided a hot, relaxing shower sounded wonderful.

After my shower, I changed into a bikini and a terry cloth cover-up and headed downstairs for a swim. Cool, refreshing night air swirled about my body after I'd escaped the doors leading out of the kitchen. Tossing the robe onto a chair, I leapt into the heated pool. The warm water hugged my skin like an electric blanket, relaxing every muscle. As I floated on my back, I gazed up into the star-filled night. Life couldn't possibly get any better.

I flipped over and dove to the bottom, touching the pool floor before pushing off to rise to the surface. Just above the water's border, a blurred figure came into sight, standing at the pool's edge. As I attempted to break through, my head slammed into an invisible barrier, trapping me inside a watery grave. A wet wall enfolded me, squeezing, crushing pain gripping my chest. My lungs compressed, like a snake coiling its wiry body around my ribs. *Air! I need air. Breathe...I can't. I have to.* Water gushed into my mouth. Flailing my arms, I floated back toward the surface, pounding my fists against the invisible barrier. The solid surface above my head shattered, and cool air grazed my fingertips. Like a grenade detonating, I exploded upward, breaking through the water and gasping for air.

The figure remained, standing above me, unnaturally still.

I wiped water and chlorine from my eyes, struggling to peer more closely at my uninvited guest. A gust of wind tossed his auburn hair over his shoulders. His hazel eyes sparkled as he grinned wickedly, exposing razor-sharp fangs. He knelt at the edge of the pool, leveling his gaze at me. "I'm Caleb." His voice was ice-cold, like a winter's chill through the air. "You must be Beth..." He curled his lips in disgust. "The human girl."

My heart plummeted. *He's going to kill me.* I swam as quickly as humanly possible to the opposite side and scurried out of the pool. My teeth chattered together as I trembled violently. Where had he gone? I scanned every inch, spinning in a circle.

A hand touched my shoulder. As the primal scream crawled up my throat, I whirled, swinging my fists wildly at the mystery man.

"Beth, it's me, Philippe!" he shouted out, his arms blocking the blow.

Hot tears burned behind my eyelids as I latched onto him with both hands. "He was here!"

"Who? I don't see anyone." His gaze scanned the empty spaces surrounding the pool.

"Caleb, your maker." As I uttered his name, chills scurried across my skin.

He frowned. "He's not due back for another week. Are you sure you saw him?"

I couldn't help raising my voice. "He introduced himself, called me the human girl."

He pulled away and searched my eyes. "What happened?"

My chest heaved, the sobs building. "He...he tried to—" my voice fell away.

He gripped my shoulders. "Tell me."

I had to force out each word. "He—tried—to—kill—me."

"He tried to what?"

Tears blurred my vision "He held me under the water."

His posture grew rigid, a vein in the center of his forehead twitched. "I'm going to find him."

I clutched at his arm. "Don't leave me."

He swept me up in his arms and carried me to our bedroom. After he'd seated me by the fire, he poured a glass of brandy and held the fiery liquid to my lips. "Drink."

I took a sip, and then another. The heat of the alcohol spread through me, calming my nerves. Stripping off the wet bikini and changing into pajamas subsided the chill. Feeling weary, I climbed into bed.

Philippe sat on the edge of the mattress and stroked my cheek. "I love you."

I took his hand, kissing it and murmuring, "I love you too."

The beauty of his eyes wavered as sleep took hold.

Sometime later, I awoke to a fire lit in the room.

"It's about time," Caleb said in his familiar, icy voice.

I shuddered with a pang of fear, shot upright, and pulled the covers up to my chin.

He sat crossed-legged at the writing desk, his fingers laced and resting in his lap.

I shoved my index finger in the direction of the door. "Get out!"

He chuckled. "Make me." He floated up and out of the chair, landing softly at the foot of the bed. His striking hazel eyes turned several shades deeper as he cocked his head and regarded me.

I darted to the opposite side of the bed and bolted toward the door—to no avail. He flew over me, descending in the perfect position to block my way. An inhuman blaze smoldered between the slits that were his eyes. My legs collapsed and I slumped to the floor, my arms splaying out as limply as my legs. This vampire seemed to control me. I couldn't move, couldn't speak, couldn't defend myself.

He shifted in the flickering light, materializing in front of me. His index finger pointed at me, and he jerked the digit heavenward. I sprang to my feet like a puppet, my head rolling to the side, my neck exposed.

My veins swelled, full and pulsating with blood, as I felt his cold breath sting my bare neck. My heartbeat catapulted into overdrive at an explosive pace. No way in hell would I allow him to drink *my* blood. Inside my head, I screamed for Philippe.

The bedroom door blasted off its hinges, sailing across the room and smashing into the wall where the wood splintered in two. Philippe charged into the room and punched Caleb square in the jaw. Caleb's compulsion spell broke, freeing me to drop to my knees. As I scurried behind the bedpost, I raked my fingers across my throat. Thankfully, I felt no puncture wounds, no wet blood. I gasped aloud in relief, sinking to the floor while I clung desperately to the bedpost.

Philippe stood rigid, glaring at Caleb. With the slice of his hand through the air, he hurtled Caleb across the room. Caleb crashed against the wall, but sprang up in the next second, brushing off his clothes, and burst out laughing. Philippe narrowed his gaze and exposed his fangs. He twirled his hand faster and faster, tossing Caleb about the room like a ping-pong ball. Caleb jutted out his arms like an airplane and hummed like a bellowing engine. When he finally came to rest, he jumped to his feet and applauded Philippe's efforts.

Philippe snarled, saliva flying from his fangs as he shouted, "You're no longer welcome in this house."

A hint of concern flashed behind Caleb's hazel eyes, before darkness fell over his face, stretching his skin taut. He flew at Philippe with preternatural speed, landing directly before him. "You cannot mean this. We're brothers. Nothing has ever come between us."

"Brothers!" Philippe pointed at me. "You tried to kill her, the woman I love. Brothers don't do such things." His arms fell to his sides and he shook his head. "I thought you valued our friendship, but your actions have proven otherwise. Look at her. You can clearly see she's terrified, so why would you torture her so when she is my life! Do know that if you end hers, you end mine as well."

Caleb charged forward, grabbing hold of my arm and yanking me to my feet. My blood ran ice cold. *Don't make eye contact.* Locking my chin to my chest, I twisted hard, pulling away from him.

He tightened his grip, painfully, as he shouted at Philippe. "You would end our friendship over a mere mortal?"

Philippe latched onto me, wrenching me away from Caleb and pushing my body behind his. "If you make me choose, I will choose Beth."

Caleb thrust his chest out in anger. "This is just a phase. You will inevitably become bored with her. She cannot fulfill your needs as an immortal would. Listen to me, Philippe."

"I will not! You constantly tell me how I should feel and disregard my true feelings. You gave me an immortal heart, but a human soul thrives inside me still. You will never understand because you willingly abandoned your humanity long ago." Philippe gazed down at me, his face beaming. "I love her. Without her by my side, I am nothing."

Caleb curled his lips into a sneer and shuddered. "She's a human, solely fated to be fed upon."

Philippe and his maker were at odds with one another over me. The rift between them was entirely my fault. I had to defuse Caleb's resentment and prove to him my love for Philippe was real, that I could be trusted, and would protect his fledgling at all costs. I approached Caleb, extending my hand as an offering of peace.

Caleb gawked at me, swatting my hand away as if it were a disgusting fly.

I didn't gasp or flinch away. I knew I couldn't show him an ounce of fear. Holding my chin high, I didn't back down and proclaimed, "I love Philippe. I've been waiting to be with him my whole life. I would do *anything* for him and would never do anything to hurt him. You must believe me."

Caleb stuck his nose in my face, sniffing like a dog. "Hmph," he protested, brushing me aside to face Philippe. "You do realize she has vampire blood inside her, yes?"

Philippe wrapped his arms around my waist possessively. "The blood is mine."

Caleb opened his mouth, but snapped it shut just as quickly, seeming to stifle his snide remark. Casting a pained look in my direction, he growled, "I suppose I can allow your infatuation with this human to play out."

Philippe exhaled a loud sigh. "She's no infatuation."

As he shook his head, Caleb added, "Your fancy with humans escapes me, but then, we all have our flaws."

Philippe lifted my hand, exposing the finger bearing his diamond. "I asked Beth to marry me."

Caleb's nostrils flared, and his face deepened several shades of red. I pictured flames exploding from his nose. In the next instant, as if he'd flipped an internal switch, he neutralized his temper. Flashing a charming smile, he asked, "Am I invited to this little ceremony?"

Philippe grabbed Caleb up in a fierce hug. "Of course. Who else could I ask to be my best man?"

"I would be honored." Caleb winked at me. "Now, let's make a toast to your little mortal."

Philippe shoved Caleb's shoulder. "Show her some respect or get out."

Caleb turned to me, sporting a devilish grin, bowing deeply in front of me. "Your highness."

I'd had enough of his arrogant attitude. Pushing past Caleb, I stalked angrily out of the room.

"Leaving so soon?" Caleb called out.

Philippe followed me into the hallway. His voice full of apology, he said, "I'm sorry. Please, ignore him. He is merely trying to get the better of you."

I folded my arms and let out a huff. "He's rude and an ass. I want him out of our bedroom, now."

Philippe kissed me softly. "Done."

My breath quickened, heat spreading through me. "However do you accomplish that, taking me from anger to pleasure in a matter of seconds?"

Philippe whispered in my ear, "With kisses, lots of kisses." He pulled me close, pressing his body against me. "I can never get enough of you."

I winked at him. "I'll be waiting in bed...naked."

Philippe's gaze roamed over my body, and he kissed me harder. "I'll be right back," he said, before hurrying into the room and seizing Caleb's arm. With fiendish speed, he hauled Caleb into the hallway and down the hall in the direction of the cold, masculine suite.

As long as Caleb kept out of my way, I didn't care where he slept. I stripped off my pajamas and slipped under the covers, my gaze focused on the broken door. We couldn't leave it like that. What if Betty or one of the maids walked by at an inopportune moment?

Philippe ran through the door, tossing his shirt aside.

"Wait," I said, pointing. "The door."

Philippe flashed over to scoop up both splintered pieces and forced them together, sealing off the entrance. "Satisfied?"

The sexy look in his eyes was all the foreplay I needed. "Yes. Now get over here and make love to me."

Philippe stumbled over to me as he removed the rest of his clothes, jumping into bed and climbing on top of me. He brushed his lips down my neck, nibbling at my skin. My legs wrapped around him as I guided him inside of me, arching my back when he slid deeper, taking me past the point of no return. Our sexual craze mounted, imprisoning our bodies with pleasure before we collapsed, laughing like teenagers.

After making love, we cuddled by the fire. Philippe propped himself up on his elbow, resting his head in his hand, and playfully tapped the tip of my nose. "So, what was it you wanted to know about Dana Karan?"

Impatient to feed my curiosity, I rattled off, "Are you the vampire in that famous photo? Was he tracking you? What's your connection? Is he still alive?"

Philippe patted my knee. "Just a tad bit eager, are you?"

"Don't tease me. You offered."

He chuckled. "Okay, okay. It was actually Caleb who was captured in the photo, but I was there when it was snapped. Yes, he often trailed both Caleb and me. His obsession with vampires is the bond which connects us. And yes, Dana is still alive."

"So he was telling the truth about the photo."

He released a long, low sigh, as if he'd held it inside for many years. "Caleb and I were hunting inside a quaint little bar in Paris one night. Caleb can be reckless and lack discretion. He's never harbored a fear of humans, believing himself to be invincible and incapable of being caught, much less disposed of."

Ahhh, I thought to myself, *Caleb loves to play God.* "Then he's playing with fire."

Philippe nodded. "And he loves the thrill of danger."

"So you protect Caleb, watch out for him."

Philippe chuckled. "Caleb needs no protection, especially from humans." He kissed me. "No offense."

I shrugged my shoulders. "None taken." I leaned forward, curiosity overwhelming me. I pressed, "So, what happened at the bar?"

"Ah yes, back to the bar. Dana tracked us there. We'd gotten rather used to him tagging along, like a stray dog. Caleb chose our victim and lured him out back, and as expected, Dana exited the bar moments later. When he spotted us, he drew near, hiding only a few feet away, but of course, we knew he was there. Caleb decided to put on a show for Dana. I advised against such recklessness, but Caleb thought messing with him would be great fun."

I couldn't keep a groan from escaping my lips. It seemed Caleb had always acted like a pompous, narrow-minded ass. The more I learned about him, the more I despised Philippe's maker. "He's so unlike you. Why do you put up with him?"

"He has his good points as well." He winked at me. "You'll see You might even grow to love him too."

I shook my head. "Not happening."

Philippe leaned forward and kissed my cheek. "Give it time."

I couldn't imagine that all the time in the world would change my mind. "Go on. So, Caleb decided to put on a show."

"It was quite the performance. Caleb hurtled our victim into the air above Dana several times before setting him on the ground and having him charge Dana with vampire speed. Next, Caleb went too far, equipping our victim with a knife."

"What?"

"Caleb thrust a knife in the man's hand. The man raised the knife over his head, stampeding like a crazed bull straight toward Dana. Dana released a petrified shriek, prompting Caleb to break into hysterical laughter before calling our victim back."

I rolled my eyes. "Like I said, he's an ass. And you think I'll grow to love him? Not a chance."

He frowned. "As I said, I don't condone his behavior, but Caleb does what he wants, when he wants, and there's no stopping him, even when he puts our lives at risk."

"And I'm assuming his little stunt with Dana did just that?"

"In a way, yes, because Dana seized the opportunity. As Caleb bit into our victim's neck, Dana withdrew a small camera from his jacket and snapped a photo before fleeing the scene. Caleb had merely roared with laughter at his action. He said, *'Now, won't that be a Kodak moment?'* Even though I implored him to go after our unwanted photographer, Caleb insisted no harm would come of it, and he didn't wish to have his meal interrupted." Philippe nodded toward his writing desk. "You know the rest of the story by reading the articles."

An unsettling feeling stirred to life inside me. I reached for Philippe's hand. "That photo ruined Dana's life. Instead of being recognized as a photojournalist, Dana's reputation was questioned. Dana has to be bitter. You're sure he's not out to get the two of you?"

"I make it my business to keep track of Dana at all times," Philippe assured me.

"Then you must know where he is now."

He eyed me. "I do."

"Well, where is he?"

For a moment, he said nothing. Stern lines darkened his brow. "He's here, in Castle Beach."

I opened my mouth but didn't get a chance to speak.

He held up his hand. "That's all I will say. Don't press me, Beth," he said in a curt tone.

I sat back, placing my hands on my hips. "You told me you could tell me anything. Why are you being so secretive now?"

"Curiosity will get the better of you; I know you too well already. You'll try to seek him out. He's unstable and dangerous. My vagueness is only for your protection."

I decided I liked being protected and that Philippe was right. If I learned Dana's whereabouts, I would undoubtedly seek him out, landing myself in a world of trouble. Leaning over, I kissed him sweetly. He picked me up and carried me back to bed. I stroked his hair until he fell asleep, lying curled into his side and watching the steady rise and fall of his chest. Slowly, sleep won me over.

When I woke, as usual, Philippe was gone. Sadly, I was growing accustomed to waking up alone. One night soon, I'd insist on joining him, but for once in a long time, I didn't possess a craving for blood. I craved food! After a quick shower, I threw my hair into a ponytail and changed into a pair of jeans and a cowl-necked sweater. My hunger led me downstairs, and I made a beeline for the kitchen. Before I could reach my goal, I ran into Betty in the foyer.

Beaming, she embraced me. "Beth, dear, I'm so happy to learn of your engagement to Mr. Delon. Congratulations."

"Thank you." I placed my hand over my heart. "I love him very much."

Her smile faded as she leaned in close and said, "I know the truth about Mr. Delon."

My breath caught in my throat. She'd just admitted to knowing Philippe to be a vampire. She trusted me. I reached out and squeezed her arm.

In a firm tone, she added, "We must never discuss this matter. We both know the truth, and that's all that matters, nothing more. Agreed?"

I crossed my finger over my heart. "Agreed."

Her eyes sparkled. "Very well. Are you hungry? May I fix you some dinner?"

I placed my hand on my grumbling stomach. "Starving. Yes, thank you."

"There's a pot of pasta simmering on the stove. How does that sound?"

My stomach rumbled again, and we both laughed. "My stomach approves."

"Wonderful."

"I feel like reading. It is too much trouble to bring my dinner to the study?"

She took my hands in hers. "No trouble at all, dear. You run along, and I'll be in shortly with a tray."

"Thank you."

I drifted down the long hallway, veering left and opening the study door. A delightfully warm fire burned in the hearth, perfuming the air with the scent of seared wood. I sighed, taking in a breath and stretching my arms overhead. While roaming the wall of books, I browsed the many titles, trying to decide which genre I was in the mood for. Concluding a mystery might be nice, I plucked one from the shelf and flipped open the cover.

"Good evening, your highness," Caleb teased, with a hint of sarcasm.

I let out a gasp, dropping the book before I whirled to face him.

He chuckled.

I shoved the book back on the ledge and shot toward the door.

"Don't leave on my account," he called after me. "Stay and chat. I suppose I should get to know you."

I froze, balling my hands into fists. Yet again, I had allowed him to get under my skin. Why? Placing my hands on my hips and facing him, I sharpened my tone. "I'm good for him. I make him happy. That should make you happy too. What is it about human beings that bothers you so? Is it because you're no longer one yourself? Are you jealous?"

His smug smirk vanished. An orange blaze leapt up inside his hazel eyes, growing brighter with each passing moment. He approached me with large, violent strides.

Blood hammered through my veins like gunfire. Why had I confronted him? What the hell had I been thinking? I could be such an idiot at times. I backed away as quickly as I could manage, my back slamming against the wall, trapping me. Mere inches separated me from the irate vampire. Shockingly, he leaned forward and kissed my mouth. Instinct took over as I jerked my head away from him.

Running a finger over my lips, he said, "I wanted to taste you," as if such a desire excused his actions. His stare hardened as he whispered, "Yes, Philippe's blood is inside you, but I also taste another's. You've been quite a busy bee."

His words echoed inside my head like exploding bombs. What could he mean, another vampire? I stared him down. "The only blood inside me is Philippe's and my own. There's been no one else."

In a malicious tone, he told me, "You're wrong. I created Philippe. I know his blood; his is blood of *my* blood." His finger rose to lift my chin. "This other blood is potent, ancient, existing before my time, even."

Was he testing me? Was his accusation a trick? "You don't approve of our relationship. You're trying to trick me, make me confess to something that isn't true."

"You're right, I don't approve, but blood doesn't lie."

"Then why didn't Philippe say anything about it to me? If you can sense another vampire's blood in me, surely he would be able to do so too," I challenged.

He shook his head, stubbornly. "Philippe remains far too human. His emotions cloud his judgment. Besides, he's infatuated with you. As they say, love is indeed blind."

I regarded him. Was I being played? The poker-faced vampire's stare offered me no clue. "What you're suggesting is impossible. You and Philippe are the only vampires I've met."

He smirked again. "Yet, you willingly accepted what he was without question. Why did you fail to ask him for proof?"

I stared at him, searching his eyes. Caleb hadn't known I was involved with Philippe, but how could that be? Philippe had entered my life so many years ago when I was just a child. Had he kept our visits secret from his maker? Was *I* his biggest secret? "Philippe never told you about me?"

His gaze scrutinized my face. "What do you mean?"

"I've known him all my life—ever since I was a small child—but until recently, he only ever appeared to me as mist."

Caleb didn't utter a single word, seemingly allowing my words to sink in. After a long moment, he took a seat by the fire and gestured to the chair opposite his own. "Please, sit down. We should talk."

Whether or not I thought such a course of action was wise, I sat in the vacant chair anyway, and waited for him to speak.

He chuckled. "I'm beginning to believe you're a vampire groupie."

My fingers drummed the chair arm, and I sighed heavily. "I'm in love with him. That doesn't make me a groupie."

"But why are you so attracted to him? When did your relationship with him begin?"

I curled a strand of hair around my finger. He was fishing, but what choice did I have? If I didn't answer him, he'd resort to poking around inside my head and take what he wanted anyway. "He's gentle and kind, and powerful, all at the same time. On my seventeenth birthday, he did something for me that bound my heart to his. On that night, I knew with certainty I was in love with him."

"Huh...and have you lived in Castle Beach all your life?"

"Yes, me and my mother. My father left when I was ten."

"Huh," he said again. "Do you know why your father left?"

I shifted in the chair, crossing and uncrossing my arms. "Not entirely."

His gaze narrowed. "You think he left because of something you may have done?"

My mind drifted back to my ninth year. I could see my mother and father standing at opposite ends of the kitchen while I ate cereal at the counter. My father's rigid posture and hateful glare drove my mother to hang her head. Her shoulders trembled, tears spilling from her eyes and striking the floor. From between gritted teeth, my father spat, "I'll never forgive you for this," before he stomped out of the room. My mother also ran from the kitchen, sobbing. Left alone in the aftermath, I had pushed my bowl away. After I'd managed to pull myself back from the past, I looked at Caleb and answered, "Yes."

"Maybe his absence was connected somehow to Philippe's visits. How often did you say he came to you?"

He was fishing again. "I didn't."

"But you did say he disguised himself as mist. Why would he do that?"

"I don't know," I said, my voice rising an octave.

He grinned. "Ah, I hit a nerve. Was Philippe truly the being hiding behind the mist?"

I ran my hands through my hair and muttered, "It has to be him. That's the only logical explanation." I fixed my gaze on Caleb and raised my voice again. "Besides, since we've been together, the mist has never returned. That alone confirms his identity."

Caleb drew his brows together and said, "If Philippe and the mist are truly one in the same, he would have no reason to hide it from you." His lips spread into a wicked grin. "Unless, of course, he has been the one who's tricked you."

I bit my lip, wishing any truth away from his words. "You're trying to plant doubt inside my head, make me cast Philippe aside."

He waved an annoying finger in my face. "Can't it be possible you're in denial simply because you believe yourself to be in love with him?"

I gave a quick shake of my head. "Not possible."

Caleb clapped his hands together with an expression of delight. "I have a brilliant idea. Why don't we just go and ask Philippe, settle the topic once and for all?"

I shot out of my chair, my fists clenching automatically. "Stay out of our relationship!"

The satisfied smirk reappeared, taking up permanent residence on his face. "So you *do* have doubts. Relax. I have no intention of getting involved. This is your puzzle to solve, but solve it fast, my dear, or hearts will be broken, and I won't abide a broken-hearted Philippe."

I glared at him with disgust. "You're a despicable creature."

He waved me away and snapped, "You know nothing about me or our race." He pointed a rigid finger at the chair. "Sit down. It's time for a little Vampire 101."

I plopped down into the chair, groaning and locking my gaze on the ceiling.

He snapped his fingers. "Pay attention."

"I'm listening," I growled, raising my voice and meeting his eyes.

He folded his hands neatly into his lap, the color of his eyes twinkling as he began. "Ten very powerful vampire gods grace this Earth. It was their blood which created the vampire race."

I leaned forward in my chair, my interest piqued, resting my chin in my palms.

"I see I have your attention," he quipped, his smile becoming prideful. "Their story is well known among our kind, but even humans have written about them." He winked at me. "Of course, being mere mortals, their versions always contain fallacies. You may have even read some of these erroneous accounts. In mythology, it's referred to as the story of Osiris, Isis, and Seth."

My mouth fell open. "I read that story in high school."

"Well now, let me tell you the real story. Seth had it out for Osiris. The jealousy he harbored for his brother drove him mad. Finally, he brutally murdered Osiris, tearing his body into fourteen pieces and scattering them throughout the land. His sister-in-law, Isis, combed the land, searching for her husband, gathering up his body parts piece by piece as she found them. Her love and devotion impressed her allies, the remaining gods, so together they resurrected Osiris, naming him god of the underworld.

"That part of the history was all the books got right. The manner in which the gods accomplished his resurrection was never accounted by any pen wielded by human hand. The truth, hidden from human knowledge, is that nine gods, to be exact, bled over Osiris' lifeless, bandaged body, chanting a spell of rebirth. Once they'd succeeded, Osiris rose from the dead a far grander god and one of blood. With his newly bestowed power and flawless beauty, Osiris seduced all nine gods, convincing each of them to join him and stand by his side for all eternity. He brought their hearts to near failure by draining each one of blood, after which he transformed their bodies with his immortal blood and awakened their immortal hearts."

I sat, gripping the edge of my seat. "Is there more? I want to know more."

Caleb's eyes took on a sinister cast. "There *is* more. Their thirst for blood knew no limits. Together, they obliterated entire cities, devouring population after population, driving the human race toward extinction. But the gods knew that without mankind, there would be no one to worship or love them. In despair, they traveled the world, seeking out twelve of the wisest human beings known to man and transformed them with their godly blood. These twelve, the gods' children, are referred to as The Old Ones or The Council. It is they who set forth the laws governing vampirism and initiated a blood lottery for The Ten."

I swallowed hard. "Blood lottery?"

Caleb sneered. "Still want to know more?"

Footsteps approached the study, and Betty peeked inside the room, her gaze traveling to mine. "There you are." She entered, carrying a tray of steaming pasta, topped with marinara sauce and parmesan cheese, and a glass of red wine placed to the right of the plate. She nodded an acknowledgement at Caleb and said, "Good evening, Mr. Keith."

Caleb returned her greeting. "Betty."

She set the tray down in front of me. "Here you go, dear."

Breathing in the aroma of fresh tomatoes and cheese distracted me. I smiled up at her. "Betty, this looks wonderful. Thank you."

She placed her hands on her hips and laughed warmly. "Enjoy." Before she turned to leave, she waved her finger at Caleb. "Behave."

He extended his palms in exaggerated innocence. "What?"

"Don't let him give you any trouble," she warned, shifting her attention to me.

"I won't."

"All right then." She left me alone with the mischievous vampire.

"The blood lottery, go on," I insisted, twirling pasta around my fork.

He was staring at the doorway, frowning. "That Betty, she's a tough cookie. After all these years, she still doesn't trust me."

With good reason, I thought. "Caleb, the lottery."

"Yes, yes," he grumbled, continuing where he'd left off. "The Old Ones set forth the blood lottery into the human world. In every town around the globe, families entered their names. Drawings were held, and those selected chose a fifth-generation family member to be offered up to The Ten on their twenty-fifth birthday."

A chill scurried down my spine. "You mean, offered up to be drained of blood?"

"Yes."

I grew queasy and pushed my food away. I was almost twenty-five. "Is there a list of the family names chosen?"

He lowered his voice and leaned forward in his chair. "The lottery was drawn in secrecy. If the ceremony were made known to mankind, The Old Ones feared the raising of an alarm which would incite a panic. Even The Ten were kept in the dark as to the chosen's identities, which were revealed only on the victim's twenty-fifth birthday and not a moment before, and some poor soul is turning twenty-five every day."

If there were any veracity to Caleb's words, I wouldn't feel completely at ease until after my next birthday had passed.

"Philippe and I aren't bound by the lottery," Caleb added. "We feed at random. Does the idea of such a thing upset you?"

In a flat tone, I answered, "It's not a choice. You must feed in order to survive."

He grinned. "Good answer. You're level-headed, and I like that." He paused, eyeing me shrewdly. "Have you told anyone about Philippe?"

I didn't owe him an answer; nonetheless, I gave him one. "Danny knows, but he's always known. He's seen the mist too. I want to tell Anna, but only with Philippe's permission."

The color of his eyes caught fire, and they burned into mine. "Who are Danny and Anna? It appears you have not been instructed about our rules."

Even though I'd hurt Danny, and he'd abruptly cut me out of his life, I still cared for him. Always would. I couldn't let a monster like Caleb go near him. Anna, on the other hand, would be a problem. She'd immediately flock to Caleb, and there would be no tearing her away. He was exactly the type she sought out—and she never gave up once she'd honed in on the scent of a challenge, and Caleb was a walking, talking challenge. "Forget about them. Besides, Danny's out of the picture. What rules are you referring to?"

"Philippe is not doing you any favors by keeping you in the dark." His tone turned impatient. "If you are to marry, you must know them, follow them."

Rules, rules, rules, who cared? What was it with vampires and their rules? "Well, why don't you list them for me?"

He rubbed his hands together and licked his lips. "No contact with humans, except to feed." He paused, letting the meaning of that one sink in.

I rolled my eyes. "Go on."

He winked at me. "Just had to gauge your reaction. Okay, moving on. Never go public with information; no interviews, photos, letters, emails, blog postings, etcetera."

I scowled at him. "Looks like you broke that rule."

He threw his head back and laughed out loud. "Touché. Where was I? Oh yes, leave no traces of your victims behind. Only exceptional humans may be turned and never anyone over the age of twenty-five or under eighteen. Respect your maker—always." He wagged his eyebrows in an exaggerated manner after stating that one. "Abide by the laws of The Old Ones. Honor The Ten. Death to any vampire who betrays his race." He waved his hand in the air dismissively and said, "There were many more over the years, but today, they are no longer applicable."

I clutched at my throat and released a tense breath. "Am I placing Philippe in danger? Will he be punished because he's breaking one of the rules?"

His face softened, and a genuine smile spread on his lips. "We've all broken a rule here and there. If The Old Ones were displeased, you'd both already know. I would know. In fact, his plan to marry appears to have aroused much excitement in them. They've accepted his portion of human nature far better than I."

"They know about his proposal already? That was fast. I haven't even told my mom or Anna. How did they find out about us?"

He snickered. "Silly girl. I told them. As you stated, he broke a rule and defied The Old Ones. I wanted to ensure Philippe hadn't placed himself in any danger."

I gazed at him in a new light. Maybe Caleb possessed a compassionate side after all.

"When it happens to you, how do you believe you'll fare?"

"When what happens?"

"Surely, you're aware of the fact Philippe doesn't age. He can't allow you to either. Once you're married, you'll be together, quite literally, forever."

The tiny hairs on the back of my neck stirred. I rose to my feet and faced the fireplace, hugging my trembling arms around my ribcage. The flames danced as wildly as the beat of my heart. "I'm not ready to think about that."

In a taunting tone, he reminded me, "Oh, no rush. You still have a few weeks to mull it over before you turn twenty-five."

I spun and glared at him. "Do you enjoy annoying me?"

He grinned wickedly and continued to twist the knife. "You'll prefer immortal life over human existence. There is no comparison. Once you're a vampire, mortality boundaries disappear. And the taste of blood..." He sighed blissfully, licking his lips, and fell backward into his chair. "...is like nothing you've ever experienced."

I balled my hands into fists and screamed, "Stop! I don't want to hear any more."

Philippe appeared in the doorway and hurried to my side. His familiar arms wound around me, pulling me close. A sense of calm spread through every limb.

Philippe's lips formed a hard line. "Why must you continue to harass her?"

Gloating, Caleb chuckled. "I was only revealing her own fate to her." He cocked his head and frowned. "She didn't appear to be thrilled by the eventual outcome."

Philippe jutted a rigid hand in the direction of the door. "Caleb, it's time for you to leave, and I don't mean to your room upstairs," he said, his tone crisp and cold.

Caleb rose from his chair and straightened his jacket. "I suppose I've overstayed my welcome. Don't bother showing me out. I believe I know the way." And then, he was gone.

Philippe seated me on the couch and knelt in front of me. He took my hands into his and said, "Beth, I know the idea frightens you, but we must address the necessity of my wish to turn you."

I dropped his hands and pushed him away. "No, not now. It's too soon. Later."

He flinched as if I'd slapped him.

I cupped his cheeks between my palms and kissed him sweetly. The thought of living forever unnerved me, unravelling every nerve so that I couldn't comprehend the idea. And then there was the blood, the *drinking* of human blood! I loved Philippe and would do anything for him. If part of that anything meant ending my human life, I would, but when *I* decided to do so and not before. Besides, I still had time. Pulling away, I locked my gaze on his and said, "I will do this for you, for us, but only on my own terms."

He released a sigh of relief and pulled me close, squeezing me against his body as though he might never see me again. "I will not mention the subject again. I have faith in you, Beth." His voice had thickened with boundless trust.

We were abruptly interrupted when Betty rushed into the study, carrying the house phone. "Beth, it's your doctor."

I clutched the phone, a sudden wariness overtaking me, and pressed the cold surface against my ear. "Hello?"

"Hi, Beth. It's Dr. Hughes." His tone carried a nervous edge. "I apologize for the late hour, but I haven't had a free moment until now. Your lab results came in, and, well, I needed to contact you."

I plopped down in the chair. "Good news, I hope."

There was a moment of silence before he said, "I'm afraid I don't have all the answers, not yet. There are perplexing abnormalities in your blood. Both your white and red counts are highly irregular. I've never seen anything like it. I'm beyond puzzled. It could be some type of new virus. I want you to come back in for further testing."

I dropped the phone, staring blankly ahead.

Philippe laid a comforting hand on my shoulder. "Beth, what is it?"

I didn't speak, my gaze focused on the flames leaping about inside the hearth. I didn't need more tests. Suddenly, it all became so very clear, all the pieces fitting together perfectly. I was slowly turning into something else, something half human and half vampire.

CHAPTER 8

Our Vegas wedding came together out of nowhere, and I welcomed the distraction, throwing my body and mind into the arrangements and brushing aside my bizarre lab results. First on the agenda had been invitations. My father didn't make the guest list. When I'd turned nine, the arguments between my parents had kicked into high gear, loaded with slamming doors, screaming matches, and ending with the silent treatment on both sides. One day my father had abandoned us—just walked out the door and never came back. There had been no phone calls, letters, or visits. It was as if he'd fallen off the face of the Earth. I'd gotten over it in time, but my mother never did. Every night, she waited on the front porch, watching for his car to pull into the driveway. She'd cry a little, mumble a few choice words, before stomping back inside the house when he didn't show. The root cause of their friction had always escaped me, but as Caleb had uncovered in my memories, my mother had done something, something my father couldn't forgive, something involving me, but what had been her crime? An affair? Was I someone else's kid? Maybe becoming a father hadn't been his thing and he wished to rid himself of the financial burden. Whatever the reason, my mother remained tight-lipped, and I got tired of asking. After he left, everything changed between us. She still took care of me, fed me, kept a roof over my head and made sure I kept out of trouble, but it was as if she'd grown incapable of showing me love and sought to constantly push me away. When I'd turned eighteen, I packed my things and ventured out on my own. She was who she was. I accepted that fact long ago, but I also figured she had a right to know her only child was getting married. So, there I sat on the bed, lost in remembrance, before I picked up the phone and dialed her number.

She picked up on the second ring. "Hello."

"Hi, Mom. It's Beth."

There was a long pause, and then in a flat, emotionless tone she said, "Hello, Beth. How are you?"

She doesn't care. Blurt it out and hang up. "Fine. I called to tell you I'm getting married."

In the same lifeless pitch, she responded, "That's wonderful. When's the big day?"

"We're flying to Vegas this weekend. Maybe you'd like to join us?" I cringed and bit my lip. Why in the world had I asked? Was I trying to torture us both? She wouldn't come, and I didn't want her to.

"Oh, Beth, I'm sorry, but it's impossible. Maybe if I had more notice, but this weekend is out of the question."

I glanced heavenward. *Thank God.* "I understand."

"When you called, I was right in the middle of something. I've got to get going. Give me your address and I'll send a gift."

"Of course." After rattling off our address, I hung up and heaved a sigh. I'd fulfilled my obligation as a daughter.

As I scrolled through my phone, Danny's number popped up. An empty feeling settled into the pit of my stomach. I knew I should call and tell him; I owed him that much. I cleared my throat nervously and tapped the screen.

A robotic voice stated, "The number you have reached is not in service, and there is no new number at this time. Please check the number and try again."

I pulled the phone away from my ear and stared, disbelieving. The automated statement repeated, broadcasting Danny's final message of abandonment loud and clear. I laid the phone in my lap. Closing my eyes, I bent forward to lay my head on my arms. I'd made a choice. I'd chosen Philippe. Danny had made a choice too. He'd closed the door on me for good.

Wiping away tears, I grabbed up my phone and tapped Anna's name, but I was positive she'd push for an explanation. The idea of a sudden wedding wouldn't fly with her. She'd argue it was too soon, ask me to wait a year or two, or tell me I was crazy. But without my mother or Danny around to offer support, I desperately needed Anna by my side—hopefully as my maid of honor. I sucked in a ragged breath when she answered.

"Hello."

"I've got news, big news."

In a playful tone, she teased, "I'm sure it's about your gorgeous billionaire."

I ripped off the bandage and blurted it out. "We're getting married in Vegas this weekend."

She barked out a laugh. "Yeah, right."

I stood and began to pace the room. "I'm serious. Please, say you'll be my maid of honor."

"Hold up. Rewind. When did this happen?"

Here we go. "When doesn't really matter."

"Like hell it doesn't. You just met the guy. Sure, he's rich and gorgeous, but you don't really know anything about him. Is he pushing for this wedding?"

"Of course not. We're in love. We don't want to wait."

"What's the rush? You're not pregnant, are you?"

Giggles flooded my mouth. She had no idea how impossible her suggestion was. I doubled over, laughing but managed to get out, 'No, definitely not." I steadied my voice. "There's no hidden agenda. We just want to get married."

"But why now?" she pressed, the volume of her voice rising.

We could spin this conversation all day and never get anywhere. I had to toss her a bone, but something reasonable, believable, and true. I sighed and confessed, "I didn't just meet Philippe. I've known him for years."

She gasped, obviously shocked. "What! You said it had been only a few months. Why did you lie about that? Did Danny know about him all those years before you broke up?"

I ran my free hand through my hair. Revealing too much would only raise more questions, but I had to tell her something. The love letters! She'd seen them, read them with me. She would believe he'd written them. "I've known him since college. Remember the love letters?"

"Oh my God, he's your secret admirer! You were with Danny then. Were you seeing them at the same time? Come on, you can tell me."

"I'll tell you everything, I promise. Just please say you'll come to Vegas and be my maid of honor. Anna, please, say yes."

"Swear you'll spill?"

"I swear."

There was a brief pause before she exclaimed, "Hell yeah, girl. You aren't getting married unless I'm there. When do we leave?"

I danced in place with the phone against my ear. "This means the world to me. Thank you. Friday, 7:00 PM. We'll pick you up at six."

"Can't wait."

After hanging up, I blasted out of our bedroom and charged downstairs, racing into the study, completely elated. Philippe sat by the fire reading a book. I plummeted onto his lap and shouted, "Anna said yes!"

He laid his book aside so he could wrap his arm around me and kiss my cheek. "That's wonderful. I know she means a lot to you."

I looked away. "We need to discuss Anna. I want to tell her about you, who you really are, what's happening to me, discuss our future."

Philippe pushed me off his lap and stood, shaking his head. He addressed me in a stern voice. "No, Beth, we have rules. Telling humans about our existence is not permitted."

I threw my shoulders back and stood strong. "Well, I have rules which govern my life too, one being that I don't lie to my friends, especially my best friend. You need to make an exception."

He arched his brow at me. "No, I don't. This isn't a game, Beth."

I stood my ground. "I never said it was, but you told me. Why can't I tell her?"

"It's not the same."

"Breaking a rule is breaking a rule. Besides, I'll need her support once I've transformed."

He widened his eyes. "You will need *me*," he declared, his tone curt. "A human cannot possibly guide you through your transformation." His expression and tone relaxed when he added, "In reality, she will most likely fear you."

I shook my head, backing away from him. "Not Anna."

Philippe's expression clouded over with gloom. "You'd be surprised by how most humans react to us." He came to me and covered my shoulders with his hands. "Listen to me. I speak from experience."

I clung to my loyalty to Anna. "I've known her for a very long time. It's true that she doesn't believe in vampires, but she believes in me. She wouldn't let anything come between us."

Philippe tugged on his goatee, regarding me. An affectionate smile found its way onto his lips. "I cannot deny you anything. You may tell her." He pointed a finger at me in warning. "But prepare yourself for disappointment. She may not react as you'd like to believe."

I threw my arms around his neck and hugged him fiercely. "Thank you. You won't regret this, you'll see. Everything will work out. I know it will."

CHAPTER 9

Jon Paul chauffeured the four of us—Philippe, Caleb, Anna, and I—to the airport. Anna couldn't take her eyes off Caleb, just as I'd predicted, and he turned on the charm, reeling her in.

Anna leaned close to me and whispered, "Caleb is absolutely gorgeous. Why didn't you spill?"

Goose bumps pinched the skin along the back of my neck. I dug my fingers into her arm and cautioned, "Because he's trouble. Stay away from him."

She waved me away and rolled her eyes before she turned to bat her eyelashes at Caleb.

An orange inferno lit inside Caleb's eyes. Pressing his lips into a taut line, he shoved his voice inside my head. "Keep your mouth shut."

I stared him down, my insides ablaze with anger. Firing back, I somehow propelled my own voice outward, slamming it inside his brain. "Was that a threat? You don't scare me. I'm going to tell her. I have Philippe's permission." My first message via brainwaves, another attribute Philippe's blood had granted me. I thrust my chin into the air, throwing my most smug expression at Caleb.

Caleb's jaw dropped, and he fell back against the seat. After recovering from the shock, he winked and lobbed more thoughts my way. "So...you can converse privately. Very impressive." Smirking, he added, "But you're no threat, Red, and your little friend here is noticeably taken with me." He licked his lips. "Her constant flirting is making me extremely thirsty."

I stared defiantly at him and secretly declared, "I will move mountains to keep her away from you."

He turned to Anna and smiled placidly. She remained utterly oblivious to our heated exchange of unspoken words, but not Philippe. He'd taken note of every word. Entering my mind, he said, "You're a quick study, Beth. There will be no limit to what I can teach you; however, I favor human nature over vampirism."

I stroked his face and poured my words into his mind. "I favor that nature too, my love."

Our lips met in a passionate kiss.

"Hello," Caleb said out loud.

We both turned in his direction.

Caleb covered Anna's eyes with his hands. "There are children present," he said, his lips nearly grazing Anna's cheek.

She giggled and gave him a playful nudge. "Caleb."

Every nerve in my body went into spasms of horror. I knew her. She was falling hard, and I had to warn her.

Philippe's voice entered my mind. "This is our day. I think it best to tell her after the ceremony."

I gave him a nod, but by no means did I agree. Anna had to be forewarned.

The terminal sign came up on our right and the car turned, pulling into the airport. Jon Paul parked the car alongside the passenger drop-off lane. He opened our doors, loaded our luggage onto a pushcart, and wished us a safe flight. We hurried off to make our way through security and board the plane. A cheerful flight attendant checked our tickets before escorting us to first class. After we'd settled into our seats, she took our drink orders. We all asked for wine—white for Anna and I, red for Philippe and Caleb.

She returned with our beverages, adding a complementary tray of assorted meats, cheeses, and crackers to our order. Her permanent grin firmly in place, she said, "If you need anything else, please, let me know. The call button is above you to the right."

"Thank you," Philippe said, giving her a polite nod.

"You're welcome," she replied, and then vanished behind the pleated curtains a few feet away.

Caleb spread his arms, released a sigh, and nudged Anna's arm. "My first time on a plane. This is going to be rather enjoyable."

Philippe raised his brows and shot his maker a keep-your-mouth-shut look.

Caleb chuckled, seeming pleased with himself.

Anna peered at him, her smile becoming a frown. "I thought you said you came to Castle Beach from Paris?"

Caleb nodded. "Indeed, I did."

She stared at him with her dark eyes narrowing before asking, "Then how did you get here?"

He flashed a dazzling smile and said, "I flew."

A sea of lines wrinkled her brow. "But you just said..."

I butted in, attempting to rectify the situation. "Caleb is always joking around. We never know when to take him seriously."

Her frown deepened as her gaze bounced back and forth between Caleb and I.

The seat belt light came on, as the pilot's voice simultaneously sounded over the microphone. "Welcome aboard, ladies and gentlemen. Our destination this evening is Las Vegas. Please, let your flight attendants know if you need anything, and sit back and enjoy the flight."

Fifteen minutes in, Caleb resumed his mind games. He touched Anna's hand, the color of his eyes sparkling as he said, "Anna, dear, did you know Philippe and I are members of a different race?"

"What race is that?" she asked innocently.

Philippe sprang to his feet and grabbed Caleb by the arm, lifting him out of his seat. "Excuse us," he said as he hauled Caleb down the aisle.

Anna watched them walk away before turning back to me. "What's going on?"

I leveled a stare full of gravity at her. "There are things you need to know."

She fidgeted with her necklace. "Like what?"

That conversation would require privacy and adequate time for Anna to get over the shock of the subject matter. "I'll tell you everything once we land and find a place where we can be alone."

She stiffened in her seat. "I don't like this, Beth."

I took her hand and squeezed it. "Trust me."

Her gaze seemed to peer into my heart. "I trust you."

Moments later, Philippe returned with a toned-down Caleb. The rest of the flight went by peacefully and without incident. We landed at 8:00 PM and went to retrieve our luggage. After crowding into a cab, we zipped through the streets like lightning, making our way to the Luxor Hotel. The black luster of the pyramid-shaped hotel, with its gleaming diamond tip, monopolized the night's sky.

My gaze roamed over the magnificent scenery when I stepped out of the cab. What a stunning location for our wedding. Philippe reached for my hand and led me past the giant stone sphinx guarding the entrance. Upon crossing the threshold, we entered a grand lobby where we checked in at the front desk. A bellboy with a crew cut, decked out in black from head to toe, ushered the four of us to our rooms—the hotel's premier suites. Anna's room was across from ours, and Caleb's was farther down the hallway. The bellboy opened the door to our suite and wheeled our luggage just inside the doorway. Entering the room and beholding the stunning red velvet sofas, hand-carved marble furniture, and floor-to-ceiling windows revealing the fantastic display of city lights, I grew beyond spellbound.

After Philippe tipped the young man generously, he closed the door. He brought the luggage into the bedroom as he said, "Beth, you're going to love this."

I glided into the bedroom as if my feet never touched the floor and laid eyes on the king-size canopy bed covered in luxurious gold fabrics, and pillows monopolizing the center of the room. A separate sitting area looking out onto the city's picturesque views was off to its right. Flopping down in one of the red velvet chairs, I stretched my arms overhead and exhaled a breath of delight.

Philippe lowered himself into the chair opposite me. "Is everything to your satisfaction?" he asked, smiling at me warmly.

I bounced to my feet and perched myself on his lap, smothering him with kisses. "It's perfect." So much so, I had forgotten all about my promise to Anna.

****

Rows of empty chairs, upholstered in light gold, filled the Luxor's regal chapel. Bronzed-colored curtains, draped like Egyptian gowns, framed the saffron altar. Philippe, Caleb, and Anna stood close to the pale walls, gazing back at me. I'd dressed in a white, knee-length lace dress, and carried a small bouquet of red roses. My lace veil was situated over my face. The "Wedding March" echoed off the walls of the room, my cue to move forward. Stepping one foot in front of the other, I traveled up the tapestry-like carpet, my gaze fixed on Philippe. His dark curls hung loose, resting on his shoulders. He looked rather debonair in his dark tailored suit, like a model straight off the page of a magazine.

When I finally reached the altar, I took his hand and let the minister's words fill my ears. Like a dream, the whole ceremony seemed to play out in slow motion. Anna handed me Philippe's ring, and I slipped it on his finger, repeating the words the minister spoke. Philippe slid my own ring into place, reciting the vows. His lips touched mine, awakening my heart to a brand-new set of fervent emotions. We had officially become man and wife. Confetti rained down on us as we ran from the chapel. I wanted the euphoric feeling to last forever, yet the daunting task of revealing our dark truth to Anna resurfaced, casting a shadow of gloom over a portion of my happiness.

Back in our hotel room, Caleb popped a bottle of champagne, filling four glasses, and passing them around. Raising his, he toasted. "To Beth and Philippe."

"To Beth and Philippe," Anna echoed.

Crossing arms and glasses, Philippe and I drank to the beginning of our lives together.

I pulled Philippe aside a few moments later and whispered, "I'm going to talk to Anna. Would you and Caleb mind giving us some privacy?"

He nodded and kissed my cheek. "If you need me, just think my name and I'll be back by your side."

I held him a moment longer before releasing him. "Thank you."

"Caleb, feel like trying our luck at the tables?" Philippe asked, inclining his head toward the door.

"I don't need luck," Caleb retorted, sprouting a devilish grin and following Philippe out the door.

As it closed behind them, I took Anna's hand and led her to the sofa. "Sit with me for a minute. I need to talk to you."

"Finally, you're going to tell me what's going on," she said, settling back against the sofa.

I scooted closer to her, searching for the right words, but none came. "I don't know quite how to say this. It's very difficult for me.'

She squeezed my hand, compassion coloring her expression. "Take your time."

I crossed my legs, uncrossed them, and crossed them again. Sweeping a strand of hair behind my ear, I started with, "You know I have always believed in vampires."

She cracked a smile. "Yes, and I've always been the one to bring you back to reality."

"Hmph. Well, the comment Caleb made about being a member of a different race, he meant it."

"Are they illegal aliens?" she surmised. "Was that the reason behind the rushed wedding? Did you marry Philippe so he could get his green card?"

I let a laugh slip out, and then bit my lip. "I wish it were that simple." *Quit stalling, just say it. Oh, to hell with it.* "They're not human. They're vampires."

Anna clapped her hands and burst into giggles. "Good one, Beth. Come on, now, what's the real story?"

"Why would I make up such a thing?"

"Are they criminals, on the FBI's most wanted list or something?"

"Of course not!"

She threw her hands up in frustration. "Well, that's more believable than vampires."

Caleb's snafu popped into my head, and I blurted it out. "Caleb said it was his first time on a plane, remember?"

"So?"

"You asked him how he got to Castle Beach from Paris, and he said he flew." I stared at her, hoping the right idea would sink in.

She shook her head. "He was joking."

"No, no, he wasn't. He flew, but not in a plane."

She began to laugh so hard, tears rolled down her cheeks and her whole body shook. Wrapping her arms around her ribs, she cried out, "Stop!"

I shouted at her. "Why in God's name would I make that up?"

"To cover up the real reason!" she shouted back.

I would admit my story was hard to believe, but I still hated being called a liar. We had known each other so long, I supposed I thought she'd take me at my word. She simply wasn't listening with an open mind. I had to do something to convince her, make her believe. Fighting to make my voice steady and calm, I told her, "When I become a vampire, you'll have to believe me."

Anna sprang off the couch and walked away with a shudder. Her next words, she spat out angrily. "Enough. What the hell is wrong with you? You've really gone too far. I used to blame Danny for all this nonsense, but he's not even in your life anymore, and you're still carrying on with these crazy stories. Whatever game you're playing, I want nothing to do with it."

Running my hands through my hair, I wanted to pull strands from my scalp and scream at the top of my lungs. Instead, I pictured Philippe's name inside my head. Certainly, he or Caleb could convince her. I stepped toward her, lacing my hands and pleading, "Anna, please, it's not a game. I know what I'm telling you sounds ridiculous, but I'm telling the truth. I swear."

She blew out a frustrated breath. "Fine, two can play this game. When Caleb gets back, I'll ask him to suck my blood so I can prove you wrong."

I cried out and ran to her. "No! Anna, you mustn't. He's ruthless. He won't care that you're joking. He'll do it. He'll kill you."

She shoved me away and spat, "You've gone overboard. There's something seriously wrong with you, and I've got a few choice words for Philippe. He's done something to you, something you're not aware of, making you crazy."

At that moment, Philippe and Caleb entered the room.

Anna marched up to Philippe and demanded, "What the hell is going on? Beth is rambling on like a mad person. She's trying to convince me of...of...I can't even say it."

Caleb stepped between Philippe and Anna. "What's the lovely redhead saying?"

Anna rolled her eyes before speaking. "That you and Philippe are vampires."

Humoring Anna, Caleb dropped his jaw and raised his brows. "She didn't! That little devil." Caleb turned and winked at me.

Anna's attention flashed back to Philippe. She glared at him. "What have you done to her?"

"I've done nothing to her," Philippe stated calmly.

Caleb chuckled and mumbled under his breath, "That's not true."

Anna pointed a finger at Philippe. "I was right. You have done something."

My shoulders slumped forward in defeat. "Philippe, she doesn't believe me. She thinks I've made it all up."

Philippe stared at Anna. "I warned you, Beth."

Anna tightened her jaw and pursed her lips. "You're in on it. Oh my God, you're such a creep."

Philippe maintained his composure. He didn't even bat an eye. "Anna, the world has always served as home to many creatures you remain thoroughly unaware of."

Anna furrowed her brow as she switched her gaze back and forth from Philippe to Caleb. "What about you, Caleb? Are you a vampire too?"

Flashing her an egotistical grin, he said, "But of course."

Anna stomped over to him. "Prove it. Come to my room tonight and drain me of my blood."

Caleb winked at her, his smile turning devious. "It's a date."

A numbing cold engulfed my body. I shuddered hard, biting my tongue. The sweet taste of blood filled my mouth, but I ignored it and ran to Anna, screaming, "Take it back! Tell him you don't mean it!"

She backed away from me, holding her hands out in front of her. "Oh, I meant every word. When Caleb doesn't show, I'll have proven how wrong you are, and hopefully, snap you out of this delusion." She threw daggers at Philippe with her eyes. "Unfortunately, you married him, and there's nothing I can do to change that."

Tears streamed down my face. "Anna, please, don't do this," I begged.

She whirled around and stormed out of the room, slamming the door.

I fell into Philippe's arms and cried. "She thinks I'm crazy. I've lost her forever."

He held me close, stroking my hair. "You'll work it out. True friends always do."

"Good night," Caleb called before slipping quietly out the door.

I turned toward him. "Wait."

He was already gone.

Cupping my face in his hands, Philippe stared into my eyes. "We just got married, and I planned a very special evening. Forget about Anna for one night."

I pushed him away. "How can you say that?" I marched to the door and threw it open. "Go after him. Make sure he doesn't hurt her."

"Keeping an eye on her is an easier task," he explained, as if her life was meaningless.

"Easier how?"

"I can simply compel a hotel staff member to stand guard at her door."

Was he insane? I quickly shook my head. "That's not good enough. *You* guard her door, and *I'll* stay in her room with her."

He disregarded my suggestion with a wave of his hand. "I will be of no protection to her." He paused and leveled his gaze at me. "Accept my offer of manipulating the hotel staff."

I drew in a breath and released it loudly. "A compelled human is no solution against Caleb. You match his strength. It has to be you."

"You're wrong," he argued and then turned away.

I grabbed onto his arm and forced him to face me. "Why are you acting this way? Why won't you challenge him and save Anna's life?"

He jerked his arm free and raised his voice. "We're governed by a different set of rules. What's done is done, and I did warn you, Beth. You insisted on telling her. Now you must suffer the consequences."

My jaw started to drop, but I clamped it shut and glared at him. Finally, one word flew out of my mouth. "Jerk!"

His expression softened, as did his voice. "Go to her. I will place someone at her door. That is all I can do."

I pushed past him and stormed out the door. With two large strides, I crossed the hall and slammed my fist against Anna's door. "Anna, open up." I pounded on the frame again. "Anna, please, open the door."

"Go away!" she shouted through the solid wood.

"I won't!" I shouted back. "And I'll keep beating on the door until you let me in."

"Stop it," she shrieked.

"Anna, let me in!"

The door flew open, and I caught a glimpse of her darting into the bedroom. A slamming thud rang inside my ears as she'd shut herself off from the rest of the world, primarily me. I could live with that. What mattered was that I had gotten inside her hotel room. I pulled the front door closed, slumped to the floor, and uttered, "Thank God."

****

The next morning, I woke in the same spot, slouched against the door. The heated argument with Anna flashed inside my mind, knotting my stomach. I jumped to my feet and raced toward her bedroom. The door stood slightly ajar. I raised my hand to knock and held it motionless in mid-air as I leaned closer, listening for the slightest sound. Eerie dead quiet filled my ears. Widening the crack, I peeked inside and called out, "Anna."

No reply.

I entered her room, my gaze drifting toward the bed. She lay with the covers pulled up to her chin. Clammy sweat coated my palms as I pulled back the comforter. She didn't move, not even a tiny flinch, and her skin seemed paler than I remembered. I stretched out my hand to touch her, and cold, stiff flesh stung my warm fingertips. A shriek fled my lungs, and I buried my face inside my palms, but not before witnessing two bloodstained pinholes marring the side of her neck. My pulse mushroomed, throbbing up into my throat. He'd gotten past me and made good on his word. Caleb had killed her. Oh God, *I* had killed her by introducing her to that monster! *Oh God, no, no, no.* My legs collapsed, bringing me to my knees, where I knelt on the floor, sobbing.

When my eyes couldn't shed another tear and full-blown numbness set in, I pushed to my feet and sat on the bed next to Anna. Caleb's mark had all but faded on her skin. My gaze traveled from her to the wall. As I stared blankly, I knew I needed to do something to sort out the mess I'd made. Picking up the phone and punching zero, I called for help.

"Front desk, how may I be of service?" a female asked, politely.

My dry throat barely produced a whisper. "My friend, she's dead. Room 502."

Ten minutes later, several police officers swarmed Anna's room, bombarding me with questions. Where was she the night before? Who was she with? Did I notice her talking to any strangers? Was she arguing with anyone? What time did I last see her? What time did I find her body? I sat mute in the corner chair, rocking back and forth, shaking my head. A glance over at Anna's lifeless body summoned a whimper from my throat. My shoulders quaked with sobs I couldn't control. I drew my legs into my chest, hugging them while I bawled out my guilt and misery. I slid off the chair and onto the floor, curled into a ball, and hid my face from the world.

A hand touched my shoulder, forcing me to look up into the face of a male paramedic with freckled skin and deep-brown eyes. "I'm going to give you something to help calm you," he said, injecting clear fluid into my vein.

A powerful fog swept over me, adding weight to my limbs. The relentless sobs crushing my chest floated away with my torment. The paramedic lifted me off the floor and set me in the chair before leaving the room. I stared straight ahead, like a zombie, swaying from side to side. The paramedic returned with two detectives, a thickset female and a male with broad shoulders. Pulling up a couple of chairs, they sat before me, whipping out their notepads.

"I'm Detective Marsh," the female said, and gestured toward her male partner. "And this is Detective Nash."

I stared straight through them.

"Can you tell us your name?" Detective Marsh asked.

"Beth Ryan. No, wait." I slowly shook my head. "Sorry. Beth Delon."

Detective Nash raised his brows but said nothing.

"When did you last see her?" Detective Marsh inquired, her gaze traveling to the bed.

She had a name. She wasn't just a dead body. My mouth felt like cotton, my tongue thick and heavy. I managed to utter, "Her name is Anna, Anna Keaton. Last night."

"What time last night?" Detective Nash asked, clicking his pen.

I turned my head toward him and blinked. *What had he just asked me?*

"Please, answer the question, Miss Delon," he ordered in a stern voice.

Detective Marsh nudged him. "Go easy. The paramedic sedated her."

He spoke a little more gently. "What time?"

Forcing out each word, I said, "I...got...married...last...night. Anna...was...my... maid...of...honor. I...was...with...her...all...night."

They exchanged glances.

Detective Nash bobbed his head. "Explains the name blunder."

Detective Marsh ignored him and asked, "She was with you after the ceremony?"

The anesthetizing haze scrambled my brain. I thought hard. Little by little, the previous evening came back to me. "Yes, we went back to my hotel room. We had champagne."

"Who else was there?" Detective Nash asked, scribbling in his notepad.

"Philippe, my husband, and Caleb, his best man."

His head popped up, and he asked, "Where are they now?"

"My husband's in our room." *Well, at least I think he's there.* "I don't know where Caleb is."

"You say you were with her all night." Detective Nash scratched his jaw. "Strange, being your wedding night and all."

Detective Marsh's gaze darted toward me. Her raised brows insinuated she'd come to the same conclusion as her partner.

"I went to check on her. She was drunk." I lied. "She asked me to stay with her." More lies. "I must have fallen asleep on the couch." *Liar!*

"Did she seem okay? Did you notice anything unusual about her actions?" Detective Nash probed.

Why yes, Detective, she was pissed off at me. Thought I was crazy. Oh, and she challenged a one-thousand-year-old vampire who I'm covering for, because he's my husband's maker. "She was fine."

"Did you see anyone near her room or hear anything out of the ordinary last night?" Detective Marsh asked before glancing at Detective Nash.

I slowly shook my head. "No, nothing."

"Beth, we need to speak with both your husband and Caleb," Detective Marsh said, her statement sounding more like an order. She looked at Detective Nash and back at me before adding, "Do you know Caleb's room number?"

I shook my head.

Detective Marsh took my arm and helped me to my feet. "Please, take us to your room so we can speak to your husband."

I leaned against Detective Marsh as I shuffled forward, leading them across the hall to our door. I patted down my dress as if it had pockets, searching for the small plastic keycard. Where was the damn thing? I stared at the door blankly. "My keycard must be inside."

Detective Nash grunted, and Detective Marsh threw him a stern look.

I raised my hand to knock and stumbled backward.

Detective Marsh caught and steadied me.

Detective Nash stood with his arms folded, shaking his head.

I didn't care what he thought of me. At that moment, the drugs had rendered me incapable of caring about anything at all.

A young, fair-skinned girl, pushing a cart full of fresh towels and linen, interrupted us.

Detective Nash held up his badge. "Excuse me, miss, please unlock this door."

Detective Marsh slanted her head in my direction and added, "She misplaced her keycard."

"Yes, of course," the maid answered, hurrying over to the door and sliding her master key into the slot. The lock popped and the door separated from its frame.

"Thank you," Detective Nash said, giving the door a good push.

"You're welcome," the maid replied before continuing on her way.

Once the door was open, Detective Marsh led me into the front room. "Please, let your husband know we're here. Can you do that for me?" she asked, speaking to me as if I were a child.

"I'll get him." I wobbled into the bedroom. Philippe stood at the end of the bed, pulling on a pair of jeans. His head jerked up, his gaze sharpening on me. "You brought the police into our hotel room? What do you think I could possibly say to them?"

My lip quivered, but the drug held my emotions at bay. "They want to speak with you," I stated flatly.

He came to me, cupping my face with his hands and peering into my eyes. "You've been drugged."

I pointed to the door. "They're waiting."

He threw on a shirt, took me by the hand, and charged into the living room where he stood with dominance, folding his arms across his chest. "Who drugged my wife?"

Detective Marsh stepped forward and introduced herself. "I'm Detective Marsh. This is my partner, Detective Nash. Your wife was experiencing extreme distress and was given a sedative to help calm her."

Philippe glanced at me before his gaze darted back to the detectives.

"Sir, we need to ask you some questions related to Miss Keaton's death," Detective Nash stated matter-of-factly.

Philippe looked at me, his eyes widening. "Death? Dear God!" He put his arm around me and turned back to the detectives. "What happened?"

A shudder ran through me. *Like you don't already know.*

Detective Nash broke into his "I'm sorry...blah blah blah" speech. "Mr. Delon, I'm sorry to inform you that Anna Keaton was murdered in her hotel room last night. Your wife found the body."

"What?" Philippe clung to me, rubbing his hand up and down my arm. "I'm...I'm at a loss for words. Yes, of course. How can I help?"

His performance sickened me.

"When was the last time you saw her?" Detective Nash asked, flipping his notepad open.

"About nine-thirty," Philippe replied. "We were having champagne here in our room."

"And your best man, Caleb. He was here as well?" Detective Marsh questioned.

Philippe nodded. "Yes."

"Did Miss Keaton leave your room alone or with your friend?" Detective Marsh pressed.

"Alone," Philippe answered firmly.

"You're sure?" Detective Nash asked, raising a brow.

Locking his eyes on the two detectives, Philippe confirmed, "Anna left, and shortly thereafter, Caleb as well. My wife went to check on Anna. She'd had too much champagne."

Our statements matched. What a coincidence.

"We need to speak with Caleb. Can you tell us what room he's staying in?" Detective Marsh asked, moving toward the door.

Philippe held out his hand. "I'll show you to his room." He turned to face me. "May my wife stay here? I believe she needs to lie down and rest."

A look of compassion softened Detective Marsh's face. "Yes, of course."

Philippe sat me down on the sofa and kissed my cheek. "Beth, try to get some rest. I'll be back shortly."

Trapped in the thick drug-induced murkiness, I focused on the tiny specks of gold running through the paint. I felt no emotion, no pain no reason—the world had become a blur of sedation. The click of the door settling into its frame echoed strangely in my ears. I looked up to find myself alone. I laid back on the sofa and rested my head on a pillow. As I stared at the ceiling, Anna's face flashed inside my mind. I flinched away from her image. My best friend was dead, and I'd helped to cover it up. How could I live with the guilt over the part I'd played in her murder? My thoughts scurried away to call forth Philippe instead. Warmth spread through me. I loved him. I loved him that much. He'd help me get through the tragedy somehow.

Sometime later—minutes, hours, I couldn't be sure—the door creaked. Philippe entered, and then Caleb strolled into the room. Pure adrenaline jolted me awake, and my rigid muscles strained against my skin. I met Caleb's eyes, staring at him defiantly. I bolted off the sofa and barreled toward Caleb, screaming as I ran. Philippe lunged for me, but I darted to the left, blasting past him and slamming into Caleb. I punched, scratched, and kicked him. He didn't move, standing statue still, allowing me to wail on him.

Philippe gripped my shoulders, sliding his hands down to pin my arms and pull me away from Caleb. "Beth, please, you must understand that Anna merely met her proper fate."

I glared at Philippe. Her fate! What the hell? I fought to free my arms so I could shove him backward. "What are you saying?"

Philippe held up his hands in surrender before taking a step toward me. "Remember, we do come from two different worlds."

"You let this happen!" I screamed.

The corners of his mouth turned downward as he explained, "When a vampire is challenged, he must accept that challenge regardless of the consequences. Anna challenged Caleb. Her life was over the minute she invited him to her room."

I flung myself at Philippe, pounding my fists against his chest. "And you did nothing to stop him. How could you do this to her, to me?"

Philippe lowered his head. "It wasn't my place."

I whirled to face Caleb, tears spilling down my cheeks as I poked my finger into his chest. "There was no challenge. Anna had no idea what she was saying. You knew that! Still, you went through with it. You got into her room, snuck by me, and killed her. You're evil, pure evil."

Caleb's composed expression remained unaltered, his voice void of emotion as he coldly stated, "*You* warned her. *You* told her what I was. She wanted proof. She asked *me* for proof. As a human, you can't possibly understand, and there is nothing I can do to ease your pain. I am sorry." He bowed his head and disappeared in the time it took me to blink.

I balled my hands into fists and shouted, "Come back here, you bastard! Face me; face what you've done! You killed an innocent girl!" I slumped to my knees and murmured, "*I* killed an innocent girl."

Philippe's arms came around me. "You did nothing of the sort. This was Caleb's doing."

I collapsed against Philippe, my chest heaving with sobs. "I went to her room to protect her. You should've helped me. If you had..."

For a moment, he said nothing, but then uttered, "I couldn't betray him."

His words pierced my heart. I cringed away from his touch. "But you could betray *me*, your wife!"

His face distorted, twisting in pain. "Beth, please, I've told you, we live by a different set of rules. If a vampire is challenged, he must accept and fulfill the challenge, and no other vampire may interfere. My hands were tied; moreover, she despised me, thought I was no good for you. She wouldn't have listened to a single thing I said, and you *did* warn her. She is the one who chose not to believe you."

The truth was that I knew very little about their way of life. Maybe Philippe really wasn't to blame. Maybe Caleb wasn't either in some twisted way, yet Anna was dead, and I only hoped I could somehow come to terms with the parts each of us had played in stealing her life away far too early.

CHAPTER 10

Philippe and I returned home the following day. Pulling onto the familiar brick drive and seeing Betty standing on the front porch gave me a glimmer of hope. Since Anna's death, Caleb had kept his distance. Bile stung my throat if Philippe even mentioned his name. He couldn't ever possibly serve any purpose in my life besides the constant reminder of my own guilt. Anna was gone forever. He'd taken her from me and her family. Her autopsy had offered them little closure, the cause of her death ruled as unexplained, extensive exsanguination. I could've offered resolution, but I'd learned my lesson. No one would ever believe me.

Jon Paul opened my door and I ran to Betty, falling into her motherly embrace.

"Beth, dear, I am so sorry about Anna."

My lip quivered, but I pushed the pain deep down inside. "Thank you, Betty."

"Can I get you anything?" she asked, releasing me and holding me at arm's length.

Anna's death had punched a large hole in my heart. The emptiness continued to drain me. What I needed most was some time to myself. "No, thanks. I just want to lie down and rest."

Her face softened. "I understand, dear."

I kissed Philippe's cheek and said, "I'm going upstairs. Join me shortly?"

He stroked my back. "I'll be up soon."

My feet dragged with each step up the stairs to our bedroom. I didn't even bother to change, just curled up on the bed and fell asleep.

Anna came to me in a dream, gliding across the floor in a flowing white gown. Her skin gleamed ghostly pale, and her eyes shone brighter than they had in life. She hissed at me, exposing ivory fangs. Blood ran from the corner of her mouth, spilling onto her chin. I froze, my heart beating its way out of my chest, my own blood thumping inside my head. She latched onto me, digging her sharp nails into my flesh. I fought back, shoving her face away in horror.

When she laughed, more blood poured from her lips. "You killed me, Beth, you and your vampire friends. Now I'm going to kill you."

I swung at her with my fists, over and over and over again, screaming for Philippe.

She squeezed tighter, pinning me against her and baring her fangs. "Your beloved Philippe can't help you. I'm just as strong now. He will soon learn to fear me."

An iron grip took hold of my shoulders, ripping me from the clutches of my nightmare. My eyes flew open, and I scurried off the bed. "Where is she?"

Philippe surveyed the room. "You were dreaming. There's no one here besides you and I."

"Anna!" I shouted. "She was here, in the room."

Philippe led me to a chair by the hearth, kneeling in front of me and taking my hands. His eyes searched mine. "You're not making any sense. Calm down and tell me what happened."

My gaze darted about the room as the madness of the dream gorged on my brain. "I don't have time to explain. Her funeral is tomorrow. I must see her. I have to see her now!"

Concern furrowed his perfect brow. "Why?"

I whispered, "I dreamt she was a vampire. It was so real."

Philippe shook his head. "Caleb didn't transform her. He didn't give her his blood. Without it, the conversion is not possible."

I shuddered and brushed the chill from my arms. "I need proof. I have to see with my own eyes." I rushed to the door and looked back at him. "Take me to Greenfield Mortuary."

Philippe regarded me for a long moment before he came to my side. "Very well. I will take you to her."

****

Jon Paul parked the car and cut the engine. Philippe didn't wait for him to the open the door, prompting Jon Paul to hurry around to his side of the car as he climbed out, confusion coloring his expression.

Philippe held up his hand. "It's all right, Jon Paul. Please, wait in the car."

Jon Paul nodded and resumed his position behind the wheel.

Philippe turned to me and offered his hand. "Come with me, Beth."

I took Philippe's hand and peered up at the building. Not a single light burned inside Greenfield Mortuary. Maybe the dead preferred the darkness. The building's haunting appearance made my skin prickle, and I glanced over my shoulder at the car. The urge to jump back inside the warm interior and flee for home itched inside my bones, but I needed to see Anna. My sanity depended on doing so.

"Come, there's not time to waste. No telling when security makes their rounds."

I mentally steeled my nerves. "I'm ready."

I tiptoed behind Philippe to the entrance. Fixated on the doorknob, his eyes began to glow with an orange tinge. The knob turned slowly, and the front door swung open. He tucked me under his arm and slipped us inside with vampire speed. Our footsteps invaded the privacy of the dead as they rang through the peaceful funeral home, empty of any other living souls. I took a small flashlight out of the side pocket of my purse and shone it along the wall.

Philippe covered the light with his hand. "Really, Beth?"

"What?"

He raised his brows. "Do you want to get caught? We don't need the light." He pointed to his eyes. "Vampire vision, remember?"

I shoved the slim cylinder back inside my purse. "Fine. Just find her."

132

We located the cold room in just a few minutes, but the vaults inside listed only numbers, not names. A sickening feeling slithered into my stomach. I gagged on rising bile. "Tell me we don't have to open each one."

"Give me a minute," he said, his gaze roaming over the vault doors. The color of his eyes seemed to catch fire, burning brighter and brighter. He pointed toward the middle row. "She's in 222."

"You're sure?"

"Positive."

I inched over and placed my hand on the metal handle, glancing at Philippe in hesitation.

"Open it," he said.

Pushing down on the lever, I popped the door. I gripped the slab with trembling hands, pulling until my efforts revealed Anna. She looked nothing like the monster from my dream. Naked, except for her covering of a white sheet, she looked peaceful, not evil. *What have I done?* I'd only failed her further, taking away what little dignity she'd had left by coming to examine her body. I quickly pushed her back inside the vault and slammed the door, my hands lifting to my face to brush away tears.

Philippe came up behind me, pulling me away from the metal door. "Let's go home, Beth."

I wanted nothing more than to leave that dreadful place.

****

Anna's funeral took place at mid-afternoon. I endured it alone, standing in the background and crying into my coat. One by one, the mourners left the burial site. I stayed behind, waiting to be alone with her. I knelt at her grave, settling a bouquet of yellow roses by her headstone. Tightness gripped at my chest as I whispered, "Anna, I'm so very sorry about everything. What am I going to do without you? You were my best friend. I need you. I'll miss you so much." Hot tears coursed down my cheeks, falling onto her grave. "If only I could see you, hold you one more time. Please, Anna."

I waited to see, if by some miracle she might appear. She didn't, of course, so I sat quietly by her side. She was alone in the dark, buried under the ground I still walked, which didn't seem fair. I couldn't bear to leave her.

A warm hand touched my shoulder. Startled, I clutched at my throat and turned to discover Mrs. Keaton staring back at me with red, swollen eyes.

"Have you been here all this time, Beth?" she asked.

"I miss her," I choked out.

Kneeling next to me, she folded her hands in her lap and breathed out a soft sigh. With great conviction, she stated, "Anna will always be with us. She'll live forever in our hearts."

Staring at the dirt covering Anna, I shook my head. "She's alone. I need to stay."

Mrs. Keaton looked up into the sky and smiled slightly. "She's not alone. She's in a much better place, surrounded by love and light. I just know it." She touched my cheek. "Anna loved you, Beth. She thought of you as a sister, and she would want you to go on with your life. Go home, dear, to your new husband. That's what Anna would have wanted you to do."

We held each other for a long while before I finally felt able to leave Mrs. Keaton at her daughter's grave.

CHAPTER 11

After Anna's funeral, I moped about, shutting out everything and everyone—even Philippe. He did his best to ease my suffering, including planning a spectacular birthday bash for me. My twenty-fifth birthday was a mere week away. I never dreamt I would be celebrating the day without her. And what was there to celebrate, really? My ever-increasing vampire attributes were taking their toll on my body. That day was no different.

I lay in bed, groggy, straining to open my eyes and keep them from closing again. Finally, close to noon, I climbed out of bed and staggered into the bathroom like a drunk to splash my face with cold water. The mild shock didn't faze me. I tried stepping into the shower and blasting my body with freezing water. I jerked away, screeching and fighting with the faucet to add hot water to the mix. A delicious warm spray rained over my body, melting away the chill.

After wrapping a thick towel around me, I stood in front of the mirror, blinking, sure my eyes were deceiving me. My hair looked thicker and shone with a richer shade of red. The rosy hue to my skin had all but vanished, and the color of my eyes had faded to a haunting transparent green. Every feature appeared sharpened, like a statue carved from stone. Holding my chin high and throwing my shoulders back, I turned to catch every angle, admiring my new reflection. So, vampire blood *did* offer some great perks. I blew a kiss into the mirror and bounced back into the bedroom. After a few moments of rummaging through the closet, I changed into black leggings, a graphic tee, and a pair of black boots. Stooping by the bed, I kissed my slumbering husband on the cheek before tiptoeing out the door and heading for the kitchen in search of a much-needed cup of coffee.

Coffee in hand, I made my way to the study to curl up with a good book. I scanned the titles as I roamed up and down the rows of books. The history section brought me to a standstill. Titles like *Vampire Legends*, *Vampires Among Us*, and *The History of Vampires* jumped out at me, screaming to be read. I took a sip of coffee and mulled over the titles. I couldn't possibly be the only person part human and part vampire. I needed to do some research. Pulling the books free and settling in by the hearth, I skimmed through the chapters. Absurd theories claimed every page. Who were these authors, and where had they dug up such erroneous material? One book actually stated that anyone with red hair who died without being baptized would be reborn as a vampire. I loved this approach: a person born on Christmas Day would, beyond all doubt, become a werewolf in life and a vampire after death. Other passages suggested that red hair and blue eyes were undeniable characteristics of a vampire. These authors and their obsession with red hair! What was up with that? I found a Hungarian legend which proposed that if one was bitten by a vampire, they could save themselves from turning by eating the dirt from any vampire's grave. In England, they believed a person born on a Sunday could never become a vampire, nor could they be chosen as a vampire's victim. My favorite by far claimed that if a black cat jumped over the body of a dead person, said dead person would awaken as a vampire.

The more I read, the more I found my circumstances to be unique. I shoved the useless books aside, rolling my head from side to side and massaging my temples, certain I wasn't going to find any answers inside those books. Accurate data and irrefutable facts were what I needed, not fiction. Someone had to have written a book about cross-species DNA.

I bolted upright, placing my cup on the hearth, and blurted out, "Haven Avenue." The street ran through downtown's more eccentric and dark business district, just the place to find a paranormal bookstore. But after nightfall, hookers, pimps, drug dealers, and cops owned the street. The place only belonged to the rest of the world while the sun was shining. Flipping my wrist over, I checked my watch. 3:00 PM, still plenty of time to make it to Haven Avenue before dark.

With large strides, I bolted from the study, breaking into a jog. In the mudroom, I snatched my jacket off its hook and slipped it on before sprinting out the front door toward my car. The flaming sun pursued me like a hateful enemy. Even through my clothes, its stinging rays assaulted my tender flesh. I armed my eyes with a pair of sunglasses, gunned the engine, and sped onto the road.

Pulling up on Haven Avenue, I tossed a fictitious coin in my mind's eye—heads turn right, tails turn left. Tails prevailed and I hung a left. Tourists mobbed the sidewalks like a herd of sheep, meandering in and out of shops while snapping photos with their phones. I slowed the car to a crawl and peered out the window, scrutinizing the storefronts and weeding through palm readers, séance parlors, and pool halls, searching for occult bookstores. None piqued my interest until *Of Unknown Origin* caught my eye. Goose bumps broke out across the flesh of my arms. I pressed down on the brake and cranked the steering wheel hard to snag the parking spot in front of the store.

Upon entering the front door, a crisp Antarctic temperature greeted me. Shuddering, I zipped up my jacket. The place sold books, not meat, right? Did the air conditioner really need to be on full blast? Not a single soul roamed the dimly lit store; there wasn't even an employee in sight. Patches of darkness lurked in every corner. The pictures on the walls displayed freakish half-man, half-beast types of creatures. Vials of holy water, rings of garlic, crosses, and wooden stakes filled a locked display case near the front counter.

For several minutes, I stood at the counter, waiting. No one showed. Shrugging my shoulders, I decided to continue exploring on my own. The back of the store served as a supernatural library, jam-packed with aged books, new books, hardcovers, and paperbacks. Straightaway, I skimmed the titles. *Werewolves and Vampires* and *The Vampire Encyclopedia* seemed like good places to start. I sat down in the middle of the aisle to read.

The author of *Werewolves and Vampires* had cleverly linked the two creatures together. He theorized that, in order to become a vampire, one must first be bitten by a werewolf. Thereafter, the werewolf protected the vampire by day and became his companion by night. Together they would stalk a shared victim. The werewolf devoured the flesh while the vampire drained the blood. During a full moon, the werewolf and vampire also possessed the power to awaken the dead, adding zombies into the equation. He believed werewolves and vampires were the creators of everything unnatural known to man. His approach, though imaginative and creative, was seriously lacking in the truth department.

The Vampire Encyclopedia read similar to the books in Philippe's study, listing the telltale signs which identified vampires: a sixth girl or boy born to a family, or twin red-haired boy born with teeth. Again with the injustice to redheads. *We are not the poster children for vampirism, people!* Shaking my head, I let out a huff before reading on. Dying in a fire, being cursed by one's parents, and being buried in unholy ground were also perfect conditions for the creation of vampires.

I'd discovered an element of comfort to the book, where the author wrote about a small number of vampires who kept their human souls and posed no threat to mankind. Doomed to suffer their vampirism, these vampires lived their lives helping others over the course of their undead existences. I pressed the book over my heart. When I transformed, this was the vampire I'd make every effort to become.

Approaching footsteps echoed through the empty store. Looking up, I found a pair of haggard eyes gazing down at me. A thin man, possibly in his early fifties, swept his bangs off his brow before speaking to me. "May I help you find something?"

I didn't answer him right away. He looked vaguely familiar, but I couldn't place where I might have seen him before.

He peered at me, wrinkling his forehead. "Vampire," he murmured, widening his eyes. Well, he was half right. "Nah," he chuckled, and then turned on the salesman charm. "Do you need help finding a book?"

"Actually, I'm interested in finding out some information about cross-species DNA," I said, my eyes fixating on his face. Where had I seen him before?

He pointed to the shelves behind me. "You've come to the right place. These walls are a wealth of information."

"I didn't find any there. Maybe you could help me?" I asked, rising to my feet.

He rubbed his hands together, grinning. "Sure. What cross-species are you interested in?"

I pursed my lips. Did I delicately bring up the subject or just blurt it out? He did work at a store full of the paranormal. I chose the latter option. "I'm looking for any documented cases on individuals who were half vampire and half human."

He didn't blink, flinch, or raise his brows. He shook his head with absolution. "There have been no documented cases."

"You didn't even look. Surely, there must've been a few over the centuries."

"Nope. Trust me, I'd know. Former FBI agent, Fringe Division. Served for thirty years."

This new tidbit of information jogged my memory, dredging up Philippe's article clippings. My mouth fell open, and I staggered backward. The man responsible for the most famous vampire photo in history stood only a few inches from me.

"Are you all right?" he asked, reaching out to steady me.

I'd come face-to-face with Dana Karan. What were the chances? It was like winning the lottery by finding a discarded ticket. Philippe's concern seemed unnecessary. He didn't look very dangerous to me. Besides, if anyone could help me find the information I needed, it would be Dana Karan. But could I confide in him, reveal the details of my circumstances? I decided to chance it, since I needed answers so badly. "You were right, you know. Well, half right."

"What do you mean?"

I leveled my gaze, staring in his eyes with sincerity. "You said I was a vampire."

His gaze darted over me, head to toe. "Are you saying...*you're* part vampire and part human?"

I answered him inside his head to prove my claim. *That's exactly what I'm saying.*

He sank toward the floor, resting his hands on his knees. "Your lips never moved. You spoke to me, but your lips never moved!" He shook off the shock and sprang upright. "Believe me, I know about vampires.

I've chased after them all my life, but I've never seen any half this and half that."

"You're sure?" I asked out loud.

"Well, I was before you walked in." His eyes bulged as he stared. "I bet you've got some stories that would blow me away. Care to share?"

I sighed heavily. "I didn't come here to swap stories. I want—I *need* answers."

As if he hadn't heard a word I'd said, he rubbed his hands together and rattled off, "What's it like? What part of you is still human? Do you have vampire cravings? Any strange kind of powers? I gotta know."

"It's none of your business," I snapped.

"This is unbelievable." He whipped out his cell phone. "I've gotta share this."

Glaring at him, I crossed my arms and huffed. I wasn't his personal show-and-tell item. Pushing past him, I headed straight for the door.

After shoving his phone back into his pants pocket, he reached out and grabbed my arm. "Wait," he said. "Please, stay."

"Let go of me!"

He released me and held up his hands in a placating gesture. "Sorry."

"I'm not some kind of trophy you can parade around." I raised my voice a notch. "Got it!"

He nodded his agreement. "You're right. Sometimes I can be such an ass. I'm just flabbergasted. I mean, you're like a walking miracle, and you show up in my store. I'm blown away, that's all."

I returned to him and shoved my finger in his face. "You need to understand this is my life, not some damned game."

"I'm sorry...I didn't think. I just reacted. Let me start over." He held out his hand. "Hi, name's Dana. What's yours?"

He seemed so sincere. I took his hand and said, "It's Beth."

In a hushed voice, he said, "I might not have a book, but boy, do I have something better...someone who can help you."

I nodded. "Go on."

"There's a club on Haven Avenue, Bloodthirst. Been open for just over a year."

"And this should excite me because?"

He smirked. "It's owned by vampires. People line up every night in hopes of being fed on by a vampire."

I narrowed my gaze, studying him. "You're lying."

"Am not."

"You're saying humans willingly go there to die?"

"Yes," he blurted out. "It's crazy. They just give up their lives. Sure, there are freaks out there who believe they're vampires, sleeping in coffins, robbing hospitals of blood, and staying out of the sun, but this club is the real deal. These vampires feed right in front of everybody."

I pressed my hands over my stomach. Sounded like a place Caleb would frequent. "And you want me to go there?"

"I think you should talk to Margarete, a vampire regular. Practically lives at the place."

He could've easily been playing me, but I chose to believe him. "So you think she can help me?"

"I can't promise that, but she's your best bet. The club opens at six, but I've got connections. I can get us in now. We can chat over drinks and wait for Margarete to show up."

I checked my watch—4:00 PM. I weighed the decision hurriedly. "I'm in."

"It's right down the block. So close we can walk."

I started moving toward the front door. "What are we waiting for? Let's go."

He trotted to the entrance like a little kid, pushing the door open for me and shooing me onto the sidewalk. As he pulled the handle to close and lock up the shop, he said, "Slow day anyway." He inclined his head to the right. "The club's down this way."

Dana hurried along the street, taking large strides. I didn't feel the need to struggle to keep up, so I followed a few steps behind. After passing several shops, he hung a sharp right before coming to a halt. He grinned and pointed. "Here it is."

The building painted in the deepest of blacks stood before us. The only splashes of color came from the gleaming gold door and brilliant-red neon letters floating above the entrance, spelling out the club's name—like a scene straight out of a horror film. I edged closer and couldn't help but smile.

Dana approached the door, punching a series of numbers into a keypad on the side. The lock popped and the door opened. A gust of freezing air rushed forward as we crossed the threshold. The club maintained its fiendish allure inside with its dark crimson walls, circular black-velvet booths, and the lingering stench of human blood. The power of the coppery scent made my head spin. I shuddered, craving a drop of the substance on my tongue.

Dana took my hand, leading me deeper into the club. He snagged a booth in front of the stage, sliding in and pulling me along with him.

I skimmed over the room. Nothing but the aroma of the blood hinted at being out of the ordinary. Two bars and a raised stage filled the space inside the dimly lit club. What was the purpose of the stage? Maybe a performance of some kind? A feeding frenzy ritual? No, that couldn't be it. They'd never get away with it, unless they played their mind games, compelling any human bearing witness to their sins to forget.

Dana spoke, interrupting my thoughts. "At six o'clock, this place is gonna be jumpin'." He gestured toward the stage. "Wanted you be up close and personal."

I forced out a sarcastic laugh. "How thoughtful of you."

Waving my cynicism away, he said, "You'll thank me later." His gaze swept over the twin bars. "What're ya drinking?"

I just might need some wine to get me through the night. "Pinot Grigio, thanks."

"Me, I'm a beer man. Be right back."

Dana jogged off to one of the bars and leaned over the counter, chatting with a female bartender who was obviously not human. The sparkle of her jewel-like eyes gave her away, as did the same attribute for the male bartender working the bar across the way from her. His eyes flickered like lanterns. My gaze traveled from face to face, observing all the fine details. Vampires bustled about the club, placing lit candles on tables, stocking the bar, sweeping the floor, and adjusting the lighting. Were Dana and I the only humans in the room?

Dana ambled back to the table, carrying our drinks. He handed me my wine, settled back in the booth, and took a swig of his beer. "Just wait until the door opens, humans will swarm the place, eager for a vampire's kiss."

Running my finger along the rim of my wineglass, I responded, "Not interested. I came here to talk to Margarete. So, where is she?"

"Relax, she'll be here." He offered me a reassuring smile. "Hey, do you mind if I asked how such a bizarre transformation happened to you?"

I unbuttoned my coat and tossed it on the seat. "Yes, I mind."

He chuckled. "I get it, you're a private person, but you have to remember that you're also kind of like a miracle. I'm so curious...were you born this way?"

I leaned across the table, shaking my head. "I'm not discussing my personal life with you. I don't even know you. I'm here for answers." I reached for my wine and took a sip. "Are we clear?"

He saluted me. "Loud and clear. Maybe I should just shut up until Margarete gets here."

I raised my glass, toasting his statement. "I think that's an excellent idea."

For the next hour, he fiddled with his wallet—flipping it open and closed, grabbed a pen out of his pocket and clicked the top until it sounded like rapid gunfire, and drummed his fingernails, annoyingly, on the table...but not a single word escaped his lips. I clamped my own together, smothering a slew of smartass remarks and requests for quiet, keeping my gaze locked on the front door and doing my best to ignore his childish antics, vying for my attention.

The long, painful wait ended at 6:00 PM sharp when the front door opened. Humans and vampires, decked out in outrageous nightclub attire, strutted through the doors like peacocks.

Dana's silence ended, and he nudged my shoulder. "Here we go."

I glanced at him briefly before focusing on the door. The masses filed in, cramming into every square inch of the club. Vampires congregated at the rear, their sparkling eyes setting them apart from the humans who wandered aimlessly about the club, starry-eyed and beaming like idiots.

The beginnings of a knot twisted my stomach. They really had come to be fed on, crossing the threshold with the full intent to die. Their choices becoming acts of suicide or murder, depending on how one might interpret it.

The front door closed with an ominous whoosh. "Welcome," a hypnotic male voice called to the patrons. "The doors to Bloodthirst are now locked."

My eyes searched for the speaker. I found him at center stage, a vampire with gleaming turquoise-hued eyes. Every human stood fixated on him, hanging in suspended motion. Had he compelled them? Were they truly present of their own free will? I turned to Dana, who tossed back a swig of his beer and winked at me. I rolled my eyes and looked away. He obviously wasn't spellbound.

"The club has a few simple rules. Vampires are free to come and go as they please. Humans may exit Bloodthirst at any time; however, once you vacate the premises, you will not be allowed to reenter. If a vampire approaches you, you may choose either to accept or refuse their kiss. If you refuse, the vampire must respect your wishes and walk away. We will guarantee your safety." His ruby lips rose in a devilish grin. "If you accept, you do so at your own risk, so please, choose wisely." He waved his hand in the air. "Let the events begin."

The crowd scattered. Off to my right, I observed a young woman in a miniskirt accept a vampire's kiss. Locking her in his embrace, he speared her neck, and she pressed her body closer against his. Her bright-red blood spattered the wall and dribbled down her neck. A howl of pure desire escaped his lips as he drained her. My heartbeat throbbed in the well of my throat, thumping fast as I sat with my gaze glued to the vampire and his prey.

Dana stood, waving wildly at a tall, skinny vampire from across the room. Her flawless face hadn't aged a day over eighteen. She slid into our booth and wrapped her arm around Dana. Brushing her raven hair off her shoulders and cocking her head, she observed me with sheer violet-colored orbs.

"Margarete, Beth here needs your help," Dana said, pointing me out with a twist of his head.

She smirked, exposing razor sharp fangs. "Why should I help her?"

Great. A teenage vampire with an attitude, just what I need.

Dana placed his hand on her arm. "Hold on now. You delve in the supernatural, and her set of unique circumstances are right up your alley. Hear her out."

She turned toward me, raising her groomed eyebrows, and asked, "What are your circumstances exactly?"

I held her gaze, determined she wouldn't intimidate me. "I'm part vampire, part human. I'm trying to find out if there are others out there like me."

Her sneer vanished, and the color of her eyes grew warmer. She took my hand and said, "What you're going through must be difficult, but you will find no others." She narrowed her gaze, her mind digging into my brain and reading me. "Your husband is to blame for your predicament. He should've taken your blood, not your body. We have rules. Making love to a human doesn't fit into our world. There would be consequences, and he chose to ignore them."

A stupid grin spread across Dana's face.

I blew out an exaggerated breath. What Philippe and I did behind closed doors was no one's business but our own, though I tried to remember it had been I who'd sought Margarete out, asking for her help. "He did warn me. It was *I* who chose to ignore the warning."

She appeared genuinely puzzled. "Then why suffer between worlds? Become whole with his blood."

Her words sent shivers down my spine. My reason for delaying the inevitable was simple. I wanted to hold onto my humanity. "I'm still part human. I'm not ready to let go of that piece of myself."

"We're not evil," she informed me with a firm nod of her head. "When we transform, we don't become monsters. In fact, we change very little. Most of us remain the same. Although, as with any race, bad seeds spring up among us, but they are few and far between." Pushing away from the table, she rose. "Let your husband help you. Transform." She turned and walked away.

Dana shrugged his shoulders and said, "Damn, I thought she would offer more. Sorry."

Caleb materialized out of thin air to stand in front of our booth, his hazel eyes burning with rage.

A gasp escaped my mouth as I latched onto Dana's arm.

Wagging a finger at me, he growled in a mocking tone, "Beth, darling, what a surprise to find you here." His flaming gaze roved over Dana. "And with my old friend, Dana. May I join you?"

He didn't wait for a reply, swiftly gliding into our booth and scooting so close to me, our bodies touched. Dana didn't budge an inch, but his hands trembled on top of the table.

Caleb took my hand and gave it a rough squeeze. "Have you forgotten about your husband waiting at home for you? I just came from there, and he is overcome with worry. Your behavior is quite lacking in consideration."

My gaze darted to my watch. "It's only eight o'clock," I answered with an angry huff.

The fierce gleam coloring Caleb's eyes intensified. "It's in your best interest to leave."

I knew better than to challenge Caleb without Philippe close by to protect me. I gripped Dana's hand. "Let's go."

Dana didn't respond, staring dead ahead. Was his silence brought on by fear? Or was Caleb controlling him? I had to do something. I scurried out of the booth and shouted, "Dana!"

The vein in the center of Caleb's forehead pulsated, and his eyes bulged. He leapt in front of me, digging his nails into my flesh and forcing me back into the booth, snarling in my ear. "If I had my way, I'd transform your pretty little ass right here, right now. Do know, I am keeping track of the company you keep."

I stared at Caleb, my breath ragged. There wasn't enough time to call for Philippe. I was on my own, with only Dana, mournfully human, by my side. He could hardly provide the protection I needed to keep me safe from Caleb. Caleb gripped my neck, jerking my head to the side. His chilly breath slithered over my skin before his fangs speared my vein.

I stiffened and let out a shriek, pounding my fists against his chest. "Get off me!"

He lingered over my neck, like a lover savoring a kiss, before finally pushing me away.

Scrunched up against Dana, I leaned farther away from Caleb and clutched at my neck. Warm blood oozed onto my fingers. Seizing Dana's hand, I yanked him to his feet. "Let us go, Caleb."

He leveled a hard stare at us both. "Fine, go, but let this be a warning to you, Beth. I could've easily killed you had I so desired."

I backed away, keeping Caleb in my sights. He merely threw back his head and exploded in a fit of malicious laughter. I didn't hang around to see what he might do next. When we reached the gold door, I yanked it open and shoved Dana outside. Dragging Dana in tow, I ran all the way to the safety of Dana's store.

As we drew near, I whirled around and scanned the street. No sign of Caleb, but he could be anywhere, watching us, ready to pounce. The vivid image of Anna's dead body assaulted my brain. I couldn't let Dana suffer her fate. The safest place I could think of was my own home. "We can't trust Caleb," I said, pulling Dana toward my car. "You have to come home with me. You'll be safe there."

The pitch of his voice rose as he blurted out, "Agreed. Now, let's get the hell out of here."

Clicking the remote, I unlocked the doors, and Dana catapulted himself inside my car, wrenching his door closed and sinking low in his seat. I knew that explaining Dana's presence to Philippe wouldn't be easy. He'd disapprove, and most likely be furious with me, but I couldn't let Caleb take another human life, regardless of the consequences. I pointed us toward home—the only place where we could escape Caleb's wrath.

The hum of the tires gripping the road became magnified in the unnatural silence. A deep frown creased Dana's brow as he stared out the window. His lips moved, but no spoken words emerged. Was he talking to himself? I tilted my head slightly toward him, straining to catch a word or two. The steady rhythm of his breath filled my ears, nothing more. I turned to get a good look at him. His lips chattered up a storm without making a sound. What the hell was he going on about?

A name flew out of his mouth. "Philippe!" Then he whimpered out another name. "Tabitha."

My foot slid off the gas pedal. Philippe? And who was Tabitha? Had she and Philippe known each other? What was their connection to Dana? Touching his shoulder lightly, I asked, "Dana, are you all right?"

His gaze remained fixed, staring ahead as if he hadn't heard me.

I nudged him. "Dana."

Still no response.

"DANA!"

He jumped and snapped his head in my direction. "Sorry, what?"

"Are you all right?"

"Seeing Caleb stirred up some old memories. I'll be fine, but I'm curious as to how you know him?"

I realized an opportunity had presented itself. I could open up the dialog, test him to see how much he knew. "My husband, Philippe, and Caleb are old friends."

His face showed no emotion, before he blinked and turned to face me. "You're married to Philippe, the vampire?"

"Yes. Do you know him?"

The muscles in his face tensed. "Yes."

"How?" I pressed.

A half-hearted smile spread across his lips. "We go way back, though I haven't seen him in years."

"When was the last time?"

"A long, long time ago."

"Were you friends?" I asked, attempting to keep my tone casual.

He barked out a laugh and shook his head. "No, he was friends with my daughter."

I stiffened in my seat. Philippe had never mentioned her when he'd told me the story of his involvement with Dana. He'd only mentioned Paris, Caleb, and the famous photo. Was he hiding the circumstances of their relationship from me? Had they been lovers?

"It'll be great to see him again," he said, settling back into his seat.

I gripped the steering wheel hard, curling my fingers around the plastic until my knuckles went white. "The house isn't much farther, just one more block." Saving Dana no longer occupied my focus. Seeing Philippe's reaction when I asked him about Tabitha had taken over.

He nodded and frowned. "Do you think Caleb went back there too?"

I took a deep breath and shrugged my shoulders. "I don't know, but if he did, he won't be staying long." I pointed to the marks on my neck. "Philippe will be furious with him for doing this to me."

"What was the point of biting you?"

"He likes to throw his weight around." I glanced at him. "Don't worry. I said I'd keep you safe, and I meant it." As we turned into the driveway, I announced, "We're here."

"The old McNally place. Nice."

After I'd parked on the circular driveway, I hurried up the steps, Dana close at my heels. As I led Dana inside to the foyer, I caught sight of Philippe pacing the polished marble with Betty at his side, attempting to calm him.

Philippe's head jerked toward me. With trembling hands, he rushed to my side, cupping my face in his palms and kissing me hard when he reached me. Then, holding me at arm's length, his gaze traveled to my throat.

"Caleb," I said simply.

Shaken, Philippe uttered, "He bit you, but why?"

I didn't get a chance to reply.

Dana stepped out from the entryway, his gaze fixed on Philippe. "We meet again."

Every muscle in Philippe's body stiffened.

I placed my hand on his chest and said, "Philippe, don't be angry. I can explain."

He pushed me away and shouted, "How dare you bring this man into our home!"

I stumbled back a couple steps, trying to regain my balance. "Remember Anna?" I shouted. "I couldn't let that monster kill another human being."

Philippe's nostrils flared as he let out a low growl. He turned to Betty and ordered, "Take Beth upstairs, now!"

She clutched her hands in front of her and approached me with hurried steps.

I shielded Dana with my body, backing away from her. "I'm not going anywhere. I swore to keep Dana safe."

Philippe pressed his fingertips against his temples, exhaling loudly. "You don't know what you've done." He pointed a rigid finger at Dana. "This man doesn't need our protection. He has manipulated you into believing he does."

"Give me some credit," I snapped. "I wasn't manipulated into anything. I asked Dana to come here."

Philippe closed his eyes and ground out his next words, "Beth, do as I say. Go upstairs with Betty, now."

I stood my ground. "Why, so you can summon Caleb? I won't let you do that. I told Dana he would be safe here."

Dana jumped in front of me, bellowing with laughter like a crazy person.

Warning bells went off inside my head, and a slew of goose bumps scurried down my arms. "Dana, what's wrong with you?"

Dana whirled to face me. "Beth, your husband is no better than Caleb. They're both monsters. They create monsters." He spun back toward Philippe and shook his finger at him wildly. "You transformed my daughter, leaving me no choice in the matter." A tremor shook his shoulders, then another and another, until his chest heaved with great sobs.

"She was dying of cancer. She asked me to save her," Philippe admitted, his voice more controlled.

Heat rushed to my cheeks. I wanted to scream at him, ask how he could've kept such a secret from me, but I chose to clamp my mouth shut and glare hatred at him instead.

A pained expression twisted Philippe's brow. "I'm sorry," he whispered.

Dana vigorously shook his head. "NO...NO...NO! She would never have made such a choice. She loved life, human life. You took hers away and forced my hand, leaving me no choice. You see, Beth, there's only one true way to kill a vampire. The age-old stake in the heart method only works in the movies. When I tried to stake Tabitha, her body healed right before my eyes. Next, I tried cutting off her head..." Hysterical laughter bubbled from his lips. "It just slithered back to her body and reattached itself."

I took a step back. He'd tried to kill his own child?

Dana began to circle the room, continuing to relay his horrible tale. "Another myth is the sun. Yes, its rays are damaging to vampire flesh, but not enough to kill one. The only way to destroy them is to burn them alive."

My stomach clenched with a wave of nausea. I took another step away from the lunatic.

A crazed gleam lit Dana's eyes as he reached into his coat pocket, calmly stating, "As you took my daughter from me, I will take your wife."

A rapid pop-pop-pop, like firecrackers, exploded inside my ears. A searing twinge of pain penetrated my chest, burrowing deeper until the agony gripped my heart, driving me to the floor. I touched something wet and warm on my shirt. Lifting my hand, I blinked at the sight of thick scarlet blood coating my skin. My blood!

Philippe's agonized howl echoed throughout the foyer, very nearly drowning out Betty's petrified shriek. Seconds drifted by before a bizarre sound, like a pile of bones snapping, went off inside my head. Dana croaked out a strangled gasp before utter silence filled my head.

Philippe's arms came around me, cradling and rocking me. Betty knelt by my side and stroked my hair. Feverish sweat soaked my body, yet I was freezing cold. A gurgling noise crawled up through my throat, cutting off my breath, forcing me to gasp for air.

Tears streamed from Philippe's eyes as he begged me, "Give me your permission, Beth. Let me turn you. There isn't much time."

I could feel the life trickle out of my body. My heartbeat slowed, and every labored breath set my lungs on fire. *Dear God, I'm dying. I can't die. I won't die. I can't leave Philippe, not now, not ever.* I latched onto his arm and cried out, "Don't let me die, Philippe. Let me live with you forever."

The words had scarcely left my lips when I felt the prick of his fangs puncture my jugular. My blood narrowly exited my body, dribbling into Philippe's mouth. Numbness began in my toes, crawling up my legs to spread into my arms, coil around my ribs, and race throughout my brain. The faint drumming of my heartbeat faded away. A feeling of nothingness consumed me, but in a pleasant way, as if I were floating on another plane, high above the clouds. I closed my eyes and welcomed the encroaching darkness.

The fierce smell of blood yanked me back from the velvety dark. The scent of salt-laced copper captured my senses, commanding my heart to beat. Air filled my lungs after. A ravenous growl ripped through my stomach, my insides hungry for the blood, wanting to drink, swim, drown in its richness. As the first drop touched my tongue, an enormous power convulsed inside me and jerked my body off the floor. My eyes flew open, and Philippe filled them. "More," I cried before embedding my newly-born fangs into the flesh of his wrist.

Philippe smiled warmly, the relief there a welcome replacement for the panic of the moments previous. "Drink, my love, drink."

And I did, until his blood spilled from my lips.

CHAPTER 12

I woke to the unpleasantness of a sticky film of clammy sweat coating my skin. I couldn't move my legs and arms; they lay limp, numb, useless. As I peered around the room, my vision zoomed in and out, like a camera lens, focusing on images with a clarity I'd never experienced before. The crackling fire, Philippe's cologne, my own perfume, the flowers in the vase on the nightstand, even the collection of scented soaps in the bathroom—every scent magnified, overpowering my sense of taste and smell. This wasn't a condition I could overcome with medication or rest. There was no turning back. My new state of being was permanent. Gathering every ounce of strength I could muster, I turned my head toward the bathroom.

Philippe stood in the doorway. He strode toward me, buttoning his shirt and running a towel through his hair. His footsteps thundered, like a giant walking through the room, jarring my head and making my ears ache.

He knelt at my bedside, propping me up with pillows and kissing my lips softly. His expression gleamed with affection and pride. "Finally, you're awake."

The memory of Dana's daughter popped up inside my brain. The smarting burn of betrayal rippled over my cold flesh. He'd kept his knowledge of her from me. He'd misled me. I turned away from him.

"Everything is a little overwhelming at first, but the intensity will settle down. You will adapt, trust me."

His words made me roll back over. I wanted to push him away, but I didn't possess the strength, so I yelled at him instead. "You told me if there was anything I wanted to know, all I had to do was ask." I paused and glared at him. "Well, I asked about Dana, and you deliberately kept the fact that you were intimately acquainted with his daughter from me. What else are you hiding?"

He exhaled deeply. "Did I or did I not already apologize?" He didn't wait for a reply. "Dana's daughter is irrelevant where you and I are concerned," he said, throwing his shoulders back in arrogance. "She's part of my past. You are my future. I saw no point in telling you about her. That being said, I haven't kept any secrets from you. You know everything about me."

I clenched my jaw. "Apparently, I don't."

He walked toward the closet, continuing to dress himself. Glancing over his shoulder, he added, "Beth, I will say this once more, I have *not* been dishonest with you."

I tried to command every muscle in my body, struggling for some type of movement—I would've settled for a twitch. Nothing happened to spare me from lying there like a corpse. I found my current state utterly maddening, remaining unable to stomp my foot, throw my hands in the air, or jump off the bed and challenge him while standing on my own two feet. My only weapon was my voice, and I hurled it at him. "If you had told me Dana had murdered his own daughter because *you* turned her into a vampire, I would have never brought him into our home. I would have never been shot. I'd still be alive, and I wouldn't be lying here in this bed turning into a vampire!"

He flinched before fleeing the room like a coward, leaving me partially paralyzed and alone.

Jerk! I uttered a whimper, which quickly turned into sobbing.

Approaching footsteps echoed in my ears. My gaze darted to the doorway. "Philippe?"

Caleb entered, a smug grin plastered on his face. "Sorry, love. It's only me."

He was the last person in the world I wanted to see. "Go away," I snapped.

He shook his head. "No can do. In your state, you definitely require a babysitter, and since you've driven Philippe away with that acid tongue of yours, I've been saddled with the job."

Sinking into the pillows, I bit my lip and groaned, helpless to improve my situation.

"Philippe's head over heels in love with you, you idiot, and you have hurt him deeply. You owe him an apology."

Adrenaline poured into my system. I felt my fingers twitch. My gaze darted to my hands. They moved. Curling my fingers into my palms, I balled my fists. "I owe *him* an apology? He lied to me. He needs to do the apologizing."

Caleb neared the bed and stood over me. "Failing to disclose the truth is hardly lying." He arched his brow. "Besides, aren't you the pot calling the kettle black? You've hidden things as well, like your mysterious mist."

Unclenching my fists, I let my hands drop back onto the bed. He had a point, and there was something else he didn't know about, something I'd uncovered while lying in my vulnerable state. Transforming had pushed me toward a new awareness, heightened senses, and a deeper insight into my own self. A blood war raged inside of me. I could feel it pulling pieces of me apart, coursing in opposing directions, one battling to conquer the other. Releasing my anger, I flicked my eyes up to search his. "Caleb..."

"Yes?"

I swallowed hard, chewing on the inside of my lip before I spoke. "You were right about the blood. It's not just Philippe's inside me. I can finally feel there truly *is* the blood of another, struggling to separate me from Philippe's and defend its territory." I scrunched my brows together. "Why did Philippe mislead me, allowing me to believe he was the mist from my childhood?"

He sat on the bed and pressed his lips into a hard, thin line. "Philippe can be rather foolhardy...and he loves to fantasize. I'm positive his intent wasn't to deceive you." He nodded thoughtfully. "You *did* want the mist. My guess is in his attempt to please you, he fulfilled the role of your mist."

Fulfilled a role? That was *my* life he'd messed with. "He should've confessed this to me before we were married. The mist meant *everything* to me. I loved him. I loved Philippe, thinking him to be my mist." I looked away and murmured under my breath, "Our love is based on a lie."

He gripped my hands. "Listen to me. Philippe loves you more than anything, more than the blood which created him. Remember that. It doesn't matter how the two of you started. What matters is now. Do you love him...Philippe?"

My chin trembled and tears moistened my eyes. "Yes."

He peered deep into my eyes and said, "You love each other. Nothing else matters."

Brushing my tears aside, I told him, "You're wrong. The mist is still out there. He matters. You don't understand what an essential part of my life he was for years, for practically my entire existence."

He leaned back and scraped his fingers along his jaw. "This poses a dilemma for us both. I knew the blood inside you belonged to another. I kept this knowledge from Philippe. He will not take kindly to learning that the other vampire, one you loved dearly, may one day reveal himself and Philippe as the imposter. The truth will undoubtedly crush his heart; nonetheless, you and I must determine the identity of the vampire behind the mist and discover what he wants from you before he comes calling. Any idea as to who this mystery vampire may be?"

"None. I truly thought it to be Philippe. I had no reason to doubt him...until now."

His typically smug expression vanished, replaced by a frown. "Why did this other vampire disguise their identity with mist to begin with? More importantly, why hasn't the other vampire returned? You're certain you know him only as mist? He never showed you his true form?"

I rolled my eyes. "Really, you have to ask me that? Of course, I'm certain. If I knew what he looked like, I wouldn't have mistaken Philippe for him."

"This is true. Something must have prevented the vampire from revealing their physical form." He said nothing for a moment and then blurted out, "The blood lottery."

"What?"

He sprang to his feet, pacing the room and talking more to himself than to me. "It makes perfect sense. The blood lottery forbids contact prior to feeding. The vampire couldn't show himself but couldn't force himself to stay away either. By concealing his true form within the mist, he could come to you without breaking vampire law." He stopped and stared at me with raised brows. "But the names in the blood lottery are kept secret, so how could he have known?"

"Known what?"

Caleb waved a hand in the air. "Let me think. The mist becomes a permanent part of your life...Philippe shows up. He marries you, turns you, and only then, the mist vanishes, but why?" He shook his head. "I keep coming back to the blood lottery. It's the only thing that makes any sense." A confident smile overtook his lips, and he snapped his fingers. "I've got it. You were chosen by one of The Ten."

I laughed. "Wrong. Nobody chose me."

"You struck some vampire's fancy so much that he risked every-thing just to be able to remain close to you."

"What risk? What are you jabbering on about?"

"Oh, there had to be risk involved. Why else would he appear to you as mist?"

"I don't know," I answered half-heartedly, growing exhausted by his endless conjecture.

"Do you have a better explanation?"

I looked up at him and pressed my lips together. "At the moment, no, but that doesn't mean you're right."

He grinned. "It doesn't mean I'm wrong either."

I sighed. "I'm not going to debate this with you. Please, change the subject."

He sat back down on the bed, boredom overtaking his expression and said, "Fine. What do you want to talk about?"

I lifted a hand weakly. "What's happening to me? Why can't I move?"

A dazed look came over him. "Philippe didn't tell you?"

"I didn't give him a chance. I brought up Dana's daughter, and we argued. He left, and that's when you showed up."

"Ah. Do you want the truth straightforward or sugar coated?"

"Straightforward."

He winked at me. "You've got it. You're not dead yet. The vampire blood is taking over, gifting you with immortality."

"That doesn't sound very straightforward. You're hiding something."

He narrowed his gaze as he added, "You want more? I'll give you more. Your flawed human organs are metamorphosing into those of an undying celestial being's. For seven days, your body will fight this process, just as it would any virus, but it will ultimately fail. The vampire blood will kill off anything human, and on the seventh day," he raised his brows in realization, "your twenty-fifth birthday, you'll be human no more. Welcome to day number one."

My stomached clenched. "Seven days of this?"

He chuckled. "Relax. I didn't say you would be unable to move for seven days. Each day will get easier, but you need to rest and let your new body grow strong. The process sounds much worse than it actually is." He spread his arms and beamed. "Immortality, my dear, is a fabulous gift. You should feel grateful."

I openly stared at him. Vampire blood killing off anything human could hardly be considered a gift. I couldn't just lie there and wait for the change to happen. Adrenaline kicked in. With the burst of energy, I threw the covers aside, swinging my legs over the side of the bed and standing on my feet. Sweat flowed freely from my pores, just before my muscles cramped and shooting pain set my joints on fire. My legs buckled, and I crashed to the floor.

Caleb's mouth flew open as he jumped off the bed and scooped me up into his arms. "What the hell are you doing? Are you mad?" He placed me back in the bed, resting my head against the pillows and pulling the covers over me. "Don't do that again."

I smiled up at him. "So, you do have a heart after all."

He put a finger to his lips. "Shh, don't tell anyone."

"Your secret's safe with me," I said. As we sat together, Dana's daughter resurfaced inside my head. I craved closure. "Will you tell me about Tabitha, Dana's daughter?"

A mischievous smile spread on his lips. "She was a feisty little thing and always loved pissing Dana off—until she became ill, that is. The poor girl lived her life in and out of hospitals, withering away to almost nothing. Philippe took it very hard. They'd forged a connection."

I chomped down on my bottom lip.

He wiggled his eyebrows at me. "A wee bit jealous, are we? They weren't lovers, Beth, merely close friends. It hurt Philippe deeply to bear witness to her suffering."

"So, he gave her his blood and turned her," I said, filling in the blanks.

He shook his head. "It wasn't that simple. She begged him for months. Philippe struggled with his decision, but in the end, he couldn't watch her die. He transformed her into the very thing Dana despised the most. Not long after, Dana truly killed her."

I placed my hand over my heart. "And Philippe? How did he take her death?"

Caleb sat quietly, a grave expression tugging at the corners of his mouth. "His guilt devastated and overwhelmed him. I offered him years of my encouragement and support before the fullness of his spirit returned." Caleb gave me a heartfelt look. "He gave Tabitha his blood so she could live. He gave you his blood because he couldn't live without you. Let go of your anger and forgive him. He lives and breathes for you and you alone."

Tears flooded my eyes, causing my lip to quiver. I did love Philippe. Maybe Caleb was right. Maybe I should let all the anger and mistrust go, forget about everything so Philippe and I could be happy together. I could do that. I wanted to do that. "The moment he returns, I'll apologize."

His shoulders slumped with relief, and he sighed heavily. "Good. And Philippe mustn't find out about the mist. I fear the truth would break him, this time for good. As I have done, you must also shield your thoughts. Let me show you how."

"I agree. Telling him won't accomplish anything but pain." I pushed upward, settling into a comfortable sitting position. "I'm ready."

Rubbing his hands together, he said, "Your first lesson on shielding your thoughts. I must tell you that all vampires use this power."

"Then Philippe must realize I can hide things from him."

"Yes, yes," he said in a sharp tone, "but you're missing the point. What he doesn't know won't hurt him. That's our focus for this task."

"Then teach away."

The color of Caleb's eyes began to change, replaced with two bright orange balls blazing between the narrowed slits. "Concentrate, Beth. Picture a box in your mind. Visualize it until it becomes real, so real that you can touch it. When the image solidifies, open the lid and store your deepest, darkest secrets inside. Shut the box, paint it black so it becomes invisible in the dark recesses of your mind, and then lock it. Only you possess the power to open it. Now, let's give it a try."

I closed my eyes and took a deep breath, letting my mind go blank. An image of a simple rectangular box slowly formed, rotating end over end inside my head. I carved out every inch of the box in my mind, adding depth and an airtight lid. I finished with a heavy coat of black paint. After I tucked the mist inside and secured the lid, I turned my key, the only key, locking him away forever. I opened my eyes and announced, "Done."

He stared into my eyes while he tunneled through my brain with his own. "Too easy," he lectured. "I popped the top and read your thoughts almost immediately. Try again."

I fell back onto the pillows. Where had I gone wrong? Pursing my lips, I squeezed my eyes shut and summoned the black box. Again, I stored the mist, pushed the lid down tight, and double locked it with a thick padlock. Looking up at Caleb with slightly less conviction, I said, "Ready."

He rolled his eyes and shook his head. "Again."

"What? You didn't even try?"

"I did and broke through with little effort. Again," he said, his tone stern.

Once again, I threw my thoughts inside the stupid box, slammed the lid, wrapped a chain around it, and locked it. "Now," I insisted.

He hung his head and groaned loudly. "No, no, no." He ran his hands through his hair, and then pointed at the bedroom door. "Beth, Philippe could walk in at any minute. You have to master this now.'

"Don't you think I know that? I'm trying really hard. I don't know what I'm doing wrong. Help me," I cried out in frustration.

Compassion flickered inside his eyes. "First of all, you have to relax. You can't force this. Secondly, this isn't simply a black box. It's personal, like a safety deposit box where one would store their valuables. These are your secrets you hold dear and must guard with your very life."

His words soothed my nerves, and the rapid fire of my heartbeat slowed to a calmer rhythm. "So, I have to make this more about me than the box."

He smiled and nodded. "Precisely." His head jerked toward the door, his body going rigid. "Philippe just came through the front door." Gripping my shoulders, he whispered, "Do it now, Beth."

My hands trembled, and tiny beads of sweat formed along my palms, but I couldn't give in to my emotions. *Get it together. Act fast, act now!* The box exploded to life in my mind. The rectangular shape shifted to form an antique chest with a gold latch and red-velvet lining. Using my newly acquired vampire speed, I tucked the mist inside the chest, snapping the lid closed and fastening the gold latch. I went a step further, draping a dark curtain across its front, concealing it from prying eyes.

Philippe skulked into the room, his shoulders sagging, head lowered.

My breath stuck in my throat as my gaze darted to Caleb.

As he stood behind Philippe, he gave me two thumbs up and wiped his brow in an exaggerated fashion. Gripping Philippe's shoulder, he gave it a comforting squeeze and said, "I shall leave the two of you alone. Good night."

Philippe placed his hand atop Caleb's and gave him a nod.

I looked at Caleb with new eyes, forged by the secret we now shared. To protect Philippe from heartache, he willingly concealed my past. For that reason, a fraction of my heart forgave him for what he'd done to Anna. "Good night, Caleb."

Caleb lingered in the doorway to smile at me, before leaving Philippe and I alone.

Philippe's blood swirled beneath my skin, making me long to feel his touch. I truly loved him, and it pained me to see the damage I had caused. Summoning all my strength, I held out my arms. "Forgive me."

Philippe's face lifted, a joyful smile touching his lips. He rushed into my embrace and pressed his body against me, burying his hands in my hair. "I'm the one who needs to be forgiven. Beth, my love for you frightens me. The power it wields is one I can't control. I have walked the Earth both as a mortal and immortal, never knowing such a love. Yes, I have loved before, but you exist as more than mere love for me. You're my spirit, my soul, my heartbeat, my breath." He laid his lips over mine and kissed me softly, tenderly, his passion building. He pulled away so he could say, "Let us never quarrel again."

As I gazed into his eyes, ripples of happiness spread out across the surface of my heart. "Agreed. Philippe, you're everything to me as well."

He grinned like a schoolboy with a crush. "I think this calls for some wine." He bounded toward the door. "Be right back."

After he'd left the room, I let out a gasp. Within only moments, I'd created my box and hidden the mist away forever. I took in a pained breath and closed my eyes. I'd argued with Philippe over keeping secrets, and there I was, hiding the existence of the mist from him. But Caleb had assured me it had to be done.

Philippe strutted through the door, all smiles, with a bottle of wine and two glasses. After he popped the cork and poured a glass for each of us, he snuggled up against me. "Small sips. For vampires, wine is a very powerful drug."

I filled my mouth with scarcely a swallow. The liquid flowed down my throat to swim through my veins, mixing with my blood. I went limp again, my entire body tingling with pleasure.

I heard Philippe chuckle. "Tell me, how do you find the wine?"

I shuddered with pleasure and laughed shamelessly. "Wonderful. I feel so relaxed."

He gave my hand a squeeze. "Would you believe Caleb fell flat on his face the first time he tried it? Wine to vampires is like honey to bees. Once you take your first sip, you're hooked for immortal life."

"Yes, I'll have wine to look forward to, but what else lies ahead of me? What must I know about becoming a vampire?"

"You will inherit an extraordinary sense of sight and hearing, incredible strength and speed. These will serve as your most valuable gifts. If you so desire, you can toy with humans by reading their minds and controlling their thoughts."

"That seems cruel to me. I refuse to play mind games with mortals," I said with conviction.

"You may live your new life in whatever manner you wish, my love. You may prefer to use your powers to move objects, fly like a bird, or alter your form. On the downside, you *will* crave and hunger after the taste of blood, and at times it can become unbearable, but you will learn to control these cravings. As you're already aware, the sun forces us to live by night and sleep by day, but only fire can kill a vampire. Lastly, try not to attract unwanted attention, and do make your private life *very* private."

"That's a rather large list."

He shrugged his shoulders. "It sounds daunting, but you'll grow accustomed to your new life in very little time. During these next seven days, I will train you on how to use your new body."

I gave him a playful nudge. "You're joking, right? I can't possibly learn everything in seven days."

"I'm serious. You already possess the power. You only require the techniques to master our gifts."

"Which are?" I pressed.

"Patience and control are all you need to help you become a powerful vampire." He kissed the tip of my nose. "Most of the time, you possess neither."

"Not true," I objected, leaning forward to kiss him.

"So true," he retorted, kissing me back. "This will be your greatest challenge during training. Overnight, your body will regain its strength, and tomorrow morning, all movement will be restored. I will begin to train you right away, but for now, sleep and allow your body to heal."

Curling up next to him, my eyelids grew heavy, and I fell into a sound, dreamless sleep.

CHAPTER 13

The next evening, I awoke to find a note resting on my pillow. As I reached for it, I realized that the dead weight pinning my limbs had vanished. I pushed the covers aside and bounced off the bed. Stretching my arms overhead, I let out a groan, as if I'd been lying in bed for days, and then flipped open the piece of paper. "Beth, my love," I read aloud as a padded through the room. "Please, join me in the formal dining room." I stared at his words a moment longer before laying the paper on the nightstand. After a quick shower, I slipped into a pair of leggings and a tank top, stepping into my flip-flops on my way out of the room.

I sauntered into the formal dining room like an arrogant housecat, parading around the massive mahogany table with my gaze locked on Philippe. He stood with his hands behind his back, smiling with his eyes. As he pulled out a chair for me, he requested, "Have a seat."

I regarded him with a tilt of my head. What was this about? I played along, sliding into the chair and wrapping my arm over the back. For added measure, I faked a yawn and winked at him.

He pressed his lips together and shook his head. "Stop fooling around. Time to get serious." He pointed to the glass vase in the center of the table, filled with bright yellow daffodils. "You must become this object. Concentrate. Use your vampire mind to move the vase."

I leaned forward, laying my hands on the table and focusing on the way the blossoms merged together. I commanded my mind to absorb the vase. The image spun around inside my brain, as if I were sculpting the vase anew from a raw slab of clay. The object kept spinning and spinning, but my mind would do nothing more. The vase didn't move, not even a slight tremor, but I maintained my focus, straining my eyes as I fixated on the stupid thing.

The ticking of the clock rattled my concentration. Why should I care whether I accomplished something so trivial as moving a vase?

"Lift the vase, now," Philippe barked out.

I concentrated anew, striving for even the slightest hint of movement. It didn't budge a millimeter. I huffed out, "I can't."

Sparks of light shimmered within his eyes. His gaze intensified, zooming in on me like a camera lens. A gentle force pushed me off my chair and set me on my feet.

"That was meant to serve as a lesson. I could have sent you sailing," he bragged. "Do you want to become an extraordinary vampire or merely an average one?"

Pouting like a spoiled child, I plopped back down in the chair. "It's boring sitting here staring at a vase."

"Would you prefer a different object? It doesn't have to be a vase." He tugged on his goatee. "Pick something else."

I slouched in my seat. "I don't think changing the object is going to help. Why can't we try something exciting, like flying?"

He scoffed. "If you can't even lift a small vase, how do you expect to lift your entire body?" The corner of his mouth twitched before stretching into a grin. Gesturing toward the door, he said, "We live right across from the ocean. Sit on the beach and become one with the seashore."

I sprang out of the chair, knocking it over in my haste. "That's a perfect idea." After righting the chair, I kissed his cheek and made for the door. "I love water. I can stare at it for hours."

"Can I trust you to go alone and complete this lesson unsupervised?"

I blew him a kiss. "Yes, Philippe, you have my word."

I hurried down the path to the beach, tasting the salty air with my tongue. At night, the ocean became a mystery, turning an impossible shade of dark blue under the moonlight. I kicked off my shoes on its shore, burying my toes in the cool sand. Lowering myself to the ground, I sat a few feet from the water's edge, tucking my legs beneath me and centering my focus on the calm horizon. Waves tumbled in and pulled away, stretching out to tickle my toes, yet never once reaching me. The ceaseless whoosh of crashing water hypnotized me. Rocking my body back and forth, I mimicked the sea's rhythm.

The water crept closer, eventually touching my feet and swelling about my waist. As I scrambled to my feet, the water rose with me. My feet were rooted into the sand, my whole body shaking, but I managed to maintain my concentration.

The waves splashed up to caress my neck and flow over my head. Still, I remained motionless, my mind fixated on the ocean. Blood rushed through my ears, the veins in my neck swelling. I could feel each muscle seize up and go rigid. Bit by bit, the water drifted away from me. An invisible barrier separated me from the sea. I ran my fingers across the glass-like surface, small flecks breaking free to gently splash against my face like a lover's touch.

I took my concentration to a new level, willing my body to rise. The powerful force of my vampire blood throbbed through my veins, turning my limbs weightless. I lifted off the ground, rising higher and higher. Like a feather on the wind, I floated above the water. Laughter bubbled up my throat, and I took my eyes off the horizon. Losing focus, I plunged onto the sand.

I jumped to my feet, eager to experience the magic of flight again. Slowly, I rose above the water, flipping my body over so I faced upward, gazing at the stars shining brightly against the black canvas of night. I spread my arms out to my sides, feeling very much like an angel from Heaven spreading its wings.

Several minutes of floating drained my strength away. I grew heavy, too heavy to fly. My dead weight landed me back in the sand. Lying in its soft embrace, I stared at the stars until the sky lightened and announced the arrival of the impending sunrise. I breathed a sigh, brushed the sand from my clothes, and dashed off to take shelter inside our home.

I found Philippe in the study, engrossed in the pages of a book. I pulled the book from his hands and I shouted, "I did it!"

He sternly pointed out, "You completed *this* lesson. Tomorrow, there will be another."

I scowled at him, but only playfully. "Killjoy."

He shot a sly wink in my direction. "If it's joy you want, then joy you shall receive."

Sweeping me up in his arms, he carried me up the stairs and into our bedroom, laying me gently in our bed. As he undressed me, he caressed every inch of my flesh, his touch driving me to demand he make love to me. And he did, adoringly and passionately, kissing my lips and whispering I love you over and over in my ears. I fell asleep, blissfully happy.

****

I stood barefoot in the desert sands of Egypt inside my dream. Pyramids soared into the heavens above me, and when I lowered my gaze, my antique chest lay at my feet, the lid thrown back, exposing my secrets—including the mist. I dropped to my knees, gripping the gold latch and slamming the chest closed. As if it had grown a mind of its own, the lid flew open, the mist rising to the surface of the velvet-lined interior. I gasped before I snapped the lid shut once more, locking the mysterious vapor inside.

The wood cracked, splintering into a thousand tiny pieces and unleashing the mist. It swirled before me, taking shape limb by limb. Out of the mist stepped an Egyptian king, his body covered by a sheer linen skirt and elaborate jewelry. His jet-black hair twisted into countless braids, cascading over his bronzed skin like ropes made of night. A beautiful light radiated from him, draining all color from the rest of the world. Not even my handsome Philippe matched his magnificence. His ancient aura touched me, passing the memories from thousands of years through my soul, yet he appeared to have aged no more than thirty years.

I stood paralyzed, gazing into the emerald-green eyes of the vampire who had truly given life to my nameless mist for nearly all the years of my human life.

In a divine voice, like a choir of angels, he said, "I am the sun and the moon, life and death, a god of gods. I am Amon, your true destiny."

Though I stood ankle-deep in the balmy sand, I shivered, staring at him mute and unable to unscramble my thoughts.

He knelt beside me and took my hand. A benevolent expression brought warmth to his face. "Soon, I will come to you. The past can no longer keep us apart."

He vanished into darkness, and my dream abruptly ended, but his commanding presence lingered. I awoke, clutching the covers in my fists, my body covered by a sheen of sweat. My gaze darted to Philippe. Face down in the pillows, arms and legs sprawling, he slept soundly. Dear God, Caleb had been right. I *was* chosen by a vampire god, and it seemed he fully intended to collect his prize. Touching my lips, I closed my eyes and called forth Amon's image inside my mind. My immortal heart soared, thumping with the strength to break free from my chest. All my life I had loved him—a heartsick, gripping, crushing love, but those raw and powerful feelings now belonged to Philippe. Or did they? Caleb's words flooded to the surface my brain—*fulfilling a role*—calling to my attention the mask Philippe had chosen to portray when he'd declared himself the mist. How could he have done such a thing? Created such complications...

If Amon came for me, I knew he would demand I end my marriage to Philippe. How could I possibly fix such a mess? One name came to mind. For the second time, I needed Caleb. Inside my head, I cried out, "Caleb, come at once. I desperately need your help. The mist has returned and revealed his true identity."

A breath after sunset, I paced the foyer, waiting for Caleb to arrive, my dream secured inside my antique chest should Philippe awaken.

Caleb burst through the front door, his eyes groggy and his hair a tousled mess. He wasted no time whisking me into the study where, in a heated whisper, he demanded, "What the hell happened? What did you do to call him forth?"

I stood my ground, answering him with venom in my voice. "I did nothing. After I fell asleep, he came to me in a dream, which I had no control over."

In a much calmer tone, Caleb said, "Tell me every detail of the dream."

"I remember more what he said than what he did. He told me his name, Amon, and said he was my true destiny, that the past can't keep us apart...and that soon he would come for me."

Caleb sank into one of the chairs by the fireplace. "I was wrong about the blood lottery. He's not after your blood, he's after you. He wants you." His hands trembled in his lap as his gaze darted about the room. "We're in trouble. Philippe falls under the rule of the Ten, and so do I." Again, he slumped in the chair, shaking his head. "I don't have a plan. I don't know how to fix this."

I fell at his feet and grabbed onto his hands. "You must know of something to defuse this sticky situation. Philippe will not care about rules. Look what he's already done to manipulate me. Besides, we're married, and I love him!"

He seemed to consider my words, pausing before he replied. "You're right, there has to be a way. I'll figure out something we can do." He pulled me to my feet. "In the meantime, continue your training with Philippe, behaving as though nothing has changed."

"Easier said than done." I stuck out my quaking hand. "Look. He's bound to sense something."

Gripping my shoulders, his gaze burned into mine. "Conceal your unease inside your black box. Do it now!"

I shoved my restless jitters into my antique chest, slamming the lid to bury my insecurity. The panicked rise and fall of my chest slowed, and a steady calm took over inside me.

A devilish smile twisted Caleb's lips as he regarded me. "You use your black box well. So many secrets for such a young vampire. Whatever shall I do with you?"

I frowned and pushed him toward the door. "Find me answers."

He bowed, retorting with a smirk, "Yes, my vampire queen."

I shooed him away. "Go. You may be the only chance Philippe and I have of staying together."

CHAPTER 14

Four days crawled by without a word from Caleb. My mind raced with wild theories, yet somehow, I managed to complete every task of my vampire training. Day four's lesson mimicked the child's game, Hide and Seek. The goal of the lesson was to learn to conceal my presence. Similar in theory to the black box, my mind could drape an invisible shield over my body, masking my location and protecting me from prying eyes. Finding my exact position inside our massive house posed quite a challenge for the seeker in and of itself. Add a cloaked vampire to the mix, and the challenge became nearly impossible. During my first attempt, I'd held Philippe off for twenty minutes before he located me. Each time after, it took longer and longer for him to discover my hiding place, which pleased him. In the end, I threw him off course, teasing and taunting him until he could stand no more, begging me to show myself.

When day five arrived with no sign of Caleb, I had to struggle with my concentration on my lesson, learning to control vampire speed. Using the upstairs hallway as a racetrack, Philippe and I stood at opposite ends. I ran straight at him, barreling forward at full throttle, gathering speed I'd mastered, but coming to a standstill was another story. Again and again, I crashed into Philippe, sending both of us crashing to the ground.

I threw my hands in the air in frustration. "I give up."

"Try again. Speed is only a matter of judgment. Measure your distance with your vampire sight. The power in your eyes is a powerful tool."

"I can't do it," I said, whining like a child.

He tapped his temple, his patience remaining intact. "Our eyes are like sensors. When an object comes too close, they send signals to the brain."

"Like a warning."

He snapped his fingers. "Exactly."

"But I'm not getting any warning."

"It takes practice."

Countless times more, I sprinted the length of the hallway toward Philippe. Every attempt resulted in a head-on collision. After the umpteenth time of picking himself up off the floor and pulling me to my feet, he said, "Oh well, it's something for you to work on."

Day six, and still no word from Caleb. Had he fallen off the face of the Earth? Even my mental summons he'd ignored. Worrying over Caleb's whereabouts drained my energy. Challenging my brain to master a lesson didn't seem remotely possible, and as luck would have it, reading minds, telepathy, and mind control were the tasks of the day, a skillset already second nature to me. Philippe canceled the lesson. We spent the night in bed, drinking wine, making love, and avoiding the elephant in the room—my final lesson. On the seventh day, my twenty-fifth birthday, hunting and draining my first victim would complete my vampire training. Entangled in one another's arms, we fell asleep as though the next day would never dawn.

****

My eyes flew open. I jerked upright, wide awake and drenched in sweat. A dull steady pain throbbed at my temples, and every nerve under my skin twitched with need. I climbed out of bed and stumbled into the bathroom. When I flipped on the light and looked in the mirror, death stared back. My skin had withered, appearing transparent and gaunt. Depleted veins stood out on my neck, starving for warm, fresh blood. My dry, cracked lips shriveled upward, exposing my fangs ripping through my gums. I staggered backward, covering my mouth and whispering into my palms, "Oh, my God."

Gnawing, churning, cramping hunger roared inside my stomach. My mind blazed with irrational, yet driven thoughts, which focused on one thing—devouring human blood. I wanted...no...I *needed* blood. I fled the bathroom, throwing my clothes on in the dark, and snuck out of our bedroom, gently easing the door flush with its frame. I snatched my car keys off the foyer table and dashed out the door, compelled by my urge to feed.

The cool night breeze encircled me. Shivering, I climbed into my car, cranking the heater full blast, and rubbing my hands over my icy, bloodless flesh. *Find blood, drink blood, devour blood* blinked on and off inside my head like a broken hotel vacancy sign. Gunning my car in reverse, I swung around and sped out of the driveway.

I drove aimlessly up and down Ocean Boulevard with the windows down, letting the intoxicating scent of blood perfume my car. Saliva spilled from my mouth, and I drooled like a starving dog. I needed to pick a place to hunt—any place, and fast. In front of a bar called High Tide, I jerked the steering wheel to the left and pulled into a parking spot, opening the door and stepping onto the street as soon as the car came to a halt. My vampire sight homed in on a crowd of humans gathered nearby. As I observed them, I licked my lips. Prowling the darkened bar for a lone victim as Philippe had done seemed a perfect strategy to follow.

I hurried to them, relishing in the continuous booming of their heartbeats caressing my ears, and the coppery fragrance of their blood tantalizing my nostrils. Under its influence, I staggered forward before quickly rooting my feet into the ground. After a moment, the dizziness cleared and I stood tall, leveling my gaze on the humans.

One by one, the walking blood-bags filed into the entrance, and I followed along. As I crossed the threshold, the intoxicating blood-bouquet seeped through the powder-blue walls, rose from dark-wood floors, swirling in the air as thick as smoke, arousing every sense in my body like the sweet kiss of a lover. I couldn't escape its call, yet I played it cool, strolling through the crowd, hoping my eyes didn't appear as wild as I feared they might. Wiping sweat off my forehead, I bumped the arm of the guy in front of me.

He turned toward me, widening his beautiful baby blues. His hand pulsating with blood touched my shoulder. "Are you all right?"

When I drew a breath in, I could taste his blood, the blood I so desperately needed. I managed a smile. "Would you mind bringing me a glass of wine, please?"

He didn't hesitate. "Of course. What kind would you like?"

My body began to quiver. "It doesn't matter."

He nodded and hurried off to the bar. He returned in a flash, bearing a glass of red wine, which smelled nearly as good as he did...almost. But when I breathed his scent in again, my lashes fluttered, and I swayed on unsteady legs.

He scooped his arm around me and led me to a table, helping me down into a chair. He sat as well, facing me and wrinkling his brow. "You look really pale. Are you sure you're all right?"

My hand shook as I lifted the glass and took a tiny sip. "I'll be okay."

"My name's Josh. What's yours?"

"Beth," I answered, the bloodthirsty vampire inside me growling to be fed.

His boyish face reddened as he swept his curly flaxen hair behind his ears. "I'm not from around here. Visiting my brother." He pointed over his shoulder to a man and woman standing at the bar. "He and his wife dragged me out here." He shrugged half-heartedly. "It's not really my scene. Hey, want to get out of here? We could sit on the beach and watch the waves come in."

I studied his features, the naïveté in his eyes. His life was mine for the taking...along with his blood, but how could I live with myself after destroying such an innocent soul? Watching the waves wasn't what would help my situation, but it did sound soothing and calming. "Yes, I'd like that."

He reached for my hand and softly enclosed it inside his. His pulse vibrated against my skin. Biting down on my lip, I called on every ounce of strength I possessed to keep me from sinking my fangs into him right then and there.

"Perfect," he said, leading me out of the jam-packed bar and down to the vacant beach.

We strolled along the shore, holding hands like lovers, and a sense of peace filled me, taking the edge off my gnawing thirst for blood.

He stopped, took off his jacket, and laid it over the sand. "Here, you can sit on my jacket."

"Thank you," I said, sitting cross-legged on the supple leather and resting my chin in my hands.

He sat next to me and offered up a shy smile. "Why were you in the bar?"

"Does it matter?"

He gestured to my left hand. "I mean, you're wearing a wedding ring."

Touching my ring made me flinch. The all-consuming blood craze had made me forget entirely about Philippe! "I didn't go there to meet guys."

He looked puzzled. "Why then?"

Oh, because I really could use a snack, and you'd do quite nicely. "Just wanted to relax somewhere new with a glass of wine."

Approaching footsteps thundered in my ears. We both turned. His brother and sister-in-law shuffled through the sand toward us.

"Josh," his brother called, "we're leaving. Gonna drive up the street to Gustavo's and have dinner. Does your friend want to join us?"

Josh's gaze darted to mine. "Will you come?"

I tapped my ring. "Can't."

He lowered his head and heaved a sigh. He offered me a warm smile that touched the brilliant blue of his eyes. "I understand. It was nice meeting you, Beth. Take care."

I handed him his jacket. "It was nice meeting you too, Josh." *I'm glad I didn't kill you.*

He waved as he joined his family, leaving me sitting alone on the beach.

"You let him live. I am proud of you."

The divine voice crept inside my brain. My cold blood ran a little faster as I scrambled to my feet and whirled around. Amon stood no more than a foot away, looking nothing like he had in my dream, dressed in jeans and a pale-blue shirt. His jet-black hair hung loose, his bronzed skin unadorned by the elaborate jewelry from before. Even without all the glitter, his flawless, dazzling beauty forced the rest of the world to slip away, as if we were the only two beings who existed. Reality crashed back with a vengeance as I remembered my husband. There was me, Amon…and Philippe!

"Happy birthday, my darling Beth."

I gasped as I stumbled backward.

He cocked his head, as if amused. "You have no reason to fear me."

"Go away," I cried. "Leave me alone. You have no right to enter my life now."

Crossing his arms, he stated calmly, "I have every right. You were promised to me by the exchange of blood."

Taking a step toward him, I challenged his statement. "Who promised? I don't remember ever offering you my blood."

"Your mother. You were only a baby, so you wouldn't remember. I have honored the terms of the promise for twenty-five years. Today, on your birthday, your half must be fulfilled."

I blinked and staggered backward again. "My mother would never do such a thing, promise me to a vampire."

He held out his hand and took a step toward me. "Here, allow me to show you."

I held my hand up in warning. "Stay away."

"I'm not going to hurt you. I didn't lie in wait for twenty-five years just to destroy you. I've watched you grow into a beautiful young woman." He placed his hand on his chest. "I love you. Have you so quickly forgotten me?"

My breath rushed in and out, mirroring the rapid fire of my heartbeat. I could never forget him. "I waited for years, begged you to show yourself. All you gave me was ambiguous mist. When Philippe…I love him now."

The color drained from his face. "And your love for me?"

Tears stung my eyes, and I wiped them away. "You can't ask me to honor that. You're too late. I married Philippe."

He glanced at my ring. "Yes, I'm very much aware, but my gifts, my cards, my visits brightened your eyes. You would spin around in circles, laughing. You couldn't wait for my visits." He searched my eyes. "Do you not remember?"

Memories flooded back, and a pang of heartbreak twisted inside my chest. I dropped to my knees. "Of course, I remember."

The color of his eyes darkened, turning cold and hard in an instant. "Then why did you shut me out and allow Philippe to take my place?" He ground his teeth together, growling out his words. "Do...you...know... how...hard...that...was...? To watch you fall in love with him because you mistook him for me?"

His words sucked all the air from my lungs, making my chest cave in on itself. A torrent of tears streamed down my face as I stood and shouted, "You're to blame for this. You led me straight into his arms."

He glared at me, his lips peeling back from his perfect teeth. "I did no such thing. You're mine, not his."

I shrank away.

He relaxed and placed his hands on his hips. "Why do you continue to fear me? I have stated more than once I mean you no harm."

"You can't just insert yourself into my life and demand my affection after all this time."

He winked at me. "I can, and I will."

"I suppose my feelings don't matter?"

He flinched as if I'd slapped him. "Of course, they matter. Your happiness is everything to me." He held out his hand. "Please, can I explain?"

I scraped my hands through my hair. "I don't see how anything you say could resolve this mess."

He came to me and took my hands, a genuinely heartfelt expression claiming his face. "Let me show you."

He wasn't going to give up. I saw no other choice but to give in. "Fine, show me."

"My blood will show you. It has lain dormant inside you for twenty-five years. I must awaken it."

I shuddered. "How exactly are you going to do that?"

His gaze radiated undeniable love, roaming over every inch of my face. "I've forgotten how easily your beauty quickens my heart. I have missed you."

I didn't say a word, but I felt the truth in my blood that I'd missed him too.

"Are you ready? A single command from me will send my awakened blood coursing through your veins."

"Why did you wait until now?" I whined again. "You should've awakened it years ago."

"You're familiar with the blood lottery, are you not?"

"The concept was explained to me, but only loosely."

"We, The Ten, created the vampire race. The Old Ones, our children, drafted vampire law by which we are all governed." His gaze added gravity to his next words. "The Old Ones do not hesitate to enforce them."

I leaned in closer. "How do they enforce laws on beings as powerful as you?"

"They singe our blood, turning it into something akin to molten lava."

I wrinkled my nose. "How barbaric."

He chuckled and nodded. "I have to agree, but unfortunately, it's the only way to keep The Ten in line."

"They attack you with fire?"

"In a way, yes. Vials of our blood are kept in a vault, always monitored by The Old Ones. If ever we break a law, our blood lights up like the lights on a Christmas tree. Without fear or favor, they light a match to the vial." He shuddered. "I can assure you, the deed stops us dead in our tracks."

"I gather you have firsthand knowledge of this punishment?"

A devilish grin crept across his face. "With every card, gift, or visit I extended to you, my vial was set afire."

Pity filled my heart at his words, along with a morbid curiosity. I wanted to know everything. "Show me. Awaken your blood."

With a twist of his hand, he said, "It is done."

"Yeah, right. I don't feel any diff..." I started, but never finished. My voice gave out. I swayed and crumpled in the sand, my gaze fixed on the stars. They began to blur together. I blinked, only to find myself standing on an unfamiliar street beside a car. Amon sat inside, along with a woman and her baby. Tears streamed down the woman's pretty face. Recognition took hold in my brain. My mother and me. I stood frozen in place, watching the scene from the past play out.

Amon leveled his gaze at my mother, speaking to her in a commanding tone. "I have come for your blood."

Her green eyes bulged with fear as she jerked on the handle, pushing open the door. "No!" she screamed.

Amon maintained deadly calm as yanked her back inside. "You do not have a choice. The blood lottery sanctions me. Were you unaware of your family ties?"

In a small, frightened voice, she whimpered, "I'm aware." She looked up at him, her eyes pleading. "But I'm not ready to die."

Amon shrugged his shoulders. "No matter. Today is your twenty-fifth birthday, and I need to feed."

My mother panicked, her gaze darting about the car as she gripped the steering wheel so hard, her knuckles became bone-white. She centered on me, asleep in my car seat in the back seat. Her lip quivered, a giant sob rippling through her chest. When she faced Amon again, she blurted out, "Take my daughter."

Her past words ripped through my present heart like bullets. Clinging to my shirt above my heart, I found myself unable to move as I gaped in horror at my mother. To save herself, she had sacrificed me. What kind of mother would do such a thing?

Amon briefly glanced into the back seat, and then waved her proposal away.

My mother lifted me out of my car seat and handed me off to Amon. "Take her!"

Caught off guard, he fumbled a bit before he nestled me in his arms. Still sound asleep, I didn't stir. A vague sound escaped him, like a gasp, as he laid his hand over my heart. He sat there, watching me, an endearing smile on his face. "I will spare your life, but only if you agree to promise your child to me. On the day she celebrates her twenty-fifth birthday, she will become my immortal companion."

There was no hesitation on the part of my mother, not even a blink of an eye. "Yes, of course. You can take her then...now. I don't care, as long as you let me live."

At that moment, everything made sense. The reason behind my father's abandonment, the indifference with which my mother had always treated me. My human life had been scheduled for termination at the young age of twenty-five. I'd never been offered a chance at a normal life.

Amon regarded my mother, his eyes full of some unreadable, clouded emotion. "The promise must be sealed with my own blood and that of your child's."

"Fine. Whatever you need to do."

Amon rocked me back and forth as he asked, "What is her name?"

"Beth," my mother said, her tears falling again.

He looked at me with pure adoration and said, "Hello, young Beth."

He pierced his finger so that a small circle of blood pooled on his bronzed skin. He gently placed the tip of his finger in my mouth, rubbing it over my gums. Collecting my thumb in his cold hand, he stabbed it as gently as he could with his fang. I awoke, screaming.

My mother wailed and turned away, clapping her hands over her ears.

Amon stroked my head and licked the blood off my thumb, his eyes never straying from mine. He kissed the top of my head, lulling me back to sleep before he exited the car. He didn't bother to look at my mother again before he disappeared into the night sky.

The vision shattered into a thousand pieces, like a broken window of time, leaving me lying on the beach, staring up at the stars. An empty, hollow sensation filled me, morphing into suffocating abandonment. Tears filled my eyes. My mother had given me up so easily. Had she ever loved me? And what of my father? Had he known exactly what my mother had done? A painful tightness swelled in my throat. I swallowed hard, pushing it back down. "My mother had no right to give me up like that."

Amon knelt next to me, the same fondness he'd bestowed on me as a baby sparkled in his emerald-green eyes. "I don't disagree with you, but I must admit, I am pleased you're mine."

I shook my head. "None of that changes anything. I'm still married to Philippe."

"You loved me once, and you'll love me again if you don't already," he assured me, a confident gleam burning in his eyes.

"You can't expect me to just turn off my feelings and up and leave him. I'm his wife," I insisted.

He didn't appear ruffled in the least. "I can give you things he cannot."

"Like what?"

He grinned and spread his arms wide. "I have a spectacular birthday gift to give you. Anna."

I choked on my own breath, trying to find reason behind his words. "Anna's dead."

The color of his eyes twinkled. "What little faith you have. Do remember, I am one of The Ten."

"How does that change her mortality?"

"There is a temple in Egypt, constructed by the gods themselves, which harbors mystical powers. Most of the structure now lies in ruins, but the hidden passage leading to the Hall of Lost Souls remains intact. Inside this room, you will find your birthday gift."

"Anna will be in this room?"

"Yes, Beth, she will. She cannot move on until she speaks to you." He rose to his feet and extended his hand. "I will take you to her."

My legs trembled, sending me tumbling backward as I attempted to stand. Amon caught me and held me in his arms. "You're weak. You must feed before we make the journey."

Nausea swelled in my stomach. "I can't bring myself to take a life."

"Then drink from me."

I touched my ring and pulled my hand away from him and into my chest. "Philippe would never forgive me."

Leaning in, he whispered, "My blood is already inside you. Drinking more of it is no sin. It will heal you, and you must drink blood tonight, either mine or a human's. You won't survive without it."

I took a deep, painful breath and closed my eyes. "I can't do this."

"You can," he pressed.

After weighing my options, I decided on the lesser of the two evils. "All right, your blood."

In true white knight fashion, he pierced his wrist and turned it over, his blood dripping under the soft moonlight. "Drink."

The rich, coppery scent rushed up into my head. The world spun around me once more. I snatched up his hand and brought it to my lips. Saliva flooded my mouth. Drunk off the scent alone, I lost all reason, piercing his flesh with my fangs and sucking furiously, gulping down his blood in mouthfuls.

Electrifying vibrations hit hard, like lightning striking and turning me inside out. I would have sworn the Earth shook beneath my feet. Pain and weakness drifted out of my body, replaced by a majestic power forcing its way through my veins, commanding my immortal heart to soar. I bit deeper, gorging on his blood, filling every inch of my body with his essence, and shuddering with pleasure.

He pulled me away with very little effort, despite my fervor, and I grumbled in protest before licking the last drops of his blood from my lips.

He stroked my hair as he told me, "My blood has made you indestructible." He lifted my face and gazed into my eyes. "And a touch more beautiful, if that were even possible." He held out his hand to me. "Come, we must go. The doorway to their world will only remain open for a short time."

Swayed by his blood, I willingly took his hand. "I'm going with you only to see Anna," I clarified.

Wrapping his arms around me, he pulled me close and whispered in my ear, "I won't let it go to my head. Hold on tight."

He blasted off the ground like a rocket, soaring into the air. With incredible speed, we flew past the moon to disappear among the clouds. The force of the wind blurred my vision, so I buried my face in his chest. Numbing cold gripped at my body, and my head rolled backward as I fell limp. Sounds faded as darkness encroached.

I awoke to find myself lying on a stone floor. Amon knelt at my side, rubbing the chill from my hands. "I apologize for traveling at such tremendous speed but was worried about the sun. I wanted to ensure our safety."

I tucked a lock of wind-swept hair behind my ear and rose to my feet. "Are we inside the temple?"

"Yes, in Egypt."

The frail stone walls lay crumbling around us in the damp and dusty room. A fine powder lingered, weighing heavy in the air.

"Come," he said, waving me forward. "We must hurry."

He led me through a genuine maze, turning left then right so many times, I lost all sense of direction as we descended deep inside the temple. The thought of seeing Anna again stirred up a slew of emotions—happiness, sadness, guilt, and remorse, all clenched at my heart. Caleb and I killed her. What could I possibly say to her? I needed to apologize. I needed to tell her I loved and missed her.

Amon stopped close to a break in the passageway, just under a lantern. He bent to pull open a trapdoor in the floor. "You will go in alone. It's you she wishes to see, not me."

I fell against the wall, shaking my head. "No, come with me."

Gently, he pushed me toward the hatch. "Don't be frightened. The souls within will not harm you."

I rooted my feet into the floor. "No."

"Go to Anna. She is waiting for you," he pressed.

"Come with me," I begged him again.

Cupping my face in his hands and gazing into my eyes, he assured me, "You don't need me by your side. Now go or you'll miss the window to enter their world."

I stepped one shaky foot inside the trapdoor and then the other, slowly edging myself downward, keeping my gaze locked on Amon until I landed on the ground in pitch-blackness. The air was so cold, it chilled my bones as it swirled around me. With my heartbeat throbbing in my throat, I felt my way along the brittle stone wall as my vampire eyes adjusted to the darkness. Several feet ahead, I caught sight of the top of a stairwell. The steep steps leading to the bottom hid what lay beneath them.

I descended the flight of stairs, only to find another long hallway, though glowing lanterns hung along the wall at intervals, lifting the darkness. The passageway appeared endless, forming many more twists and turns. Ultimately, it led me to an open door. When I crossed the threshold, I entered a fluorescent room. The light source originated from thousands of illuminated souls floating around me. Their transparent hands swept over my flesh before shrinking away and aimlessly roaming the room. I was not the person from which they sought salvation.

"Beth," Anna's soft voice sounded in my ears.

Hearing her call out my name left me breathless. I whirled to find Anna standing there, smiling at me.

Tears flooded my eyes. "Anna," I whispered.

She neared me, shaking her head. "If only I had listened to you."

That fatal night played out inside my head. "Anna, don't. I'm to blame. I'm so sorry. How can you forgive me? Please, forgive me."

Her smile brightened. "No one's to blame. Events just played out as they did because I wanted to tempt fate. But please, know I don't care about any of that now. I just wanted to see you one more time and let you know I feel at peace."

I turned away.

"Look at me, Beth."

I did, focusing my gaze on the light shimmering inside her.

"It's okay to be happy, Beth."

My lip quivered, as a continuous stream of tears fell from my eyes.

Her light grew brighter. "I really am happy now too."

I reached for her but grasped only air. "I will always love you, Anna," I cried.

Tears appeared to pool in her eyes as she floated upward. "I will always love you too, Beth."

Her candle-like flicker grew into a radiant flame burning inside her. She blew me a kiss,

waved a final goodbye and vanished into the warm light waiting for her near the ceiling of the chamber.

CHAPTER 15

With vampire speed I fled the room, raced down the passageway, and burst through the open trapdoor. For the first time, I seemed magically equipped to gauge distance while using the power, coming to a stop inches shy of Amon.

His emerald-green eyes softened as he gazed down at me and smiled. "How was your visit?"

His kindhearted gesture of revealing the Hall of Lost Souls had left me speechless; although, I couldn't help but have my suspicions. Was this an attempt to sway my love away from Philippe? Were his intentions truly selfless or was he trying to manipulate my affections? Searching his face, I tried to read him.

He furrowed his brow in response. "If you have a question, why not just ask it?"

"Why did you bring me here?" I blurted out "And don't just make up something you think I want to hear."

He raised his brows. "I have no intention of making false statements. It serves no purpose. I assure you, my intentions are all driven by honesty."

"Then answer my question."

Shrugging his shoulders, he said, "I could sense you needed to make peace with yourself regarding Anna's death. That is the only reason I brought you here."

I eyed him sharply. "You had no hidden agenda?"

Crossing his arms over his chest, he exhaled loudly. "I am a vampire god, superior to Philippe. Neither a competition nor trickery is necessary. I feel quite certain you will come to the same conclusion, and relatively soon."

"I love Philippe," I reiterated.

He held his head high. "I don't expect you to stop loving him. You will come to love me more all on your own."

"You're overly confident. You can't propose to know how I will come to feel."

His self-assured smile grew. "We'll see."

I rolled my eyes. His persistence was most annoying, and I was through debating with him. I wanted to go home to Philippe. "Take me home. I'm ready to leave."

His smug expression vanished, and he took a step toward me. "I was hoping to take you to the pyramids where vampirism began and disclose the details of that very day. We have time, Beth."

He looked vulnerable, even slightly human...and he had given me closure with Anna. What could it hurt to hear his tale? Although, Philippe was probably being driven out of his mind with worry, wondering where I was. I felt tempted, but a part of me knew his distress would only intensify once I arrived home, as I felt fairly certain Amon would refuse to leave my side. Prolonging the inevitable seemed a better choice at the moment. "Very well, Amon."

"Thank you."

The location to which Amon led me was the very one from my dream. We sat opposite each other in the warm desert sand. A sorrowful glaze clouded his eyes, and he clasped my hands, lacing our fingers. His gaze combed the horizon as he began to speak. "We were powerful gods, ruling the world, fearing nothing and no one." His eyes met mine. After a long pause, he continued. "Seth changed our lives forever. He murdered Osiris, his brother and my best friend, ripping his limbs from his body and spreading them throughout the land. Isis, Osiris' wife, was overcome by her grief. We thought she'd gone mad, roaming the Earth, searching for her husband's remains. When she returned three days later, she had collected every piece of his body and called for a gathering of the gods. She convinced us that her own powerful magic, Khnum's magnificent sorcery of life, and Hathor's powers of love and birth, could all be used together to bring Osiris back from the dead."

"So all of you went mad at the same time?" I asked, interrupting him.

He chuckled. "Perhaps, but we were gods. We believed we could do anything, even bring someone back from the dead." He released my hands and pointed to a mound of sand off to the left. "A temple used to stand in that spot right over there, and inside it, we pieced Osiris' body together on the stone floor. Slicing our flesh, we bled power and life back into his body as Khnum, Isis, and Hathor chanted their mythical spells. New skin grew to connect his severed limbs, healing his wounds. His heartbeat awakened, thundering anew inside his chest. Air rushed from his lungs once again as his eyelids flew open, but he merely stared at us, his voice hauntingly silent."

The hairs on my arms rose. I found his tale to be more than a little creepy, especially given that the incredible facts he relayed were true. I drew my legs in and hugged them close.

The color of his eyes darkened as he continued. "The next morning, Osiris was gone, and two gods lay dead, completely drained of blood. We searched everywhere for Osiris, but it was as though he had disappeared into thin air.

"That night, none of us slept as we awaited Osiris' return. He came to us late in the night, surprised to find all of us awake. He dropped to his knees, lifted his hands to the heavens and roared, 'I am no longer Osiris, Emperor of the Dead. A new god has arisen. A far grander god. A God of Blood.' He began to wail and plead for his life. Isis ran to him, attempting to comfort him by assuring him we had no intention of destroying his new form. We all gathered around him as he spoke of his boundless power. He claimed he could see the smallest of creatures up to hundreds of miles away and hear the tiniest scratch as each scurried about. He believed his strength surpassed Hercules by one thousand times, and we could all see his beauty exceeded the splendor of the very stars. He warned us that the flaming sun, once considered a golden jewel, had become his sworn enemy, its sweltering beacons of light blistering his pale flesh, burning his fair eyes, and restricting all his travel to the night.

"Intrigued and seduced by his chronicle of adventure, power, and beauty, Isis demanded Osiris drain our bodies of blood and convert us with his own immortal blood." Amon turned to me, his expression beaming with excitement. "We all agreed, and Osiris couldn't have been more thrilled himself by our wish to join him. Shortly before sunrise, vampirism breathed new life beneath our skin and gifted each of us with immortal hearts."

Rising onto my knees, I rattled off, "Tell me more. What of The Old Ones and the blood lottery?"

Undeniable love shimmered in his eyes as he gazed upon me. "Your curiosity pleases me." He laid back in the sand, resting his weight on his elbow, a stream of moonlight illuminating his face. "The Egyptian people worshiped us. Realizing we needed blood in order to survive, the mortals offered their lives to us without hesitation. As gods, we knew no restraint. We drank, caring only about the ecstasy of the blood, devouring city after city." He frowned. "Continuing down such a path of destruction and extermination troubled us. We knew we must stop, yet we found ourselves powerless to do so. We needed to be controlled, to be governed, to be held accountable. We searched the globe for twelve of the wisest men and women, and once found, we transformed those dozen with our godly blood. They became The Old Ones, our children. Over the years, they became known as The Council, as they were the individuals responsible for writing vampire law and instituting the blood lottery."

"What about my mother's family and their ties to the blood lottery?"

He shrugged his shoulders. "The inner workings of the lottery are kept secret. We are given a name and a location, nothing more. Your mother's family name descends from O'Ryan. That is all I know."

The name didn't mean anything to me, but I didn't know much about my mother's ancestry. I stared at him, at the god sitting before me. I was a mere human when he chose me, and unworthy of his love. "Why did you let my mother live and pick me as your companion?"

The color of his eyes sparkled when he placed his hand over his heart. "Your heartbeat. It thumped with such fearless power, commanding my attention, as if you were already immortal. As I held you, it grew louder, alternating its rhythm to beat in perfect time with my own. For nearly five thousand years, I felt no other mortal to be worthy of my blood...until you. You were my mirror image in spirit."

The glamour of his words enfolded my heart, squeezing gently. It tingled inside my chest, beating out the rapid gunfire of pride before slowing its rhythm hijacked by reality. I shook my head. "No, I'm more like Philippe. We share a human bond. You've never been human, so you can't possibly understand that connection."

"I may not have been human, but I am humane," he declared. "You never feared me. You loved me! I saw it in your eyes, especially so on the night I left my note on your pillow. *If I had to choose whether to breathe or to love you, I would use my last breath to tell you that...I love you.* Do you remember? You cried when you read it."

I clutched my stomach. Of course, I remembered. It was the moment in time when I knew I'd fallen in love with him. "This is all your fault," I cried. "If I was truly yours, why didn't you reveal yourself sooner? Why did you let me meet Philippe?" I bolted to my feet. "Why did you let me marry him? Now I'm suffering, you're suffering, and after Philippe learns of your existence, he too will be suffering."

Amon's face iced over. Slowly, he balled his hands into fists and slammed them into the sand, making the grains dance around us in a wide circle. "Both the promise and the blood lottery rules held me prisoner. My hands were tied. I could not lawfully reveal my bodily form to you until your twenty-fifth birthday."

The ground continued to shift beneath my feet, and I struggled to keep my balance.

Amon flew to his feet and stood before me. His whole body shook with rage. "You're hardly blameless in all of this. You carried on with Philippe, knowing *my* blood was inside you."

I shrank back, my gaze transfixed on him. "I never realized your blood was inside me. I wasn't a vampire; I knew nothing of your laws. How was I supposed to figure that out on my own? I thought Philippe was you—my mist—so he is to blame for his part in this mess as well. But it doesn't change the fact that he won my heart with his deception, and I fell in love with him. We can't undo the past. Now, Philippe has claimed my heart by marriage."

Gritting his teeth, he slammed his fist into his chest. "A piece of paper creates no *true* bond. Your heart belongs to *me*. My blood flowed inside your veins before Philippe's—since you were an infant. Nothing can change that."

I glared at him and shouted, "And nothing can change the fact that I now have feelings for Philippe." *Except maybe his deceit and robbing us both of our true blood bond,* a too-insistent voice suggested inside my head. Slumping into the sand, I cried, "How do you expect me to fulfill such a promise? It will kill Philippe." Was I more concerned about hurting Philippe than acknowledging my true feelings?

Amon dropped to his knees and embraced me. Brushing a loose strand of hair behind my ear, he kissed my forehead. "Forgive me. We will find a way to please everyone, even Philippe. And though it pains me, I find your loyalty to him commendable. If anything, it makes me love you more. Come, we must return to Castle Beach and flesh out the truth of the matter."

CHAPTER 16

I stirred and forced my eyes open. I was home, lying on the sofa in our living room. I jumped to my feet, my gaze darting into every corner. Where was Amon? Dear God, was he with Philippe? Heated voices thundered through the house, ricocheting off the walls. Cocking my head, I homed in on the vibration. The study! With vampire speed, I dashed down the hall, charging through the door with such force, it rebounded off the opposite wall.

Philippe stood with his legs planted wide, clenching and unclenching his jaw. Caleb paced behind him, rubbing at the back of his neck. Amon sat by the hearth, his arm hooked over the back of the chair, yawning. None of them noticed my entrance.

A crazed glare darkened Philippe's expression. "I don't give a rat's ass who you are. Ten or no Ten, you have no right to barge into our home and demand I allow you to take her."

Caleb shoved Philippe out of his way and faced Amon. "Your majesty."

Amon jerked his head in Caleb's direction. "I am not a king."

"Forgive me. Your Holiness."

Amon sighed with exasperation. "Call me by my name, Amon."

Caleb nodded. "Yes, of course, Amon. Philippe speaks from a place of anger. He knows not what he is saying."

Philippe slowly turned his head and threw a hard squint at Caleb. "I know exactly what I'm saying." He whirled to face Amon. "You cannot claim her as your personal property. She's a free-thinking person. Treat her with the respect she deserves."

Amon blinked. "But she *is* my property."

Philippe's eyes protruded from their sockets as he spat, "No. She is my wife."

Amon waved him away like an annoying fly. "Sadly, you are mistaken. She was promised shortly after her birth to be my immortal companion, bound by my blood."

Their ceaseless bickering made my head swim. At full volume, I shouted, "Enough!"

As if their heads were bound together by wire, each snapped in my direction. When I had their attention, I lowered my voice. "This back and forth is getting us nowhere. We'll have to work together if we want to resolve this."

Amon rose from the chair, his posture statuesque, his narrowed gaze targeting Philippe. "She knows. Confess to her," Amon ordered.

Philippe stumbled backward, fear carved into his features. "I cannot," he uttered.

Amon's expression became unreadable. "She already knows you deceived her. Tell her so we can end this."

Philippe stood his ground and demanded, "Why are you doing this? What purpose does it serve?"

Caleb gripped Philippe's shoulder. "He is one of The Ten, Philippe!"

Philippe didn't respond.

"The night of your chance encounter, you read Beth's mind, learning of our history and how I appeared to her as the mist. You seized your opportunity and baited her with that very form," Amon stated in a calm and level tone.

Caleb's eyes grew large as the truth sank in. "I surmised you were merely roleplaying to please her, but pretending to be one of The Ten? And you did this with full knowledge of your own deception? Are you mad?"

Philippe strong-armed Caleb out of his way and faced me. "Beth, please, let me explain."

A small noise came from inside my throat, my legs desperately wanting to collapse, yet I held my body tall when I spoke. "You looked me in the eyes and told me you'd never been dishonest with me, but that's not true. I can think of several lies you told that very first night." I trembled as I fired off his fabrications. "One cannot control the choices of the heart. My beauty captured you, even when I was child. You left France to be near me, disguising yourself as mist in fear of rejection, Danny forcing your hand. Those were lies...all lies!"

"I...well, not entirely," Philippe stammered. "They were your thoughts. I merely pulled them from your mind."

My solid stance faltered, and I stumbled back a step. "You took advantage of me. You used me."

Philippe dropped to his knees and grabbed my hands, a pained look twisting his brow. "No, I didn't. I would never hurt you. Yes, that night I watched you, completely overcome by your beauty and the sweetness inside your heart. I had to know you." He squeezed his eyes shut. "So, I read your mind." He swallowed hard. "I said all those things because they sat at the forefront of your mind, and I wanted the chance to get to know you. But I swear that I didn't know about Amon, only that an unknown vampire had become a part of your life." He looked up at me. "I wanted to be that vampire. I wanted to be part of your life."

I sank to the floor. How had my life grown so horribly complicated? My chin quivered, and hot tears spilled over my lower lashes. I swept my fingers at them, but more came to take their place.

Amon knelt at my side, reaching for me.

Philippe pushed him away. "No. I have to fix this."

Amon nodded reluctantly. "Very well."

Philippe sat on the floor next to me, reaching for my hand. I jerked mine back and accused, "You kept up the charade. I don't even know who you really are. You've had thousands of chances to tell the truth, but you haven't. Why?"

He cleared his throat. "I never planned on telling you. When I overheard the conversation between you and Caleb, I considered owning up to what I'd done, but I just couldn't."

I shivered as my body caved in on itself. I wanted to flee the room, but my legs refused my command to rise.

Guilt sprang up in Caleb's expression, but he didn't utter a word.

"You both questioned whether I was truly your mist," Philippe explained, "If I revealed to you that I wasn't, I feared I'd lose you forever. I love you more than anything. If I were to lose you..." He paused, his shoulders quaking. His eyes filled with tears, and he struggled to control his voice. "Please, Beth, forgive me. You're my life. Without you, I have no purpose, no will to go on."

In front of us all, he sat there, humbled, vulnerable, spilling his heart out to me and pleading for my forgiveness. I wanted to hate him, but my heart wouldn't allow it. We were both guilty of keeping secrets. Caleb's words from long ago sprang up inside my mind. He had suggested we ask Philippe whether or not he was the mist, but I had rejected the idea. Maybe because I'd always known as Amon stated. Maybe fear had played a role in my refusal. If only I had asked, but dwelling on things I couldn't change wouldn't alter the present. The one thing I was certain of, despite all Philippe had done, was that I loved him. I touched his face and said, "I want to forgive you. I will try to forgive you."

He released a restrained breath and turned my hand over to kiss my palm. "Thank you."

Amon pulled me to my feet, separating me from Philippe. He shook his head and pointed out, "The dilemma remains unchanged." His gaze traveled to Philippe. "You masqueraded as another in order to sway her affections, but Beth has always been my love, and only mine."

Philippe stood and challenged Amon. "You're wrong. We love each other. She married me."

Amon peered sharply at Philippe. "She believed you were me; therefore, she actually married me, not you."

I pushed the two of them apart and raised my voice again. "Enough! None of that changes the facts. I'm married to Philippe. Amon, you have to understand that."

Caleb slumped down in a chair facing the fire and groaned. "This is not going to end well."

Amon's expression remained firm as he regarded me. "I am not blind, Beth. I don't deny that you retain strong feelings for Philippe, but you also felt those same kinds of feelings for me." He glared at Philippe and arched his brow. "And I have done nothing underhanded in an attempt to sway your heart."

Philippe's voice buzzed with hostility. "I've apologized for what I did."

Amon shouted, "But that does not remedy the situation or right your wrong! Tell me, Beth, if Philippe hadn't interfered, would we be standing here debating? I think not." His composure fell apart further by the minute. "Why? Because for *years* you loved *me*, not him!"

I threw my hands into the air, feeling more and more helpless as the conversation continued. "You're never going to give up, are you?"

Amon glanced at Philippe, hatred twisting his expression. "He should be the one to give up, not I."

Philippe clenched his jaw defiantly. "Not going to happen."

Amon regarded us for a long moment. After a brief pause, he shrugged his shoulders and said, "I am willing to share you with Philippe."

I felt as though I'd been punched in the stomach. I blinked and stared at the arrogant vampire in disbelief. Was he serious? How could he possibly think I would go along with such an arrangement?

Philippe's temper built in every quivering muscle. "Are you out of your mind?" He turned to me. "He's out of his mind."

Amon executed a dismissive wave of his hand. "I'm not thrilled with the idea either, but I've waited twenty-five years to be reunited with Beth. I don't intend to just walk away." He raised his brows at Philippe. "It doesn't appear that you intend to either, so I'm open to suggestions."

Philippe cut his hand through the air. "Absolutely not. She is my wife. Deal with it."

Amon stretched his fingertips to form a steeple. He frowned before stating, "We are at an impasse. I can think of only one solution."

"Which is?" Caleb interjected.

Amon stated matter-of-factly, "Philippe and I must fight to the death. The one left standing will claim Beth's hand."

When I finally found my voice, I cried, "No!"

Caleb flew out of his chair, shielding Philippe with his own body, a defiant stare plastered on his face. "You'll have to kill me first."

Philippe's face paled to a ghostly white. "You're a god. I don't stand a chance against you."

I shouted, "There's got to be another way to solve this!"

Amon's nostrils flared as his gaze raked the room. "Whether you're willing to admit it or not, I'm the one who has been wronged, not any one of you." Slightly composing himself, he suggested, "Work with me. Offer me some viable options."

Caleb stepped forward. "Kohath is my maker and head of The Council. I say we take this matter before them."

Amon clapped his hands together. "Splendid idea. I wish I'd thought of it myself. The Council will see I have done nothing wrong." He pointed at us. "On the other hand, you three have participated in the assumption of my identity and attempted to hide my existence within a black box inside your mind. The Council doesn't take kindly to dishonesty."

"We will let them decide for themselves," Caleb said with a firm nod of his head.

Amon grinned. "Indeed. We shall leave at once for Scotland." He turned to me and offered his arm. "Beth, shall we go?"

Philippe stepped in front of Amon, offering his own arm. "She travels with me."

My gaze ping-ponged between the two of them, and then I crossed my arms over my chest, expelling a huff. "Don't play me as if I were a chess piece. I won't travel with either of you."

"No one is going anywhere for now." Caleb pointed to the clock on the wall. "The sun has risen. We're stuck here for the day."

Amon rubbed his hands together and laughed gleefully. "Lovely. I shall retire for the day. Please, prepare my room."

Philippe narrowed his eyes. "I'm not your damned servant. Go upstairs and pick a room yourself."

Betty charged into the study, placing her hands on her hips. "What is all the yelling about? I can hear you all arguing clear into the kitchen."

Amon transported himself in front of Betty in an instant. Glowering over her, he licked his lips. "Marvelous, a food vessel." He extended his hand. "Come, my dear, allow me to feed from you."

Betty scowled at Amon and slapped his hand away. "I'm not a drinking fountain. I'm Philippe's caretaker." She sized him up, her eyes fearless, and huffed, "And who might you be?"

Giggles rose in my throat, easing the tension of the previous moments. Leave it to Betty to put a god in his place.

A look of sheer horror overtook Caleb. "He's a god. Show some respect."

Philippe groaned as he gestured to Amon. "Betty, this is Amon."

Amon stood tall, puffing out his chest. "I am one of The Ten."

She crossed her arms stubbornly. "That doesn't excuse your rudeness."

She turned her back on Amon to face Philippe. "Will he be staying? Shall I prepare one of the guest rooms for him?"

In a lukewarm tone, Philippe responded, "Yes, Betty, he will be staying with us...today."

"Very well," she said, eyeing Amon with distrust.

"Thank you, Betty," Amon said. "And my apologies."

She offered him a polite nod before she left the room.

Amon turned to me, offering his arm again. "Will you join me, Beth? I would love to catch up over a bottle of wine."

"You've got to be kidding me," Philippe blurted out, throwing his hands in the air.

"I'm quite serious," Amon stated, furrowing his brow.

I went to Philippe and touched his cheek gently. "I'll be okay. Don't worry. Go to our room, and I'll be there shortly."

He grabbed my arm and pulled me close. "I'm not leaving you alone with him."

"He brought me back to you, Philippe. He's not going to hurt me. I'll be fine. Go."

Philippe didn't budge. "No."

Caleb placed his hand on Philippe's shoulder, kindness warming his complexion. "She'll be all right." He turned to Amon. "I will contact Kohath and inform him of our impending journey."

Amon seemed pleased, a smile touching his lips. "Please, let him know we will arrive at their haven before tomorrow's sunrise."

Caleb nodded, nudging Philippe toward the door. "Leave them."

Philippe's gaze fixated on me. He planted his feet firmly and crossed his arms. "I said no."

Caleb collected his shoulder in his iron grip and dragged him out the door, pushing it shut behind them.

"Thank you," Amon said once they were gone.

"I didn't stay for you. I stayed for me. Tell me about my mother. I have to know why it seemed so easy for her to give me up."

A kind and gentle light brightened the color of his eyes. "She was young and frightened. She made a choice to save her life. I'm sorry if her choice causes you pain."

My voice came out choked by tears. "She was twenty-five. *I'm* twenty-five. What kind of mother willingly hands their child over to a...a..." I couldn't say the word.

He finished for me. "A vampire."

"I didn't mean it like that." I walked over to one of the chairs and slumped into it, shaking my head. "I just meant...well, she couldn't have loved me to do something like that."

He sat next to me, quietly stroking my hand.

His touch soothed me, and when I turned my head toward him, his expression reminded me of the boys in movies gazing with love at a childhood sweetheart. I belonged to him; I could feel it. I'd always belonged to him. I leaned over to kiss his cheek. "Did you know her, my mother?"

His hand lingered on his cheek where I'd kissed him, and he gazed longingly at me, as if I'd offered him the world. After a moment, he folded his hands in his lap and responded. "Before that night, no, but over the course of our visits, I came to know her quite well." He looked thoughtful for a moment before he continued. "Let me rephrase...I knew her thoughts well. Her decision to give you up weighed heavily on her soul and that of your father's."

I hand flittered to my throat. "Was he a part of the decision too?"

"No, but she confessed to him what she had done. He was furious. Said he could never forgive her, nor could he bear the pain of losing you on the appointed day. He chose to distance himself from the pain by leaving."

His actions finally made sense.

"She couldn't live with the guilt of her choice, so every day she pushed you further and further away."

The sting of tears burned behind my eyelids, but I held them back. She didn't deserve my tears. "She stole my life. I never even had a choice as to how it might turn out."

He stroked my hair, absolute devotion shining in his eyes. "I always wanted to give you everything she refused you."

I shuddered, my heart aching for him. He'd waited every minute of twenty-five years for me, and I had gone and married Philippe. I took his hand and said, "I don't know what to say or how to fix this."

For some time, he gazed at me, his voice a gentle tone when he assured, "The Council will decide for us."

CHAPTER 17

A few hours before sunrise, Amon, Caleb, Philippe, and I arrived at The Council's haven. A towering wrought-iron gate, paired with a solid wall of purple trees, surrounded the massive fortress. In contrast, delicate flowers in every color of the spectrum lined the cobblestone walkway. Splaying my fingers over my heart, I exhaled a breath.

Amon rested his hand on the small of my back. "It's beautiful, don't you think?"

"Breathtaking," I said, unable to pull my eyes away.

Philippe stepped between us, forcing Amon to one side. "She's my wife. You'd do well to remember that."

"So you keep saying."

"Someone's coming," Caleb said, pointing to the crest of the hill.

A golden stream of moonlight illuminated a woman's silhouette as she glided along the long pathway leading from the summit of the haven. Her white gown dragged upon the ground in the breezeless night, swaying as if it possessed a will of its own. When she reached the bottom, she pulled open the gate and stepped outside. Her angelic, pallid skin and platinum hair glistened under the moonlight. "Welcome. I am Teresa, an apprentice here." She kissed Amon's cheek with her cherry-red lips and gestured us forward. "Come. The Council is expecting you. The others have already arrived."

Amon arched a brow. "Others?"

A becoming smile touched her lips as she answered him. "The remaining members of The Ten have arrived. They grow anxious to see you."

"This is truly a wonderful surprise, but I never contacted any of them."

"Kohath summoned them. He thought this would please you." Again, she urged us forward. "Come. They are waiting."

Amon clutched at my hand and pulled me along. "Beth, this is fantastic. I have bragged about you to all of them for years. Now I can finally introduce you."

I glanced over my shoulder at Philippe.

A pained expression pinched his face, yet he waved me forward, following a few steps behind.

Inside the gate, more of the purple trees dotted the landscape, and between them, an enormous water fountain of dancing medieval knights stretched across the lower level of the property. Everywhere I looked, different types of trees, flowers, and other foliage sprouted up out of the Earth, garnishing the landscape. Simply strolling across the cobblestone walkway made me feel like royalty.

Caleb rushed ahead, slipping his arm under Teresa's, and escorted the beautiful blonde up the path, chatting up a storm as they walked.

When we topped the hill, a dove-colored brick fortress loomed before me. I stood small and insignificant, feeling like an ant next to the massive structure with its high arches, towering peaks, and cemented-covered windows. How could I, a newly born vampire, cross their threshold, stand in the presence of such ancient power and ask for help?

As she opened the arched wooden doors, Teresa said, "Please, come inside."

Amon led me, because my feet seemed to have lost the ability to move on their own. As I stood within the circular foyer, standing on European marble tiles, my gaze wandered, drinking in the magnificence. Teardrop chandeliers illuminated the ornate gold ceilings, and from several points in the room, vibrant green vines tumbled toward the floor like living waterfalls. A stone arch announced entry to every dark passageway, but in spite of all the embellished architecture, not a stitch of furniture could be found.

"This way," Teresa said, taking my arm and guiding me away from the foyer.

"I'm sorry, I can't..." I wrenched my head around further. "...stop staring."

She pushed her shoulders back, a gleam lighting the color of her eyes. "We take great pride in our home. Many of us never set foot outside its walls. Everything we may need is kept right here."

"And what do you do for blood?"

She picked up her pace at my words. "The Council will answer all your questions."

Philippe caught up to me, slipped his arm around my waist, and whispered, "This place is a little..." He examined the space once more. "...overwhelming." He brushed his lips against my cheek and pulled me closer. "I'm frightened that The Council may change our lives forever."

I spun my wedding ring and answered, "Don't say that. We'll be fine."

Amon pushed between us. Scowling, he crossed his arms over his chest. "Out of respect, I have refrained from displaying any outward affection toward Beth. Please, show me the same courtesy I've shown you, Philippe."

Philippe forced a smile. "She is *my* wife, but I guess we're all victims of this mess." He reluctantly stepped away from me. "I'll honor your request, for now."

Amon relaxed visibly. "Thank you."

Philippe's tension eased off as he replied, "You're welcome."

"Please, everyone," Teresa urged. "The Council will gather soon. We must move along."

"Very well," Amon said, gesturing toward the hallway. "Please continue, Teresa."

"This way," she said, leading us down a long, dark hallway.

Ivory statues carved into the forms of mythical gods stood by each doorway, their watchful eyes observing us as we passed. The power radiated by their superior expressions humbled me. Should I lower my eyes and bow at their feet? I looked to Teresa. Staring straight ahead, she ignored those beautiful creatures set in stone. Each one I passed, I acknowledged with a fleeting glance.

Near the end of the hallway, Teresa stopped to light two hanging lanterns. The warm glow revealed a solid black door trimmed in silver.

My hands trembled, so I tucked them behind my elbows, attempting to play it cool. What, or who, would I find on the other side? The question sent a flutter of panic to brush over my heart. The Council? The Ten? What would such regal beings think of a nobody like me?

Teresa turned the latch and pushed the door open.

And I entered at last, crossing the threshold into a room full of flawless, elegant, timeless beings. No human being I'd ever met had matched their magnificence. *Oh God, The Ten.* My legs turned to lead, and I backpedaled slightly. I couldn't let them see me as a blubbering, awestruck baby vamp. Forcing my chin up and my shoulders back, I stood as tall as I could, staring directly into their jewel-like eyes while inching my way over to Philippe. At his side, my gaze traveled the length of the vast room. Twelve regal high-backed chairs, tucked underneath a lengthy marble table, remained vacant. Those must've belonged to The Council.

Amon embraced a female with long golden curls streaming beyond her shoulders with great affection. Her rose-colored lips turned upward to form a seductive smile as she warmly returned his greeting.

"Hathor, I have missed you," Amon said after kissing her pale cheek.

She laughed flirtatiously, gently pushed him away. "And I you."

After taking her hand, Amon led her in my direction.

My heart swelled in my chest, firing a rapid thump-thump-thump into my ears.

"Hathor," Amon said, gesturing toward me. "I'd like you to meet my Beth."

Her turquoise-colored eyes examined me up and down, her head tilting slightly to the side. She held out her hand. "I have heard so much about you, Beth. Finally, we get to meet in person."

I'd found myself to be at a disadvantage. I knew nothing of her, of any of them for that matter. As I took her hand, I said, "It's nice to meet you, Hathor."

Philippe stuck his hand out and said, "I'm Philippe, Beth's husband. It is an honor to meet you, Hathor."

Amon stood, holding his hands loosely behind his back. "Oh yes, forgive me. I should have introduced Philippe as well."

Her flirtatious laugh returned, and she turned her full charm on Philippe. "The pleasure is all mine."

Caleb strolled up to give Hathor a brief hug. "Hathor."

She winked at him when he pulled back. "Caleb."

He knew her. Oh, how I craved a peek inside Caleb's black box

"The reunion of The Ten calls for a celebration," a male, with shaggy brown hair and mischievous brown eyes, shouted out. He glanced at Teresa and added, "Teresa, my dear, would you be so kind as to retrieve several bottles of your finest wine?"

She nodded. "Of course, Osiris."

I turned my head to better observe him. So, he was the famous Osiris, the one who set vampirism into motion.

Gesturing to the many chairs scattered throughout the room, Teresa said, "Please, be seated. I will return shortly with the wine, and The Council will arrive soon to greet you." As she left the room, the gods scattered, selecting their chairs.

Osiris chose the seat on Amon's left, while Hathor claimed the one to his right. The others lifted their chairs, carrying them closer to Amon, Hathor, and Osiris, forming a row of gods. I chose a chair by the marble table, while Philippe and Caleb chose seats on either side of me.

Amon bounced out of his chair and glanced in my direction. "I must continue my introductions." Walking the row of gods, he made his way to the first chair and stopped behind the god seated there. Resting his hands on the back of the chair, he said, "This is Isis, Osiris' beautiful wife." He shifted to the second chair. "This is her sister, Nephthys."

Turning her headful of jet-black hair toward Amon, she queried, "Am I not beautiful as well, Amon?"

"Breathtaking, my dear!" Amon boasted, indulging her.

She beamed, her eyes settling on me.

Elaborate jewelry bedecked both sisters. They sat arm in arm, their long, straight, jet-black hair flowing down their backs, both sets of gray eyes fixed on me, without a trace of smile to their plum-colored lips.

Amon approached the third chair. "This dashing lad is Horus, Iris and Osiris' son."

Horus swept his sandy-colored bangs out of his navy-blue eyes and studied me without a word.

I shifted in my chair. Their intimidating stares dissected me as if I were a frog in high school Biology. I refused to play the victim in their game of attempted intimidation. Tossing my hair over my shoulder, I lifted my chin, offering each a welcoming nod of acknowledgement.

Amon's eyes danced as he gazed at me. He gave me a playful wink before continuing on to the fourth chair. "Here we have the first vampire to walk the Earth, Osiris."

Osiris chuckled, ignoring me completely as he nudged Hathor. "Amon is just as handsome and charming as ever. Wouldn't you agree, my dear Hathor?"

She replied with her own charming smile and flirtatious laugh.

Amon boomed out over-the-top laughter, strutting like a magnificent lion behind Hathor. He placed his hands on her shoulders and gave them a squeeze. "You already met the lovely Hathor."

She touched his hand. "Amon, you're too kind."

A burning sensation inched up my neck, spreading heat onto my face. If she barked out that exaggerated floozy laugh one more time, I might puke. I was so unlike her. What could Amon possibly see in her? Wait...what did I care anyway? I'd married Philippe. I loved him, yet my gaze followed Amon with relentless fervor.

At the seventh chair, Amon regarded the seated god with a smirk.

Suave and debonair and clad in a traditional black suit, white linen shirt, and scarlet tie, the god ignored Amon's presence, smoothing his slicked-back hair farther away from his marble-smooth face.

Amon chuckled. "This is Anubis, our Hollywood vampire."

Thrusting out his chest, Anubis spread his dramatic, maroon-colored lips into a sneer. "I'll have you know that Hollywood copied me, not the other way around."

Amon scoffed at Anubis' arrogance, progressing down the row and placing a hand on chairs eight and nine. "Sobek and Khum, our somber, grim comrades, meet Beth."

They bowed their blonde heads in tandem, acknowledging me as best they could with their dark, deadpan eyes.

Amon exhaled a loud sigh as he came to the tenth and final chair. He extended a warm smile to the god seated below him. "Last, but certainly not least, my dear friend, Ptah."

Ptah stroked his neatly trimmed beard, winked at me with his almond-colored eyes, and said, "It's lovely to meet you, Beth."

I nodded and said, "And you as well."

Amon took a step back, spreading his arms wide. "And there you have them, The Ten." He ambled back toward his own chair but paused. "Forgive me." He raised his hand and gestured toward our trio. "Caleb, who most of you know, is seated to Beth's right, and that is her husband, Philippe, on her left."

Caleb and Philippe received a few nods, a couple winks, and several hellos—a much more receptive response than the flat looks and hard stares I'd received. I tapped my foot on the floor, observing The Ten. Why the catty behavior? Did they disapprove of Amon's feelings for me? Or could there be resentment regarding the power I held over Amon? That didn't seem possible, yet something had aroused indifference toward me among the majority of them.

Teresa came through the door bearing a silver tray, laden with bottles of wine and glasses. Setting the whole array upon the table, she filled every glass and offered wine to each of us. "Enjoy," she said before leaving the room.

Amon lifted his glass toward his allies. "Thank you all for coming. Your support means the world to me."

Hathor rested her hand on Amon's arm and leaned into him. "You are mistaken. We haven't come to aid you. We have come to prevent you from making a regrettable mistake."

I grabbed onto Philippe's arm, my brain scrambling to understand. Was I the regrettable mistake?

A cold glare swept over Amon's face. "It was *you*," he accused in a low, gruff tone. "You persuaded the others to turn their backs on me."

Her eyes widened, yet she furrowed her brows. "Yes, my heart aches for you," she confessed, spreading her fingers over her heart like a fan, "but I did nothing to sway them. We are united in our decision. This infatuation with Beth has corrupted you, clouded your judgment."

Amon scowled at her, venom infecting his voice. "I have not changed. This is your jealousy speaking for you, Hathor."

Osiris gripped Amon's shoulder. "You must listen to Hathor. This fixation of yours must end. Let Beth go."

Amon sprang to his feet, sending his chair flying into the wall. "What are you talking about?" He faced the gods with utter exasperation, raising his voice. "There is no infatuation—no fixation. Why do you refer to our blood promise as such?"

Isis gave a nod toward Philippe. "She has married. The promise no longer carries weight."

Amon centered on Isis, his nostrils flaring. "Isis, when you needed the strength of my blood to save Osiris, I offered it freely. Now you turn your back on me!"

Her hand flew to land upon her chest. "It was you who turned your back on us."

My heart ached with the weight of her words. Because of me, they'd turned against him. I fell back in my seat, my energy drained.

Philippe glanced at me, absorbing my emotions. The cords in his neck strained against his skin as he rose to his feet.

Caleb grabbed his arm, attempting to force him back down. He pressed his finger to his lips momentarily. "Now is not the time to defend Amon, Philippe."

Amon slumped into his chair in a similar fashion, his fingertips pressed to his temples. "Where is this line of thought coming from?" Realization shaped his lips into a vicious sneer. "You mean Hathor—I turned my back on Hathor."

Absolute silence crept over the room for several minutes.

Anubis was the one to finally speak. "Your obsession with this girl has caused grief for all of us. Let her be. Her common attributes cannot compare with your own magnificence. Come back to us, to Hathor."

Amon's gaze blazed murderously. Raising a fist, he shouted, "I refuse to be manipulated like this!"

Hathor clutched at his chair arm with both hands. Genuine fondness filled her eyes as she begged, "Please, Amon, a life together would be best for everyone. Come back to me."

Amon sat speechless, words seeming to mount behind his lips. In a single breath, he let them fly. "I will NEVER come back to you."

She flinched as if he had struck her, the color draining from her face. Collapsing into herself, she buried her face in her hands.

Amon ignored her, guzzling his wine in one massive gulp. Leaning forward and resting his elbows on his knees, he assumed an air of self-assurance before speaking. "We will allow The Council to determine the fate of my blood promise."

His blood surged and withered again and again inside me, like a fish gasping for air. Seeing him defeated, hunched over in his chair, wounded me. His vampiric family had abandoned him because I'd been deceived—*I* had abandoned him.

Ptah deserted his chair to stand at Amon's side. Relief swelled in my lungs as I watched him rest his hand on Amon's shoulder and declare, "I will stand by you."

Amon released a pent-up breath, reaching for his friend's hand and squeezing it. "Ptah, I am grateful. Thank you."

Ptah eyed the remaining gods, his brows pinched together. He turned his back on them and faced Amon. "You know I don't play by their rules. I've always created my own."

The gentle tap of a slipper brushing the stone floor outside the room thundered inside my vampire ears. I held my breath, eyeing the door. The latch turned agonizingly slow. A subtle gush of air filtered through as the door swung wide. One by one, they entered, light-footed and angelic. An illusion of kings and queens danced before my eyes as the statuesque immortals glided across the floor toward their twelve seats of power.

My fingertips turned ice cold, lying limp in my lap with dead weight. I eyed my wine, craving a sip, yet I couldn't summon the strength to reach for my glass. I glanced over at Philippe to gauge his reaction toward these twelve beings. His back melded against the chair cushion, staring at The Council with eyes as large as saucers.

"Welcome," a flaxen-haired male called out, standing behind the center seat at the table. With a powerful rotation of his cloak, he gestured to the eleven immortals standing beside him. "Be seated."

As one, the members around the table claimed their seats, placing their hands upon the table and looking to their leader.

His olive-colored eyes combed the room when he spoke next. "I am Kohath." He gave a brief nod of acknowledgement to Caleb and Hathor, before returning his attention to the room. His thick, bushy brows furrowed as his gaze roamed over the rest of us. "I sense profound tension amongst you. We must remedy this immediately. I believe a warm carafe of human blood will help to put everyone at ease." He turned toward one of the seated members and said, "Adam, please retrieve several carafes from the blood lounge and serve our guests. They are in need of its magic."

I glanced around at the others, blinking in surprise. Had he said human blood? Was that what Teresa meant when she'd told me, 'everything we need is right here?'"

A male with long red hair, seated at the far end of the table, rose to his feet. "Certainly," he responded, before exiting the room.

Kohath stepped away from his seat and approached Caleb, his eyes filled with warmth as he extended his arms. "Caleb, my child, it is good to see you. Let me embrace you."

"Wonderful to see you again too," Caleb responded, wrapping his maker in his arms.

They hugged each other, appearing as father and son, and in a way, I supposed they were.

Kohath gripped Caleb's shoulders and stared into his eyes a long moment after pulling away. "It has been too long, my son."

Caleb bobbed his head in agreement. "I know, I know. I'll make it a point to visit more often."

Kohath beamed. "I would like that very much." He turned from Caleb, and with the grace of a king, approached Hathor. He bent to kiss each of her cheeks. "My dear Hathor, it is always a pleasure to have you in my presence."

She stroked his cheek tenderly and said, "You look well, my child."

The red-haired male returned, carrying a serving tray stacked with carafes and goblets. The polished goblets looked to be centuries old, embellished by gold leaves twisting down the stems. I couldn't ignore the delicious smelling swirl of steam rising above the rims. I licked my lips and sniffed the air, taking in the intoxicating scent of blood as it perfumed the room.

He proceeded around the room, handing out goblets of blood. After all were served, he returned to the table and took his seat.

Kohath made his way back to his throne of authority and raised his goblet. "Please, everyone, drink."

With haste, I brought the goblet to my lips and filled my mouth with blood. The thick, warm liquid flowed down my throat and into my veins, caressing my body with its seductive heat. A sense of power surged inside of me, igniting my soul. I closed my eyes, enjoying the ecstasy the blood extended to every cell of my body.

"This is the first time I've seen you drink blood. The life of a vampire suits you. That makes me very happy, and you even sexier," Philippe whispered into my ear.

I opened my eyes and turned toward him. He smiled at me as though we were the only two vampires in the room. I took his hand and held it inside mine. Kohath was right, the blood seemed to be lifting everyone's spirits, altering the atmosphere in the entire room for the better.

"Shall we begin?" Kohath suggested, lacing his pale fingers on top of the polished marble and eyeing each member seated around the table.

"The purpose of meeting within The Council's gathering chamber is to settle disputes, convene and deliberate, and if necessary, conduct trials. Who here has called upon the wisdom of The Council and to what end?"

Amon was the first to stand and face them. "I shall begin. A blood promise I entered into has yet to be fulfilled." Amon strayed from The Ten and wandered into the center of the room. "I, and others in this room, seek guidance from The Council regarding this matter."

"Amon, you may return to your seat," Kohath said, motioning toward his chair.

"I prefer to stand," Amon replied, folding his arms.

Kohath nodded in agreement. "Very well. Is there anyone else here who would like to speak?" he asked, glancing around the room.

Amon's gaze found me, his head inclining slightly toward The Council.

Slowly, I rose from my seat. Upon standing, my legs quivered, and in a small voice I said, "I, too, am here because of the same blood promise."

Philippe shot out of his chair, grabbing up my hand. "The blood promise has brought me here as well."

Hathor clasped her hands and stood tall, gesturing in the direction of the remaining seated gods. Conviction rang in her voice as she addressed the room. "I speak for The Ten. We have all come forth to challenge the validity of this blood promise."

Ptah jumped to his feet, marching over to Amon and declaring defiantly, "Do not include me in this vendetta of yours, Hathor." He faced Kohath. "I stand with Amon. He speaks the truth. The blood promise made must be upheld."

Raising his brows, Kohath asked, "Is there anyone here who has come before us with other business?"

The room fell silent.

"Let us begin," Kohath announced after waiting a moment longer. "All members of The Council must state their name and your intention to either agree or disagree to this inquest. I, myself, am in agreement."

Around the marble table, the members voiced their replies in turn.

"Daniel, agreed."

"Adam, agreed."

"Tamar, agreed."

"Dinah, agreed."

"Athaliah, agreed."

"Japheth, agreed."

"Luke, agreed."

"Miriam, agreed."

"Samuel, agreed."

"Cain, agreed."

"Peter, agreed."

"The decision is unanimous," Kohath announced with a firm nod. He looked to Amon and said, "Amon, you may continue. Please, present the details of your argument."

Amon regarded the twelve wise faces. He moved forward, placing himself at the head of the table. Glowering in Hathor's direction, he began. "Less than twenty-five years ago, a promise was made to me and sealed in blood—my own blood, as well as Beth's. Beth was bound by this promise to become my immortal companion on her twenty-fifth birthday."

Kohath interrupted Amon to ask, "Who made this promise to you?"

Amon gave me a heartfelt look before answering. "Her mother."

Kohath stiffened. "And why would she make such a promise?"

"Her mother is a descendant of Danny O'Ryan," Amon replied. "As you're well aware, theirs was one of many families chosen to participate in the blood lottery." Amon tucked his hands behind his back as he paced the length of the table, coming to a halt at the opposite side. "A messenger from the blood lottery provided me a name and a location. My designated prey was Beth's mother."

Kohath's expression remained unaltered. "Am I to assume you didn't follow through with the choice provided you by the blood lottery?"

"You assume correctly. She begged for her life, and I let her live."

Kohath tilted his chin downward and frowned. "And why would you do such a thing?"

Amon turned toward me, that same look of undeniable love becoming so familiar to me brightening his face. He smiled at me before returning his attention to Kohath. "She offered me her daughter's life in exchange for her own. Beth is that daughter."

Kohath shook his head, his expression revealing the depth of his disgust. "Continue."

Amon shrugged half-heartedly. "I had no interest in a baby, until I held her." He placed his hand over his heart. "I felt her heartbeat! The rhythm mimicked my own, thumping with the strength and will of a god. At that very moment, my immortal life changed forever. I knew she was fated to become my immortal companion. So, you see, I *had no choice* but to accept the blood promise and allow her mother to live."

Even though I knew every detail of the story, the words still smarted, like bullets drilling into my flesh.

Kohath pressed Amon further. "Describe the particulars of this blood promise."

Amon rattled off the details, like he was reading a grocery list. "Until the age of twenty-five, Beth would remain with her mother. I was not to interfere with those years. On the day of her twenty-fifth birthday, she belonged to me, and I would be fully within my rights to come and collect her."

Hathor's composure crumpled, and she shot from her chair, pointing a rigid finger at Amon. In an accusatory tone, she shouted, "But you did interfere! You never left her alone. You manipulated her, changing the course of her life by appearing to her in an altered form."

Kohath demanded, "Is this true, Amon?"

Before he could reply, Hathor stormed forward to answer for him. "Of course, it's true. Why would I say so otherwise?"

Osiris launched across the floor, landing next to Hathor and wrapping his arm around her. "While we believe Amon interfered with Beth's life, the more pressing matter is whether or not the blood promise actually ever existed."

Ptah threw up his hands and let out a groan. "You can't be serious. Amon would never lie about such a thing."

"The blood promise occurred just as I described," Amon uttered, speaking through gritted teeth.

A commanding impulse surged in my blood, pushing me to my feet. "He's telling the truth," I blurted out. "I witnessed the past through Amon's memory with my own eyes."

Hathor glided across the floor, her face inches from my own. Leveling her hate-filled gaze, she spat, "Gullible child! You bore witness only to what Amon wanted you to see."

I stood my ground, even daring to take a step closer to her. "You're wrong. The visions came to me from his blood. Blood doesn't lie. I watched my mother willingly give me up. You can't imagine how hard that was to see."

She laughed with arrogance, waving a dismissive hand at me. "Oh, please. What could you possibly know about visions and blood? You're just a baby still in training wheels."

This vampire was maddening, pushing all my buttons. I threw out a statement, hoping to push one of hers. "I also *drank* Amon's blood which further substantiates his claims."

Philippe's mouth fell open, his stare disbelieving. Moving close to me, he whispered in my ear, "You drank his blood?"

Great. My husband cared more about the fact I'd drank another vampire's blood than the fact I'd been bartered away by my own mother. I shooed him away. "Not now."

Hathor huffed out an angry breath. "Amon's playing you, you fool."

I shoved my finger in her face. "You're the fool. You're jealous and desperate and would do anything to get him back, even lie to The Council."

She tossed her blonde locks over her shoulder, her hands perching on her hips. "Jealous! I'm the Goddess of Love. Men fall at my feet, whether they be mortal or immortal."

I shrugged my shoulders, my head inclining to indicate Amon. "Not that particular immortal."

A mixture of mischief and pride twinkled inside Amon's eyes as he winked at me.

A nasty scowl curled Hathor's lips away from her fangs, and she raised her hand to strike me.

I flinched, but my feet remained rooted into the ground with my chin held high.

Amon leapt in front of me, blocking the blow. She pounded on his chest, screaming at the top of her lungs like a child throwing a temper tantrum.

Rising from his seat, Kohath boomed loudly, "Enough!" He strode into the center of the room and glared at the grappling pair. "We are not barbarians. We are civilized immortals, and such behavior does not become us."

Hathor whimpered and lowered her head, prompting Kohath's gaze to soften, further reiterating his point.

"Kohath," Amon said, smoothing his rumpled shirt, "Hathor is your maker. Please, assure me her outburst will not sway your decision. Can you judge the validity of the blood promise without bias or would you recommend that you step down from this one case?"

Kohath's stance revealed no tension brought on by Amon's suggestion. In a calm voice, he stated, "She will receive no special treatment from me. My decision will be based on facts alone. I will not be swayed by any sense of loyalty."

Hathor swept her arm through the air with exasperation. "I don't bend the rules for anyone, nor would I interfere with the laws governing the blood lottery, but Amon did both. That alone should be the deciding factor in this case."

Philippe stepped in front of her and said, "I, more than anyone, stand to lose everything because of this blood promise, but Beth would never lie. I believe her. What The Council must focus on is finding a fair solution for everyone involved."

Caleb stood and placed his hand on Philippe's shoulder, grinning proudly. "I agree wholeheartedly with Philippe."

"And I," Ptah assented, folding his arms across his broad chest.

Hathor's gaze darted to Kohath. "I created you." Her beautiful face twisted hideously. "My blood is inside you. If I were to speak untruths, you would sense it."

Kohath pulled her into an embrace and smoothed her hair. "The Council must examine the case from all sides, my dear," he said softly.

She collapsed into his arms and wept.

Kohath clenched his jaw and raised his voice, barking out orders. "Adam, Dinah, take Hathor to the slumbering cellar. Have her drink her fill of wine. Ask one of the scholars to remain with her."

Adam and Dinah hurried to Kohath's aid, gathering up the distraught Hathor. Her arms drooped over their shoulders, her head flopping back and forth as they escorted her from the chamber. Kohath's gaze followed the three until Hathor had disappeared from sight, after which he returned to his seat, running his hands through his long, flaxen locks before reinstating his calm nature. "The hour has grown late. The journey to our haven, long. Everyone is exhausted and emotions are heightened. We must adjourn for the day and continue with our inquest tomorrow."

Osiris came forward, offering a curt nod. "I will do no such thing. I challenge The Council to continue. I see no need to draw this matter out further than necessary."

The eleven other council members rose from behind the table to join Kohath, standing tall as to defy Osiris, the mighty creator of the undead. Kohath took the god's hands into his own, compassion filling his eyes. "Dear Osiris, you desire resolution and you will have it, but not on this day. Everyone needs their rest."

Osiris continued to argue. "Tomorrow cannot be a rehash of today. This kind of chaos is a hindrance and cannot continue. We need to end the session by coming to some kind of productive conclusion."

Kohath's thick brows came together. "Osiris is right. We need proof to verify the blood promise truly exists."

"Kohath, show me the respect I deserve. I am a god, a member of The Ten. I would never fabricate such a promise," Amon asserted.

"Relax, Amon," Kohath spoke in a soothing tone. "I have the upmost respect for you. Whether I believe your story or not is irrelevant. In order to come to a decision, The Council must be shown concrete proof. It is the only way to resolve this matter in an unbiased fashion."

"And how do you plan to find such irrefutable proof?" Amon queried.

Kohath furrowed his brow as he stroked his chin. His gaze suddenly brightened, and he snapped his fingers. "The mother!" He whirled to face the other members of The Council. "Luke, Samuel, at sunset this evening, set out to collect Beth's mother and bring her here at once so we may question her."

I shuffled back a step, slowly shaking my head. "What? No. My mother can't be involved in any of this. I won't have it."

Kohath set an alert gaze on me. "My dear child, your mother is already involved. The details suggest she initiated this chain of events which are the source of so much trouble and unhappiness for you all."

CHAPTER 18

Teresa escorted us out of The Council's gathering chamber, down a dark hallway, and up a spiral staircase as if she were herding sheep.

Dragging my steps and twisting my ring, a slew of cold chills plagued my skin. My mind conjured up images of vampires plucking my mother from her home, whisking her off into the night sky, and dropping her into the middle of a vampire compound. On the other hand, laying eyes on her and knowing the truth of what she'd done, seemed far worse. And could I look her in the eyes, speak to her, hear her flimsy excuses? Time would tell, but really, what choice did I have? My unwillingness to see her hadn't been a factor in The Council's decision to bring her here in the least. Damn that blood promise all to hell.

A council member met Teresa at the top of the stairs. With a smile that touched her radiant dark-brown eyes, she pulled Philippe and me aside. "Take the others to their rooms, Teresa. I will show Beth and Philippe to theirs."

Teresa bowed her head. "Yes, Miriam." She turned back to Caleb, Amon, and the remaining members of The Ten, urging them forward. "Come. This way, please."

Amon glanced at me over his shoulder as Teresa led him down the hall. I watched him disappear around the corner of the hallway and then faced Philippe and the female vampire.

"I am Miriam," she said, leading us a few feet farther down the hallway before coming to a stop at a door on her right. She ushered us inside, gliding across the hardwood floor and gesturing to our surroundings. "This will be your slumbering chamber for as long as you remain with us." She pointed toward a kitchenette in the corner of the room. "There is a small refrigerator and microwave for storing and warming blood. My apprentice, Thomas, will be by shortly to stock it for you. Is there anything else you require?"

"Wine," I blurted out.

She came to me and squeezed my restless hands. Human compassion emanated from her angelic face. "You're in need of its power to heal. I will see to it that Thomas brings wine to you as well."

"Thank you," I said, releasing a huge breath.

After she left us, I explored the room she'd referred to as our slumbering chamber. Antique furniture garnished the massive bedroom. The largest piece, an ornate four-poster bed, occupied a quarter of the room. Covered in rich, gold fabrics, the bed's dressings perfectly matched the gilded dressers, decorative throw pillows, picture frames, and stately chairs occupying the room.

Philippe stood next to me, running his finger along my cheekbone. "Are you all right?"

A knock at the door prevented my reply.

Philippe left my side to answer it.

A young male vampire with deep-set eyes and bushy blonde hair waited in the doorway. A tray bearing both blood and wine rested on his right palm. "I am Thomas," he said. "Miriam sent me. May I come in?"

"Of course," Philippe replied, stepping aside.

Thomas hurried into the kitchenette, placing several bags of blood inside the refrigerator, as well as an additional bottle of wine. Like a flicker of light, he moved into the sitting area. On the table between the two chairs, he placed a carafe of warm blood, two goblets, and the first bottle of wine. "Is there anything else I can get you?"

Philippe looked to me.

I shook my head.

"No, thank you," Philippe told him.

As Thomas neared the door, he faced us one last time. "If you should need anything at all, you need only to think my name, and I will come to you."

Philippe nodded. "Very well. Again, thank you, Thomas."

"My pleasure," he said, offering us a slight bow before leaving us alone.

As the door settled into its frame, I grabbed the bottle of wine and popped the cork so I could fill a goblet. The minute the rim touched my lips, Philippe pulled it away.

"Remember, wine is a very powerful drug for us." He set my wine back on the table, pouring blood from the carafe into a goblet and handing it to me. "You must be starving. Please, drink this first."

The steam floating above the goblet's rim hypnotized me. My stomached growled, begging to be fed. Ripping the goblet from his hand with a frenzy I couldn't control, I downed half its contents, finding I craved the wine even more. Abandoning the blood goblet and reaching for the wine, I emptied it in one gulp. I filled the wine goblet three more times. Blissfully numb, I fell back into one of the chairs.

Philippe knelt in front of me, placing his hands on my legs and peering into my eyes with concern. "Talk to me. How are you feeling?"

I looked away from him, staring off in the distance. Thoughts of my mother occupied every cell in my brain. "Mothers are supposed to protect their children," I rambled. "My mother cared more about protecting her own life than that of her child." I threw my hands up to cover my face. "And tomorrow, in front of everyone, I'll have to hear the story of how she gave me up all over again."

"I'm sorry," he said, his voice just above a whisper. "What can I do to ease your pain?"

Again, a knock sounded at the door. When I looked up, Philippe stood before the opening, hanging his head and emitting a groan.

Amon stood in the doorway, his eyes transfixed on me. "How is she?" His question directed at Philippe.

Philippe's shoulders drooped. "She's suffering, but I don't know how to help her."

"May I come in?" Amon asked, his tone suggesting he would no matter the answer Philippe gave him.

Philippe continued to block his path. "Can you help her?"

Amon nodded, his expression confident. "Yes."

Philippe opened the door wide and said, "Then do come in."

Amon rushed inside, placed a chair directly in front of me and eased himself into it. His gaze drifted over my face as he stroked my hair. "Look at me, Beth...into my eyes."

I obeyed.

Brilliant orange flames danced there. The blaze grew more and more powerful. It captivated me, held me hostage.

"Feel the power of my love...Philippe's love," Amon said, his voice mesmerizing. "Our love will never abandon you."

A warm and soothing sensation tingled into my toes, spiraled out through my arms and legs, rushing upward to enclose my heart. I moaned and sank deeper into the chair.

Amon kissed my forehead. "Rest now, my love."

My eyelids grew heavier, my body sinking to a new level of calmness.

Amon scooped me up into his arms and carried me to the bed. Pulling back the comforter and slipping me underneath its soft goose-down, he promised Philippe, "She will sleep now."

****

Summoned by the evening's newly born moon, my eyelashes obediently fluttered open. It seemed only moments before they had closed. I laid in bed, alone. The faint sound of water tapping against tile filled my ears. When I sat up, the room whirled around me. A dull ache throbbed at my temples, and I was sure I was going to be sick. I fell back onto the pillows, grabbing the comforter and jerking it up to my chin. In spite of the thick fabric, I shivered, knowing only blood could warm my perpetually cold body and cure my hangover. The thirst for blood tore at me with a vengeance. My body struggled to rise, ignoring the temptation to remain in bed. Hugging myself with my own arms, I wept.

Philippe hurried out of the bathroom, wrapped in a towel. "Beth, what is it? Are you all right?"

"I feel sick," I sobbed.

He threw some clothes on and sat on the bed beside me. "How can I help?"

Burying my face in my hands, I cried, "My head is pounding from the wine. I feel shaky and weak."

"In the moment, wine paralyzes our torment, only to double back cruelly and bring its own." He vanished into the kitchenette, returning seconds later, carrying a mug. "Here, the blood will help."

The heat radiating off the mug warmed my icy hands. I swallowed half the contents with a desperate gulp, took a breath, and drained the mug dry. Blood pumped through my parched veins, driving the dreadful chill away. My body relaxed and I closed my eyes, exhaling a deep sigh.

"Better?"

"Much better," I said, handing him the empty mug. I cocked my head. "Where do you think they get the blood?"

"I'm told it's donated."

"By whom?"

"Humans. Supposedly, the number of donors is considerable, so very little blood is taken from each."

I shuddered. "Are the humans kept here?"

He shrugged his shoulders. "The members say no. Humans are brought here, donate their blood, and are sent on their way, the haven's location erased from their memory."

"I don't believe that. Do you?"

He smirked. "I think The Council rigged some kind of system for themselves, as they did for The Ten with the blood lottery."

I nodded. "That's much more likely." Feeling alive once again, I sat upright. "I think I'll take a nice long shower."

He grabbed my hand. "Wait."

I scooted closer to him.

His expression grew serious. "Amon helped you last night, and I'm grateful. I couldn't stand to watch you suffer like that. I owe him."

"He's not going to cash in if that's what you mean."

He sighed. "Yeah, I know."

I gazed at him and touched his face. "I love you."

He gave me a boyish smile and kissed my cheek. "I love you too."

What if The Council took me away from Philippe? If I lost the chance to gaze into his eyes every day? I latched onto him.

He moved closer, studying my face. "What's wrong?"

"Promise me something," I whispered.

"Anything," he whispered back.

"If The Council determines I must uphold the terms of the blood promise, I couldn't bear to never see you again. Ask Amon to share our home, to share me." My eyes implored him. "Promise me."

He broke loose and held me at arm's length. "I would do that for us, but I have to know...do you still care for him?"

In a gentle tone, I confessed, "I will always love him. He watched over me my entire life." I cupped his face in the palms of my hands. "But now, I love you too."

Fire sparked in his eyes, and he pressed his lips against mine.

A knock at the door ended our kiss.

Philippe held me a moment longer and kissed me again before leaving my side to answer the door.

Caleb entered the room, tension locked along his jawline.

Philippe's expression turned grim as he asked, "What is it?"

Caleb let out a nervous breath. "Beth's mother has arrived."

A sudden chill scurried down my spine. *And so it begins.*

CHAPTER 19

I drug my feet across the stone floor as we neared the gathering chamber. At the door, my hands seemed to turn to ice. I'd find my mother on the other side, and I felt nowhere near prepared.

Philippe slipped his arm around my waist, pulling me close and whispering, "Remember, I'll be right next to you."

I didn't look away from the ominous door as I squeezed his arm and murmured, "Thank you."

Caleb grabbed the latch, offered me a fleeting, kindhearted smile, and threw open the door. Several bottles of wine occupied the center of The Council's table. The members conversed in the far-right corner of the room, while The Ten gathered in the same row of seats they'd filled the day before. Hathor had returned, her body poised gracefully, her beautiful head held high, seemingly oblivious to her earlier, childish outburst. Amon and Ptah seemed to be the only two missing.

Somewhere in the room, my mother began to whimper, the sound exploding inside my head. I reached for Philippe's hand.

Locking our fingers together, Philippe asked, "Are you ready for this?"

"Yes." I lied, my gaze zooming in on my mother sitting near The Council's table. She'd swept her hair up into a neat and tidy bun, so tightly wound, it pulled at the delicate skin at her temples. Clutching her hands in her lap, she stared straight ahead, trembling every so often. She hadn't even noticed me. No surprise there. She'd pushed me into the background and kept me there my entire life. Well, no more. Straightening my spine, I took a step toward her.

Amon and Ptah strolled into the chamber, their arms wrapped around each other's shoulders, bellowing with laughter. Amon's gaze fixed on me, and he came to me at once, kissing my cheek when he reached my side. "Are you feeling better?"

My mother stole away my chance to respond. She jerked her head in the direction of Amon's voice, her eyes focusing past me as if I weren't even there. Recognition flashed in her eyes, and they doubled in size. She thrust a finger at Amon as she jumped to her feet. "You! We had a deal. I gave you my daughter. What more do you want?"

An eerie silence fell over the room. My mother had just confirmed the blood promise without one iota of prompting.

I let out a gasp.

My mother's eyes met mine.

She choked on her own breath, her face crumpling. "Beth," she blurted out. Her gaze darted about the room mechanically. "Why is my daughter here? What's going on? What do you creatures want from me now?" she demanded.

Her words cut through me like a knife. Balling my hands into fists, I stormed over to her. "Thanks to you, I've become one of those creatures."

She blinked several times before fixating on me. A scowl built slowly along her brow. "I no longer have a daughter. Get away from me," she spat.

I shrank away, my shoulders quaking. The tears fell, thousands of them, and they just kept coming.

Amon stood at my side in an instant, his lips to my ear. "She doesn't deserve your tears."

Philippe claimed my other ear. "Ignore her," he said, stroking my hair and pulling me away from Amon.

Kohath rose and clapped his hands. "Silence! Everyone, take your seats. The sooner we begin, the sooner this issue can be laid to rest and all of you can live your lives in peace."

The Council came together at the table, taking their seats. My mother recoiled, but I did nothing to comfort her. As she had so coldly stated, I was no longer her daughter. Taking my seat, I glared at her, but held my tongue as Kohath had requested.

Kohath looked on my mother with kindness. "May I offer you a glass of wine?"

Words seemed to fail her. She merely stared at him, openmouthed.

Kohath glided across the floor and knelt before her, taking her hands. Gently, he caressed each finger. Genuine compassion laced his voice as he said, "Don't be afraid. You're only here to validate information about a case we're investigating. What is your name, dear?"

My mother looked up at him, her gaze trusting. "Joanne, Joanne Ryan."

He nodded and patted her hand. "Joanne, may I bring you a glass of wine?"

"Yes, please."

Kohath waved his hand in the air, but his eyes remained on my mother. "Cain, please pour a glass of wine for our guest and bring it to her."

Immediately, the vampire seated in the third chair from the end of the table rose. His blackish-blue hair was pulled back into a neat ponytail, exposing his chiseled jaw and gleaming jade-colored eyes. He selected one of the bottles and filled a glass to the rim. "Drink," he implored her as he handed the goblet over.

Kohath smiled up at him. "Thank you, Cain."

He nodded and returned to his seat.

As my mother brought the glass to her lips, her hand quivered. Kohath steadied her goblet. She managed a brief smile, pressing her lips into a thin taut line an instant later. She took a swig of the wine. "I'm better now, thank you."

"Very well," Kohath said, leaving my mother to return to his seat, where he sat in stoic silence.

Every creak of furniture, bustle of clothing, and thump of a heartbeat magnified inside my head. I shifted in my chair, swiping sweat from my brow and eyeing the wine on The Council's table. Did I dare rise and disturb Kohath's thoughts to retrieve a much-needed glass of wine?

Suddenly, Kohath waved me forward. "Come."

Heat warmed my cheeks as I rose from my chair and neared the table.

Kohath poured the goblet of wine himself and handed it to me. "Drink."

"Thank you."

Kohath bowed his head in acknowledgment, and then shooed me away.

I returned to my seat, where I took a generous swallow of wine.

Philippe leaned over and touched my arm. "Small sips, remember."

To hell with small sips. Drowning and deadening my torment mattered. My life going back to normal, as normal as life could get for a vampire, mattered. But most of all, going home mattered. Lifting the glass, I swallowed another mouthful.

With a wave of his hand, Kohath said, "Let us begin."

My mother sank deeper into her chair, her hand flying to her throat.

"We have gathered today to verify a blood promise made between Amon and Joanne," Kohath announced with a nod in their respective directions. "As Joanne clearly stated earlier, said blood promise was contracted. Now, we must determine how to proceed." He looked to my mother. "Joanne, is he indeed the vampire with whom you made the blood promise?"

"Ye..." her voice cracked, and she took another drink of wine. After clearing her throat, she looked at Amon and said, "Yes. He came to me on my twenty-fifth birthday."

I glanced at Hathor. Her polished exterior had begun to splinter and crack.

"Your family is tied to the blood lottery?" Kohath pressed.

She nodded her confirmation. "Yes, on my father's side. Beth and I go by Ryan, my father's name, not my ex-husband's. When he left us, I gave up his name."

"Then you were fully aware that on your twenty-fifth birthday, your life would be sacrificed to one of The Ten?" Kohath asked, probing further, not a hint of empathy in his voice.

After a long pause, she answered. "I was aware, but I didn't believe my father. I thought the whole story was just an old wives' tales until... that night."

Kohath leaned forward, his gaze narrowing. "Tell us about that night."

Amon rose from his chair, his voice touched by annoyance. "Is that really necessary? She's already confirmed the existence of the blood promise. Isn't that why we're here? Why make her..." He glanced at me, "...as well as Beth, relive the details?"

As I nursed my wine, a faint numbing sensation washed over me. I sat back, allowing the wine to take hold.

"The details matter, Amon," Kohath explained. "I need to hear Joanne tell the story in her own words. Please, be seated and let her speak."

Philippe, too, rose to his feet, his blue-gray eyes blazing. "I agree with Amon. What difference could the details possibly make at this point? Haven't we heard enough?"

Caleb's eyes widened, and he sprang out of his chair, clutching at Philippe's arm. "What the hell are you doing?"

Philippe shook Caleb off, his gaze darting back to Kohath. "We're all victims here. Dredging up the past is only going to inflict more torment. There's only one question here: does the blood promise stand to be honored or not?"

Kohath rubbed his brow as if to ward off a headache of gigantic proportion. "As I said before, the details do matter. No more interruptions, please."

With a great deal more force, Caleb shoved Philippe back into his chair. "Sit down and keep your mouth shut," he growled.

Philippe clenched his jaw, lobbing a fierce scowl in Caleb's direction. "I have every right to speak my mind."

Caleb shook his head and in a low voice said, "Philippe, pull yourself together. Challenging Kohath will only make matters worse. Trust me, I know."

Philippe heaved a sigh and glanced at my wine. "Are you going to finish that?"

I handed it over. "I've had enough. Here you go."

He finished the remaining wine off in one swallow.

I leaned over to touch his shoulder softly. "Calm down."

His eyes searched mine, the anger slowly fading away. He took my hand and brought it to his lips. "I'm only worried about you."

"I'm okay, so don't worry."

Amon stared daggers in our direction and threw up his hands. "Do I dare say more?"

"Everyone, please remain calm and have patience. I assure you, we will remedy this situation." Kohath focused his gaze on my mother. "Continue."

Amon mumbled something under his breath and sank back into his chair.

My mother swallowed the last of her wine. "May I please have another?" she asked, raising her glass.

"Cain, please refill Joanne's glass," Kohath said.

Once her goblet had been filled, my mother took a rather large swallow, and another. A glazed, slack expression claimed her. Had the wine finally taken over? She sat upright and locked her sights on Kohath. "I don't know what you expect to hear. That vampire appeared out of nowhere. I was young, frightened, and I didn't want to die. Beth was asleep in the back seat. I saw a way out. I offered him Beth."

The blade of truth plunged deep into my heart once more. I cringed under the weight of her confession, and I wasn't the only one. Hathor apparently wore her emotions on her sleeve. The blood drained from her face, her turquoise eyes growing large and vacant.

Without so much as a glance in my direction, my mother continued. "My proposal annoyed him. He couldn't be bothered with a baby. In desperation, I forced her into his arms. Then he looked at her. Awe filled his eyes in a way even mine had never done. He couldn't stop staring at her. Moments later, he agreed to my proposal."

"You're certain you made the offer of your own free will?" Kohath pressed.

Amon flew from his seat. He stood rigid, glaring at Kohath. A vein bulged in the center of his forehead. "Careful, Kohath," he warned, his tone sharp and crisp. "Do not call me a liar. If I so desired, I could demolish the entire room in the blink of an eye."

Kohath leveled his gaze, matching the animosity in Amon's tone. "I have not forgotten."

Amon arched a brow and fired back, "Yet you accuse me of lying."

"No, I'm merely clarifying," Kohath refuted.

"I see no need for clarification. I have stated the facts. My description of the events should've sufficed, and yet you chose to question this human, to take her word over my own. Me, Amon, a vampire god."

I gripped the arms of my chair, certain the bones in my fingers would break, fixated on Amon and Kohath. Neither one appeared ready to back down.

Kohath stood tall with his chin raised, his penetrating gaze aiming for Amon. "And I am Kohath, the Old One, created to govern The Ten by The Ten, and leader of The Council." Their eyes locked for several minutes, as if engaged in a battle of the minds. Resuming his calm nature, Kohath evenly stated, "Amon, I hold you in the highest regard, but I must hear all sides to the story as everyone in this room has staked some kind of claim they wish to be honored, involved with the making of this blood promise."

"This blood promise has proved most exasperating. I've had to plead my case to Beth, to Philippe..." He spun, his gaze spewing venom at The Ten. "...and even to my own allies, which appear to have severed their ties, and now we stand divided." Again, he faced Kohath. "Now I have to prove my story to you."

"Not to me..." He gestured toward the members seated with him around the table. "...to us. Have faith, Amon. We *will* come to a resolution."

"Kohath is right," Ptah said, rising from his seat to stand next to Amon. "Please, my friend. Let The Council continue their investigation."

Ptah gripped Amon by his shoulders, inching him backward. Amon resisted, fighting every step of the way, until Ptah plopped him back in his seat, standing over him like a guard dog.

"I'm fine," Amon scoffed.

Ptah slowly sat down, keeping Amon locked in his sights.

My mother raised her hand like a student in class. "Should I answer the question or not?"

"Please answer," Kohath urged with a wave of his hand.

"I made the offer, but he set the terms."

"And what were the terms of your agreement?"

I observed the members of The Ten. They sat noble, like kings and queens, but each wore pinched expressions. Hathor especially, with her nails embedded into the chair arm.

"He swore he wouldn't return or interfere in her life until her twenty-fifth birthday," my mother replied.

Hathor sprang from her seat and pointed at Amon. "But he did interfere. He never left her alone. He..."

Kohath held up his hand. "Hathor," he interjected, "just as I have asked Philippe and Amon to refrain from outbursts, I expect the same restraint from you. Now please, sit down."

Her turquoise eyes darkened several shades darker as she glared at Kohath. "I will not."

Osiris stood, tucking his arm around her waist so he could pull her back down. "Hathor, do as he asks."

She settled back into her chair with an air of refinement, but a firestorm of rage lit her eyes.

Kohath returned his focus to my mother. "Please, carry on, Joanne."

"She's right." My mother bobbed her head in Hathor's direction. "Even though we never saw him, he was always leaving Beth some kind of token of affection."

My hands fell limp at my sides. She knew. All this time she'd known about his visits and never said anything.

"Because of my...choice, Beth never had much of a family life." My mother gestured toward Amon. "He made her happy, so I let him interfere. There's not much more I can tell you."

Hathor slid down farther in her seat, the flames of rage inside her eyes dimming slightly.

Kohath turned his attention on me. "Beth, may I hear from you now?"

A tingling wave of nerves crept over my skin when Kohath addressed me. I glanced at Amon.

"Tell them," he said quietly.

I cleared my throat and focused on Amon instead of The Council. "What more can I say that hasn't already been said? But I married Philippe. I don't see how the blood promise can be honored. I am sorry."

Philippe sighed with relief.

A glowing expression brightened Amon's face as he gazed at me. Had he heard the words I'd spoken? He came to kneel before me and took my hands. "Tell me, Beth, if you hadn't met Philippe on that cold winter night, would we be here today, seeking resolution from The Council?"

Philippe closed his eyes and turned his face away.

Caleb placed his hand on Philippe's shoulder, giving it a firm squeeze.

Hathor, Osiris, and Isis rose from their seats, their gazes hardening.

Ptah smiled impishly at the three gods.

Kohath leaned forward in his chair.

I became the center of the room's focus. A kaleidoscopic of prying orbs judged me, weighing my unspoken response. I couldn't bring myself to give them one.

Ignoring everyone else in the room, Amon set his sights on me. He kissed my hands, and then pressed them over his heart, holding them there. "If *I* had come to you *that* night and asked you to become my imortal companion, would you have hesitated?"

Memories flooded my brain—the visits, the gifts, the invisible touches. My heart fluttered with a fervent ache I couldn't deny. I pulled my hands away. "It's not a fair question. Hypothetical what ifs are irrelevant."

"Quite the opposite, Beth, they are most relevant. Answer the question," Kohath insisted, his tone stern."

Philippe turned to look at me, a haze of anguish dulling his gorgeous blue-gray eyes. I brushed my fingers over the top of his hand and said, "I love you, Philippe. My answer doesn't change that."

He sat a little taller, yet the misery clouding his eyes remained. "I understand. Go ahead and answer him."

I offered Kohath the most defiant stare I could muster. "I would not have hesitated to accept Amon's proposal and become his immortal companion."

Amon kissed my hands once more. "Thank you," he said before standing tall and returning to his chair.

"Nooooo," Hathor cried, throwing her head into her hands.

Kohath hurried over to console his maker.

Osiris scooped her into his arms, his eyes wide. "We must do something. Her heart is breaking."

One of The Council members called out, "Fill her with wine. It will ease her pain."

Kohath rushed back to the table, returning to place the glass to her lips and forced her to drink. When the glass was empty, she demanded more. I lost count of the times Kohath handed her glass after glass. Drunk beyond measure, she moaned with pleasure, falling limp in Osiris' arms.

A deep wrinkle cut through Kohath's forehead as he addressed The Ten. "Why is Hathor affected so drastically by this blood promise?"

Isis spoke up. "She has never gotten over her love for Amon, even after their separation. She has been in denial for many years, yearning for a reunion of their hearts. It is now evident Amon has no intention of reuniting with her."

Her words sank in, like needles piercing my skin. Had I stolen Amon from Hathor?

Sympathy filled Kohath's eyes. "She still loves him after all these years?"

Isis sighed heavily. "Unfortunately, yes."

Kohath took Hathor by the shoulders and shook her gently. "This is absurd. You must forget him."

Hathor pushed him away, muttering something unintelligible under her breath.

Kohath looked to Osiris for assistance. "Keep her in her chair for now. We will tend to her later."

"Forgive her, Kohath," Osiris said, as he set Hathor back into her chair. Isis scooted her chair closer to Hathor's, and each of them took up a hand, cooing kind words and stroking her arms in an attempt to soothe her.

"One thing at a time," Kohath muttered. "I must return my attention to the matter at hand. Then I will deal with Hathor."

After Kohath made his way back to his seat, he folded his hands upon the table and asked, "How was the blood exchanged to seal the blood promise?"

"He pricked his finger, drawing blood and rubbing it inside her mouth," my mother answered, "and then he did the same to her, licking her blood off her finger."

Kohath looked down the row of seated members, his gaze settling on a female with long blonde hair. "Athaliah, affirm for us the Rule of Blood."

Athaliah's navy-blue eyes flickered like flecks of glitter, catching the light as she spoke. "The offering of blood, other than creating life, paired with the receiving of blood, is a promise of shared eternity."

Her words played again and again inside my head, yet they seemed a photocopy of what had already been said.

"The exchange of blood customarily signifies consent to a union of immortality," Kohath stated. "However, Beth was far too young to understand the implications of such a union, and so, her mother offered consent as her proxy. We must determine whether this blood promise can be upheld by vampire law under the circumstances."

Amon snorted in impatience. "Nonsense. The mother fell well within her rights to make such a promise. How was I to know there would be any debate so many years later?"

Kohath arched a brow at Amon. "Had you known, would you have chosen differently?"

Amon held me in his gaze while shaking his head. "Beth is irresistible, beautiful, passionate—my weakness. Without her love, I would willingly breathe my last breath."

Again, my heart fluttered wildly inside my chest.

I felt Philippe's eyes on me, but when I turned my head, I found him staring into the palms of his hands.

Kohath folded his arms, looking at the three of us in turn. "But Beth has stated she loves Philippe."

"Yes, but what she hasn't said is whether or not she still loves me," Amon added.

I couldn't take any more. Not one more word. "Everyone is suffering. Haven't you heard enough? End this now. Give us your answer."

Kohath stared at the other members of The Council with intense focus. The twelve distanced themselves from the table, gathering in front of the gold door, collaborating in muted tones, a frequency unknown to the rest of us.

My immortal soul resembled a wishbone about to be splintered apart. No matter what their decision, I feared irreversible damage loomed over us. I couldn't even say I felt uncertainty over the choices I'd made as none had been my own. My entire life had been arranged, and this set of circumstances appeared no different.

Breaking apart, The Council returned to their chairs. "We have come to a decision," Kohath stated with authority.

I pressed my hand against my stomach, as if to hold my quivering insides together, and with the other, I reached for Philippe's hand. Our fingers interlocked with an iron grip.

"You, Beth," Kohath continued, "are not bound by the blood promise, but your mother is."

Gasps echoed in my ears. I sat motionless, mental numbness weaving throughout my brain. What had he said? Something about my mother? Consciousness came in waves. *Not bound...blood promise...mother is...*Dear God, had he meant death! My gaze darted to my mother. A mask of fear spread across her face, her eyes bulging from their sockets.

Amon bolted from his chair, determined to confront The Council. "What do you mean? This solves nothing."

The gods followed suit, leaping to their feet in an uproar, blathering with one accord.

Philippe sank his chin to his chest and muttered, "Will this ever end?"

"You can't be serious!" Caleb shouted at Kohath.

Amon paced the length of the table. "I challenge your decision."

Kohath relaxed in his chair. "This is indeed our answer."

Order had fled the room. A free-for-all erupted before me—flailing, crying, grimacing, rambling—The Ten succumbing to juvenile behavior and The Council...their decision was pure madness. I, too, sprang to my feet and cried, "What about my mother? What does your decision mean for her?"

"Her contract with the blood lottery stands. Your mother must sacrifice her blood and her life," Kohath clarified.

I jutted a rigid finger at him. "You stated you weren't barbaric. What do you call this?"

"Vampire law," Kohath countered. He regarded me intently before he spoke again. "You still have the option of fulfilling the blood promise, which will terminate your mother's obligation."

My mother clamped her hands over her ears, shaking her head and wailing.

"I will not feed off her," Amon stated in defiance.

Kohath had to be bluffing. Surely, he would never allow my mother's life to waste away in the center of their gathering chamber. I stepped forward and pleaded for his compassion. "Please, this is my mother. She gave me life. I can't take away hers. There must be another way to resolve this."

Philippe appeared at my side, wringing his hands. "Even I cannot abide by these terms." He turned to Caleb. "Do something."

Caleb wore a bleak expression when he addressed The Council. "I know all of you to be fair and compassionate immortals. Please, Kohath, offer some kind of judgement which helps all of them."

"I cannot alter the rules, my son," he said in a commanding tone. "Our decision is final."

Amon stood his ground. "Well, I refuse."

My mother's wailing morphed into pitiful howls, each shriek carving out a piece of my heart. "Amon will not comply," I shouted at The Council. "It's over."

"We will merely ask another member of The Ten to feed off her," Kohath confirmed without remorse.

Amon curled his lips back, baring his fangs, his eyes wide. Every inch of his body trembled as he slowly advanced on Kohath, like a panther stalking its prey. The battle of wills between Amon and Kohath were the least of my concerns. The invitation to feed off my mother drew my gaze toward The Ten. Sobek and Khum had already set their sights on her, their eager tongues darting across their lips. I whirled to face The Council, throwing up my hand. "Stop!"

Noise evaporated from the room as all eyes encountered mine.

Tears streamed down my face. *To love is to sacrifice*, I thought. This was my sacrifice to make. The alternative was unthinkable. I pushed my shoulders back as I addressed The Council. "I will fulfill the blood promise."

My answer unleashed a new wave of weeping, shouting, and stumbling about from the immortals. The aftermath of my words surrounded me in a suffocating fashion. I turned away and focused on my mother, the only one I could save.

"Joanne, your daughter has once again saved your life," Kohath announced. "We will return you safely to your home." He turned to the rest of his cabinet and named two vampires as escorts to accomplish the task.

"Wait," my mother cried, rising to her feet and turning to me. She reached out to touch me, before some instinct pulled her back. "Beth, please, forgive me."

An inner peace filled me as I witnessed the relief radiating from her body. I'd done my duty as a daughter and saved her life, but as an immortal, she would no longer be a part of mine. "Take her away," I whispered.

Luke and Samuel, the vampires designated to be my mother's escorts, gathered her up and whisked her away, forever removing her from my sight.

Philippe suddenly burst into injured sobs. He staggered past me, collapsing in front of Amon and clasping his hands. "Don't take her from me," he begged. "I cannot bear it. I will share her, I will."

With genuine compassion, Amon said, "We both love her." He offered his hand, helping to pull Philippe to his feet. "My offer still stands. We will share Beth's love."

I had become a shared trophy—a possession. Bowing my head, I let my hair hang in my face, hiding my eyes.

Kohath's voice rose above the turmoil as he declared, "It gives me great pleasure to unite Amon and Beth under the edicts of our immortal world. Athaliah, bring forth the ceremonial blood dagger and goblet for the binding ritual."

I jerked my head upright. What the hell was a binding ritual?

The blonde immortal bolted from the room, returning before the door closed. In her hands, she held an ancient golden goblet. The tip of a sterling dagger peeked just above the rim.

Amon came to my side, his emerald-green eyes sparkling like jewels dancing in the sunlight. "Don't be afraid," he assured me.

His voice sent warmth spilling throughout my body, calming every nerve. "I'm not afraid." *I'm committing a crime, entering into a second marriage while my first husband bears witness.*

"Beth, Amon, come forward," Kohath commanded.

As we approached the table, everyone in the room seemed to speak at once, the noisy hum of voices overlapped, commingling their words.

"Silence!" Kohath roared. His gaze darted about the room. "Hold your tongues, or I will conduct this ceremony in private."

"Wait," Philippe shouted, rushing toward the table.

Caleb hurried after him, attempting to pull him back. "Philippe, there is nothing you can do."

Philippe ignored his words and faced Kohath. "You can't do this. Beth is my wife!" he screamed in a panicked voice.

Kohath emerged from behind the table and neared Philippe, placing his hands on his shoulders. "This must be difficult for you, but you must accept the union between Beth and Amon, or your grief will tear you apart. Amon has extended kindness, allowing your marriage to Beth to continue, but you'd do well to remember that your union was one consecrated in the human world, not that of the immortal world."

Philippe's voice rose with sheer desperation. "I don't know how to do that."

Caleb embraced Philippe fiercely. "We'll find a way, and I will remain at your side to help you in any way I can."

Wincing, I looked away from him. There was nothing I could do, and part of me argued the fact that Philippe had brought all this misery upon himself—upon all of us—when he'd made the decision to deceive me.

"You're strong, Philippe, a powerful vampire," Kohath told him with great conviction. "Do not fear their union. Beth holds love in her heart for you. Fight for that love."

I cast a fleeting glance at Philippe.

He regained his composure and stood tall. "I will fight."

Kohath trailed away from a much calmer Philippe to take his place next to Athaliah. "Beth, Amon..." He urged the two of us forward. "Place your left hands on the table, face up. Athaliah, spear their palms with the dagger."

Amon cupped my chin in his right hand and turned my head toward him. "Keep your eyes on me. It will all be over before you know it."

But I couldn't look away from the sterling dagger meant to stab my flesh.

Athaliah's dainty fingers curled around the handle, and she jerked the blade overhead with tremendous power, hurling it down into Amon's palm before I could blink.

Amon winced but held his ground.

A wild gleam sprang up in Athaliah's eyes as she held his palm over the goblet, allowing his blood to drip inside.

The potent scent of his immortal blood perfumed the air, its fragrance filling my head with light and color. Intense desire stirred within the pit of my stomach, causing my knees to weaken. I latched onto Amon, searching for balance. He wrapped his free arm about my waist, steadying me.

Athaliah released Amon's hand and turned to me. "Your hand," she demanded.

A sour taste filled my mouth as I cautiously offered up my hand. With what I would've have sworn to be a bit of delight, she stabbed my palm. A stinging force plunged into my skin, reaching all the way down to the bone. I shrieked and tried to jerk my hand back.

Athaliah tightened her grip, clamping down on my wrist and twisting my palm over the rim of the goblet. I turned away as my blood trickled freely to mix with Amon's, burying my face in his chest. He kissed the top of my head, just as Athaliah released my hand. I yanked it back with a glare.

She used the dagger to churn our blood, stopping briefly to inhale the elixir of immortality. Appearing satisfied by the scent, she lifted the goblet, approaching me and placing the rim to my lips. "Drink until I tell you to stop."

Obediently, I opened my mouth so she could fill it with our blood. Upon my first swallow, I swayed uncontrollably. Sinfully sweet and powerfully seductive, our commingled blood coursed through my entire body, awakening every nerve. I growled like a crazed animal, gulping down the blood with insatiable need.

"Stop!" Athaliah ordered.

I nearly defied her, gripping harder at the goblet. A second later, I relaxed my fingers, reluctantly pushing the divine concoction away.

She smiled kindly at Amon and lifted the goblet to his lips. "Drink until the cup is empty."

With one hand still encircling my waist, Amon drank. He trembled and moaned, pulling me closer. As Athaliah tilted the goblet, allowing the last drops of blood to flow into his mouth, his eyes rolled back into his head.

Raising the golden goblet above her head, she proclaimed, "It is done."

Drunk on blood, I couldn't focus. The voices around me echoed inside my head, while the walls warped and blurred, rushing straight at me. The floor seemed to shift beneath my feet as the room spun around me, sucking me down into a dark hole. I crumpled to my knees.

Strong arms came to my aid, lifting me up. The soft brush of lips graced my cheek, my forehead...Amon's lips.

Philippe's muffled grumble reached me from some faraway place. "Stop kissing her!"

"We agreed to share, remember?" Amon fired back.

My vision flickered like a dying candle, catching fleeting glimpses of my surroundings. Amon carried me in his arms, weaving through a darkened hallway. Philippe marched along at his side. My eyelashes fluttered, finding only more darkness. A door creaked, and their footsteps grew hushed afterward. *Carpet. We're on carpet.* The soft caress of a mattress hugged my body. The hiss of a match sizzled within my ears. I could make out the soft glow of candlelight to my right. Was I back inside our bedroom? I reached out my hand. "Where am I?"

Fingers closed around my left hand, and then my right.

"My slumbering chamber," Amon informed me.

"Philippe?" I called out.

He squeezed my right hand. "I'm here."

Sleep rose up to claim me, the two men in my life holding my hands as I drifted away.

CHAPTER 20

I awoke to find myself alone. Where had they gone? Had something else happened to take them away? I climbed out of bed and hurried to the door. As I stepped into the passageway, Hathor blocked my path. The fine hairs on the back of my neck stirred, knowing she saw me as the obstacle to her future with Amon. I had no intention of confronting her. Stepping to the side, I blasted past her, hurrying down the hall.

"Wait!" she called out. "I must speak with you."

I came to a standstill and turned to face her. "What do you want?"

"Not here," she whispered, glancing over her shoulder. "Follow me. I will take you to a place where we can talk."

I realized I'd be an idiot to follow her alone. "No. Tell me what you have to say right here."

"I won't harm you. Please, you must come with me. I have further news regarding the blood promise."

"The blood promise?" I parroted back.

"Yes." She waved me forward. "Come."

Every inch of my brain screamed at me to stay away, but I ignored my own warning and followed her.

She led me outside and into a spectacular garden overflowing with dark-red rose bushes in full bloom. Their subtle fragrance hung in the crisp night air.

Graceful as a ballerina, she glided across the brick walkway and lowered herself onto a marble bench. A statue of a praying angel loomed above her, his lowered head and clasped hands suggesting he offered blessings for anyone who sat beneath him on his bench.

I sat next to Hathor and waited for her to speak.

She stared straight ahead, her posture rigid. "Amon was never meant to be your immortal companion," she told me in an icy tone. "For centuries, I dazzled him with my powers and beauty. Now, I mean nothing to him. He desires something more, something more human, someone like you." When she faced me again, she placed her hand over her heart. "Because I am not human, I no longer please him. Because you lived the life of a human, you now please him."

What was her point? "Do you have something important to tell me or not?"

Fierce hatred blemished her beautiful face. "I can't fathom what he sees in you. You were a mere mortal, only recently transformed. I match his grandeur, his power. You can't even begin to compare."

"Look," I said, pushing to my feet and throwing my hand onto my hip, "if you brought me here to insult me, I'm going to leave."

She grabbed my arm and pulled me back down. "You will stay and listen," she commanded. I flinched away, so she softened her tone. "Your mother robbed us both of the lives we chose, but what you did for her was touching, unselfish...but you and I both deserve to spend our lives with our true loves. Lovers we don't have to share. I've organized a plan."

A knot twisted my stomach. What was she up to? "What plan?" I pressed.

A cunning gleam flashed in her eyes. "The Council was wrong. There is another way."

I drew in a breath and searched her eyes, looking for some truth. Vacant darkness was all she mirrored back to me. "Aren't you too late? Amon and I are now bound by blood."

She nodded. "My plan is complicated. Many parties are involved, including Philippe."

My heart stopped beating when she spoke his name. I flew into a rage. "If you've done anything to hurt him, I swear I'll—"

She silenced me by holding up her hands. "I will get to Philippe's role, but first I must describe yours."

I clutched at my wedding ring. "Tell me where he is!"

"Relax, he is safe. He's with Osiris and Isis," she revealed, her voice void of emotion.

"Why would he be with them? What are the three of you up to?"

"Isis has cast a spell of magic."

I blinked. "Magic?"

Annoyed, she snapped, "Must you repeat everything I say? Yes, magic."

I pinched the base of my throat, worry filling me like a poison. "What have you done?"

She grinned. "Isis conceived a plan, a rather brilliant plan if I say so myself."

"For heaven's sake, tell me," I blurted out.

Staring up into the night, she spoke softly. "It is a spell of love. Isis has crafted a powerful elixir of love. It will bind us."

I laughed out loud. "A love potion? You can't be serious. Amon will never be overpowered by such nonsense."

She raised her brows. "My dear, you underestimate my conviction to win back Amon's affections, as well as Isis' magic."

I could see from the certainty in her eyes that she meant every word. I stood, backing away. "I won't be a part of this," I asserted firmly.

She sneered at me. "You already are a part of it. Soon, Amon will come to you. He will profess his love for me and release you from the blood promise, freeing you to live your life with Philippe."

"You say you love Amon, but love doesn't use trickery to get its way," I argued, trying to reason with her. "How can you betray him this way?"

Her incandescent eyes dulled slightly. "It is the only way to regain his love." Her eyes welled up with tears as she revealed, "Unfortunately, the spell has its limitations. One day, it will lose its power. When it does, he will awaken and run back to you."

"Then why cast it in the first place?"

"If it's a fleeting moment, day, or year, I don't care, as long as whatever time is granted to me, I can spend in his arms," she explained in a voice heavy with sorrow.

"Don't do it," I pleaded, my voice shrill. "He will think Philippe and I played some part in this. He will kill us both."

She took my hands. "No, he will hold Osiris, Isis, and I responsible," she assured me.

She must've gone mad. "You need to let him go. Move on with your life."

"I cannot. He is my life in the same way Philippe is yours." Her gaze turned unwavering. "Now, for Philippe's role in all of this. When Amon returns, Philippe must be strong enough to challenge Amon for your hand. Osiris is transforming Philippe as we speak, transfusing him with his godly blood, making him indestructible."

I gasped, the small sound dying away inside the still night. "Philippe would never jeopardize his human soul, the bond we share...what makes the two of us whole. He would never agree to deceive Amon either."

She laughed softly, shaking her head. "My dear child, you're so naïve. He has already agreed. Now you must do your part and allow Amon to free you."

Her words pierced me like an arrow. Had Philippe really agreed to such a thing? His selfishness had driven him to deceive me before. Had he done so again? Did he wish to claim me so badly that he would alter his very being? To say nothing of his disrespect for The Council's order, the binding ritual, or the sacrifice I made so that my mother could live. "I won't betray Amon this way. I won't," I screamed at her. "I'll warn him. I'll tell him everything."

Her self-assurance didn't waver. "He will not believe you. The spell cast by the elixir is too powerful. It rules his mind, even now." She rose to her feet and kissed me on the top of my head. "I must leave you. Amon is near. I can feel him. Good luck, dear Beth." Without another word, she vanished.

I couldn't breathe, and my legs had lost all power to keep me standing. I crumbled onto the bench, hugging my arms and rocking back and forth. *He will believe me. He has to.*

A gentle breeze brushed across my cheek, and I looked up into Amon's sparkling, emerald-green eyes. I gripped his hands in mine, my voice rising in desperation. "Amon, there's something I must tell you."

He pressed his finger to my lips and shook his head. "Me first." He released a long, low sigh. "I've lied to you, kept you in the dark. I brought you here on false pretenses. You believed I needed The Council's help to ensure the blood promise, but in truth, I came to see Hathor."

I shook my head fervently, shaking his shoulders in an attempt to wake him from the spell. "No. That's what Hathor wants you to believe, but it's a lie. They've tricked you. They've put you under some kind of spell."

He stared at me, his eyes vacant. "There's no spell. You and I, we're different. Your soul is human, and I am not of this Earth. We were never meant to be. I caused you and many others so much pain, and for that, I am truly sorry. I've made terrible mistakes, mistakes I must now fight to correct, but at least I have the power to free you from this blood promise."

"Listen to yourself!" I screamed, still hoping to shatter the trance he'd fallen into. "You're not making sense. For twenty-five years, you waited for me to become your immortal companion. Twenty-five years! We exchanged blood. Why would you suddenly give up on me?" And why was I suddenly horrified by the idea of living without him?

"I can't give up what really wasn't there to begin with."

I ran my hand through my hair. I was failing him. What could I do to sway his altered mind? "Hathor, Isis, and Osiris are behind your change of heart. They used some elixir to put you under their spell."

He looked up and away from me, into the star-filled night. He sighed, louder this time, and hung his head. "You're clutching at straws, Beth. Jealousy does not become you."

After all he'd put me through—me and Philippe through—I couldn't help but lose my temper. "I'm not jealous. I'm trying to make you see what they've done to you. I'm trying to save you from making a grave error by leaving with Hathor when you don't truly love her."

He gestured toward The Council's haven and said, "You belong with Philippe, not with me. I hope someday you will be able to forgive me for all I have done. I will agree to our dissolution of vows. I set you free."

A whimper swelled in the base of my throat. Would I be able to get through to him? Resting my hands on his chest, I tried once more. "Do you remember these words? *If I had to choose whether to breathe or to love you, I would use my last breath to tell you that...I love you.* Do you remember? Tell me that you do."

He trembled, and for a fleeting moment, the undeniable love I'd grown accustomed to flickered inside his eyes, before vanishing completely. "Beth, you're not making this any easier. Go to Philippe. Your heart unquestionably resides with his."

My voice choked on my brimming tears. "You're m—making a t—terrible mistake."

His form altered, became translucent, before becoming my familiar mist. "Goodbye, my darling Beth."

Amon slipped through my fingers and floated up and into the wind. I ran after him, crying, "Amon, don't go, please!"

He'd left me...again.

I plopped down on the bench, slumping forward and covering my face with my hands. As I cried into my palms, I whispered, "I failed you."

Footsteps rushed in my direction. I clutched my chest and muttered, "Please, please, please, let it be Amon." Rising off the bench and lifting my head, I caught sight of Philippe running toward me.

"Beth," he cried, "I've been looking all over for you."

I glared at him and spit out one name. "Osiris!"

"Did Osiris hurt you? He turned, his gaze searching the shadows of the dark garden.

"How could you?" I cried, pounding my fists against his chest.

He gawked at me. "What are you talking about?"

"Hathor told me everything. You drank Osiris' blood. You knew about their plans to betray Amon." I glowered at him and shouted, "You helped them trick him into living his life as a lie."

His eyes grew large and his jaw slack. "I didn't." He placed his hand over his heart. "I value my human soul too much. It's the bond that you and I share between us. I would never do anything to break that bond."

My hands trembled, and I sagged against him in relief. What a fool I'd been. How could I ever suspect he would jeopardize our bond? "Forgive me," I said, wrapping my arms around him. "I believed Hathor. I should've known better."

He pressed his lips against my cheek, his arms pulling me closer. "I told them I wanted no part of their plans to deceive Amon. I walked out on them."

I pulled away to gaze lovingly at him. "I'm so happy you did."

He smiled and kissed me as though he might never get the chance to kiss me again. "Yes, I am too." His eyes wandered about the garden again. "Where is Amon? Did you see him?"

A hollow sensation passed through my core. All I could do was nod.

He eased me down onto the bench. "Did he drink the elixir?"

I nodded again.

"So they went through with it anyway."

"Yes," I managed through my tears.

Philippe's hands dropped into his lap. "I can't believe they did it, took his life from him like that."

After taking several deep breaths, I finally regained control of my voice. "I couldn't reach him. I tried, but the spell, it had a hold of him and wouldn't let go." I paused before adding, "He released me from the blood promise."

Philippe's head whipped in my direction. A smile began to form on his lips, but quickly vanished. In a flat, emotionless tone, he said, "We are free because of a spell."

"Yes," I breathed, sharing in his gloomy outlook.

More hurried footsteps approached.

"Beth, Philippe," Caleb and Ptah called out, reaching us in an instant, their faces haggard and taut.

Philippe rose to his feet, while I sat motionless, my heart aching.

"Where the hell have you been?" Caleb demanded, embracing Philippe. "I feared the worst when I couldn't find you."

Philippe peered down at me, sorrowfully. "Do you want to tell them or shall I?"

"Tell us what?" Ptah demanded, his voice on edge. "And where is Amon? I couldn't find him either."

My lip quivered, and I cleared my throat. "He's gone."

Ptah frowned. "What do you mean, gone?"

That wretched feeling when I'd failed Amon resurfaced, punching me in the gut like a stone fist. I winced at the pain. "Osiris, Isis, and Hathor took matters into their own hands. They brewed up some kind of love spell. Amon left with Hathor, falsely believing himself to be in love with her."

Caleb's jaw dropped. "What?"

Ptah clenched and unclenched his fists rapidly. "That damned little witch! I knew they were up to something. Always off in some corner, whispering." Fortitude flared in his eyes, and his jaw set in a hard, determined line. "We must undo this spell."

"I tried. I couldn't get through to him. The spell's too powerful." I patted Ptah's arm in a gesture meant to calm and comfort him. "All we can do is wait."

"Wait?" Caleb sneered in disbelief.

Ptah's face brightened, and he snapped his fingers. "You mean the spell will eventually expire?"

I nodded and reached for Philippe's hand.

Philippe squeezed my fingers and brought them to his lips. His eyes searched mine when he said, "I'll do whatever you want to do."

I met their eyes, one by one, in turn. Vengeance laced my voice when I spoke. "When the time comes, Amon will return to me. He will seek revenge against Osiris, Isis, and Hathor for stealing away part of his life. And the four of us will stand by his side and help him."

Ptah extended his hand, an unwavering gaze blazing within his eyes. "Agreed."

Caleb placed his hand atop Ptah's and smirked. "I'm in."

Philippe followed suit. "Me too."

With renewed strength, I placed my hand over Philippe's, pledging myself, along with the others. "And so, we wait."

About the Author

LAURA DALEO is a multi-genre author, specializing in Dark Fantasy, Urban Fantasy, Supernatural fiction, Science Fiction, and Young Adult Fiction. Immortal Kiss, her best-known vampire series, explores the Egyptian pantheon that gave rise to vampires. Currently, she is working on her eighth book, I am Wolf, an urban fantasy.

A native of San Diego, California, Laura now lives in Tucson, Arizona with her two dogs, Rose and Cooper.